SHARE
the
Music

M c**GRAW-HILL**

AUTHORS   Michael Jothen   Barbara Staton

Vincent Lawrence   Merrill Staton

Jeanne Ruviella (Knorr),
Contributing Author

McGraw-Hill
School Division
New York   Farmington

SPECIAL CONTRIBUTORS

CONSULTANT WRITERS

Dr. Betty W. Atterbury
Mainstreaming
Gorham, Maine

Mary Frances Early
African American Music
Atlanta, Georgia

Alex B. Campbell
Choral Music
Lakewood, Colorado

Dr. JaFran Jones
Ethnomusicology
Toledo, Ohio

CONSULTANTS AND CONTRIBUTING WRITERS

Dr. Clifford D. Alper
Towson, Maryland

Nancy E. Ferguson
Tucson, Arizona

Jane Pippart-Brown
Lancaster, Pennsylvania

Dr. James Anthony
Towson, Maryland

Donna Brink Fox
Rochester, New York

Edwin J. Schupman, Jr.,
of ORBIS Associates
Spokane, Washington

Teri Burdette
Rockville, Maryland

Dr. Judith A. Jellison
Austin, Texas

Cynthia Stephens
Ellicott City, Maryland

Gregory Clouspy
Reisterstown, Maryland

Tom Kosmala
Pittsburgh, Pennsylvania

Mollie G. Tower
Austin, Texas

Ruth Landes Drucker
Baltimore, Maryland

Carl J. Nygard, Jr.
Fleetwood, Pennsylania

José A. Villarrubia
Towson, Maryland

Dr. Robert A. Duke
Austin, Texas

Belle Ortiz
San Antonio, Texas

McGraw-Hill School Division

A Division of The McGraw-Hill Companies

Copyright © 2000, 1997 Macmillan/McGraw-Hill, a Division of the Educational and Professional Publishing Group of The McGraw-Hill Companies, Inc.

McGraw-Hill School Division
Two Penn Plaza
New York, New York 10121

Printed in the United States of America
ISBN: 0-02-295374-4
2 3 4 5 6 7 8 9 004 03 02 01 00 99

ACKNOWLEDGMENTS

Grateful acknowledgment is given to the following authors, composers, and publishers. Every effort has been made to trace the ownership of all copyrighted material and to secure the necessary permissions to reprint these selections. In the case of some selections for which acknowledgment is not given, extensive research has failed to locate the copyright holders.

Arc Music Corp. for *Book of Love*. © 1957 (Renewed) Arc Music & Windswept Pacific. All Rights Reserved. Used by Permission.

Boosey & Hawkes, Inc. for *Birth of Kijé* and *Wedding of Kijé* from LIEUTENANT KIJÉ SUITE by Sergei Prokofieff. © Copyright 1936 by Edition A. Gutheil; Copyright Renewed. Copyright and Renewal assigned to Boosey & Hawkes, Inc. Reprinted by Permission.

Bug Music for *River* by Bill Staines. © 1978 MINERAL RIVER MUSIC (BMI) / Administered by BUG. All Rights Reserved. Used by Permission.

Dunvagen Music Publishing Inc. for *Floe* from GLASS-WORKS by Philip Glass. Copyright © 1982 Dunvagen Music Publishing, Inc. Reprinted by permission. All rights reserved.

Folk-Legacy Records for *All the Good People*. © 1987 KEN HICKS, FOLK LEGACY RECORDS, INC. Sharon, CT 06069.

Hal Leonard for *La Borinqueña*. Music by Felix Astol. Lyrics by Manuel Fernandez Juncos. Copyright © 1957 by Edward B. Marks Music Company. Copyright Renewed. International Copyright Secured. All Rights Reserved. Used by Permission. For *(Life Is a) Celebration*. Words and Music by Rick Springfield. Copyright © 1976 Songs of Polygram International, Inc., 40 West Music Corp., Children of Charles Music and 212 Music. International Copyright Secured. All Rights Reserved. For *Milk and Honey*. Music and lyric by Jerry Herman. © 1961 (Renewed) JERRY HERMAN. All Rights Controlled by JERRYCO MUSIC CO. Exclusive Agent: EDWIN H. MORRIS & COMPANY, A Division of MPL Communications, Inc. All Rights Reserved. For *Only You (And You Alone)*. Words and Music by Buck Ram and Ande Rand. TRO–Copyright 1955 (Renewed) Hollis Music, Inc., New York, NY. International Copyright Secured. All Rights Reserved Including Public Performance For Profit. Used by Permission (Canadian rights only). For *Our World*. Words by Jane Foster Knox. Music by Lana Walter. Copyright © 1985 by Jenson Publications. International Copyright Secured. All Rights Reserved. For *Run Joe*. Words and music by Dr. Walt Merrick, Joe Willoughby and Louis Jordan. Copyright © 1947 (Renewed) CHERIO CORP. International Copyright Secured. All Rights Reserved. For *Together Wherever We Go*. Words by Stephen Sondheim. Music by Jule Styne. Copyright © 1959 by Norbeth Productions, Inc. and Stephen Sondheim. Copyright Renewed. All Rights Administered by Chappell & Co. International Copyright Secured. All Rights Reserved.

HarperCollins Publishers for *Backward Bill* from A LIGHT IN THE ATTIC by SHEL SILVERSTEIN. COPYRIGHT © 1981 BY EVIL EYE MUSIC, INC. SELECTION REPRINTED BY PERMISSION OF HarperCollins Publishers.

Julian Harvey for *Drum Song* from FOUR CHINESE FOLK SONGS. © 1994 by Julian Harvey and Lucy J. Ding.

Hollis Music, Inc. for *Consider Yourself* and *Food, Glorious Food* from the Columbia Pictures–Romulus Film OLIVER! Words and music by Lionel Bart. © Copyright 1960 (Renewed) Lakeview Music Co., Ltd., London, England. TRO–Hollis Music, Inc., New York, controls all publication rights for the U.S.A. and Canada. Used by Permission. For *Only You (And You Alone)*. Words and music by Buck Ram and Ande Rand. TRO–© Copyright 1955 (Renewed) Hollis Music, Inc., New York, NY. International Copyright Secured. All Rights Reserved Including Public Performance For Profit. Used by Permission.

Henry Holt and Co., Inc. for *Bravado* from THE POETRY OF ROBERT FROST edited by Edward Connery Lathem. Copyright 1947 © 1969 by Henry Holt and Co., Inc. Copyright © 1975 by Lesley Frost Ballantine. Reprinted by permission of Henry Holt and Co., Inc.

Hinshaw Music for *A la nanita nana*. Copyright © 1995 by Hinshaw Music, Inc. Used by Permission.

Irving Music Inc. for *I Get Around* © 1964, Renewed 1992 Irving Music Inc. (BMI) All Rights Reserved. International Copyright Secured. Used by Permission.

Julie Music Corporation for *Mi Caballo Blanco*. Words and music by Francisco Flores. Copyright © 1971 Julie Music Corporation (BMI) Administered by Next Decade Entertainment, Inc. All Rights Reserved. Used by Permission.

The Lorenz Corporation for *I Hear America Singing* by André Thomas. Copyright 1993 Heritage Music Press, a division of Lorenz Corporation, All rights reserved. Reproduced by Permit #327661.

Music Sales Corporation for *The Ghost Ship* from REFLECTIONS OF A LAD AT SEA by Don Besig and Nancy Price. Copyright © 1982 by Shawnee Press, Inc. (ASCAP). International Copyright Secured. All Rights Reserved. Reprinted by Permission. For *Take These Wings*. Music by Don Besig. Lyrics by Steve Kupferschmid. Copyright © 1984 by Shawnee Press, Inc. (ASCAP) International Copyright Secured. All Rights Reserved. Reprinted by Permission. For *Tonight* from WEST SIDE STORY by Leonard Bernstein. Lyrics by Stephen Sondheim. Copyright © 1956, 1957 (Renewed) by Leonard Bernstein and Stephen Sondheim. Jalni Publications, Inc., U.S. & Canadian Publisher. G. Schirmer, Inc. worldwide print rights and Publishers for the rest of the World. International Copyright Secured. All Rights Reserved. For *Un bel dì vedremo* from MADAMA BUTTERFLY by Giacomo Puccini. English version by John Gutman. Copyright © 1964 (Renewed) by G. Schirmer, Inc. (ASCAP). International Copyright Secured. All Rights Reserved. Reprinted by Permission.

David Parker for *I've Got a Robe*. Musical arrangement by David Lee Parker.

Random House for *April Rain Song* and *Dreams* from THE DREAM KEEPER AND OTHER POEMS by Langston Hughes. Copyright 1932 by Alfred A. Knopf, Inc. and renewed 1960 by Langston Hughes. Reprinted by permission of the publisher.

Marian Reiner for *Rainbow Writing* by Eve Merriam. Copyright © 1976 by Eve Merriam. Reprinted by permission of Marian Reiner.

(continued on page iv)

Acknowledgments (continued)

Silver Burdett Ginn for *The Golden Vanity*. © 1974 GENERAL LEARNING CORPORATION. All Rights Reserved.

Jerry Silverman for *Freedom Is a Constant Struggle*. Arranged by Jerry Silverman. Somerset Press for *In Stiller Nacht*. Arrangement © 1985 by Somerset Press (A Division of Hope Publishing Company), Carol Stream, IL 60188. All rights reserved. Used by permission.

Songs of Freedom Publishing (ASCAP) for *Climbing Up to Zion*. Words and Music by Wintley Phipps.

Sundance Music for *Can You Hear the Music?* by Linda Worsley. Copyright Sundance Music. For *70 Times the Speed of Sound* by Linda Worsley. Copyright Sundance Music.

J. Weston Walch for *Eraser Piano Tees* from ZOUNDS by Dorothy Gail Elliott. Copyright © 1994 J. Weston Walch, Publisher. Used by permission.

David Ward-Steinman and Susan Lucas Ward-Steinman for *The Web*. Copyright 1976 by D. Ward Steinman.

Warner Bros. Publications for *Believe* by Elton John and Bernie Taupin. © 1995 Williams A. Bong Ltd. (PRS) & Hanis (ASCAP). All Rights administered by WB Music Corp. (ASCAP). All Rights Reserved. Used by Permission. For *Cum Sancto Spiritu* edited arrangement by Patrick M. Liebergen. © 1991 Studio 224. All Rights Reserved. Used by Permission. For *La Cigarra* by Ray Perez y Soto. © 1958 Promotora Hispana Americana de Musica S.A. © Renewed/controlled by Peer international Corp. (BMI). All Rights Reserved. Used by Permission. For *Love Song*. Music and lyrics by Stephen Schwartz. © 1972 Stephen Schwartz. All Rights administered by Jobete Music Co., Inc. & EMI Mills Music, Inc. All Rights Reserved. Used by Permission. For *That's What Friends Are For* by Burt Bacharach and Carole Bayer Sager. © 1985 WB Music Corp. (ASCAP), New Hidden Valley Music (ASCAP), Carole Bayer Sager Music (BMI). All Rights jointly administered by WB Music Corp. (ASCAP) & Warner-Tamerlane Publishing Corp. (BMI). All Rights Reserved. Used by Permission. WARNER BROS. PUBLICATIONS U.S. INC., Miami, FL 33014.

World Music Press for *Zol Zain Sholem*. © 1994 World Music Press, P.O. Box 2565 Danbury, CT 06813.

ART & PHOTO CREDITS

CONTENTS

UNIT 1

EXPLORING MUSICAL STYLES

Detail from *The Ghent Altarpiece*, Jan van Eyck, CATHEDRAL OF ST. BAVON, Ghent

Figure of *Horn Player* (Benin bronze, Nigeria). Courtesy of MUSEUM OF PRIMITIVE ART, NY

1

INTRODUCTION TO STYLE

Musical styles differ throughout the world. The many styles of music reflect the cultures and people who created them. Becoming familiar with a variety of music can help you identify the source of a specific type of music.

- As you listen, look at the pictures on the previous pages. Follow the pictures that represent the musical selections in "Style Montage."

 "Style Montage"

A Caribbean Style

Musical styles are often made up of elements from several cultures. Styles of music today also reflect the influences of the latest technology. These influences may be heard in the instrumental and vocal tone colors, the types of rhythms used, the interplay between voices and instruments, and the overall form of a musical composition.

- Listen to a piece based on Jamaican musical traditions. What instruments do you hear? What vocal sounds do you hear? What musical elements can you identify that you have heard before?

Lucky Dube

 "Serious Reggae Business" by Lucky Dube

Raft on the Rio Grande, Jamaica

- Tap the steady **quarter note** (♩) beat with your foot, and clap the rhythm pattern as you listen again. Make a silent palms-up motion on each **quarter rest** (𝄽). The **repeat signs** (𝄆 𝄇) mean play the pattern again.

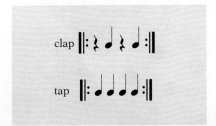

Making music at Montego Bay, Jamaica

3

- Play this melody on a recorder or keyboard instrument. Each **half note** ($\downarrow$) sounds as long as two quarter notes.

- Play these chords on a keyboard instrument. A **chord** consists of three or more pitches sounded together. To play **B♭** (**B-flat**) on the keyboard, find the black key to the right of **A**.

Refrain

F		B♭	C
C	C	F	G
A	A	D	E
F	F	B♭	C

- Listen to "Serious Reggae Business" again. Play the melody above during the Verse and the chords during the Refrain.

Ziggy Marley

Bob Marley

4

Reggae

"Serious Reggae Business" is an example of the musical style **reggae** (re'gā). This style developed during the 1960s on the island of Jamaica in the Caribbean. Reggae has since become very popular in the United States and other parts of the world.

Reggae grew out of the Jamaican **ska** music. Ska was a fast, lively style that featured the trumpet, trombone, and saxophone. Over time the ska ensemble grew to feature a prominent rhythm section of electric guitar, bass guitar, and drums. Eventually some ska songs became slower, and rhythms and melodies became catchier. Reggae is one of the few styles to feature the bass guitar. The guitar sounds, combined with reggae drum patterns, give the music its distinct rhythmic style. The electric guitar generally plays a simple off-beat strum, while organ and brass instruments are often used to punctuate and fill out the sound.

Michael Rose

The first song to name this musical style was "Do the Reggay," recorded by Toots and the Maytals in 1968. Reggae music in the United States can trace its popularity to a 1973 film "The Harder They Come." The film starred Jamaican singer Jimmy Cliff, who was one of the creators of the reggae music used in the film's popular soundtrack. Bob Marley made reggae popular in the 1970s with his unique vocal melodies, full harmonies, and lyrics containing political and social statements. The reggae style influenced rock groups in America and Britain—most notably The Police in the 1980s.

In addition to creating reggae music, Jamaican culture contributed to the creation of rap. As early as the 1960s, long before rap was developed in the United States, Jamaican disc jockeys would improvise rhymes over recordings of instrumental music. This practice was called "toasting" and was linked to a musical style called **dancehall**. Dancehall survives in Jamaica as a more melodic style of rap. Dancehall and reggae have continued to be influential in American music. Prominent reggae performers today include Michael Rose (formerly the lead singer of Black Uhuru), Shabba Ranks, Buju Banton, Ziggy Marley, and Beenie Man.

Buju Banton

STYLE MAKES THE DIFFERENCE

- Listen to *Bwala,* a dance from Uganda, and the Kyrie (kir′ ē-ā) from the Mass in G Minor by Ralph Vaughan Williams. What characteristics of each composition might help you identify its origin?

Bwala (dance from Uganda)
Kyrie from Mass in G Minor, by Ralph Vaughan Williams

In different cultures many things vary. The people may speak different languages. The foods they eat and the clothes they wear also may be different. The art and architecture produced by different cultures also have their own unique characteristics.

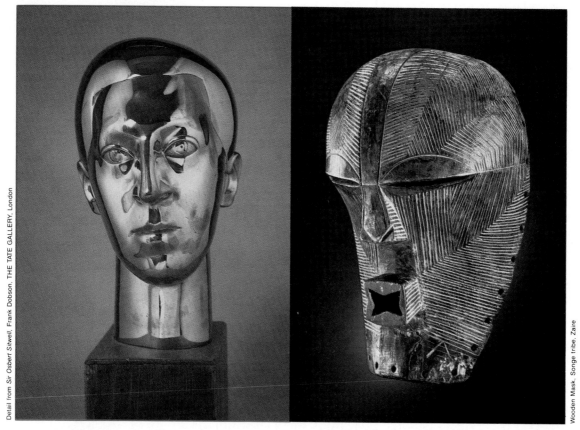

Detail from *Sir Osbert Sitwell,* Frank Dobson, THE TATE GALLERY, London

Wooden Mask, Songe tribe, Zaire

The sculpture on the left is by a twentieth-century English artist. The sculpture on the right is by an artist of the Songe tribe in Zaire. Although they both have the same subject, their styles are quite different.

Music from different times and cultures sounds different. The **style** of a culture is a unique mixture of its characteristics. The style of a musical composition is the unique mixture of its musical and cultural characteristics.

In *African Sanctus,* a new musical style results from combining the musical characteristics of different cultures. *Bwala* with its percussion, strong steady beat, and accents is combined with the choral singing tradition of Western cultures.

- Listen to *African Sanctus.* As each number is called, decide whether the music sounds more African or more Western. In which sections is it hard to make a choice?

 African Sanctus, by David Fanshawe

The style of *African Sanctus* is unique. The musical characteristics of two cultures have been combined to create music in a new style.
- Tap the steady quarter-note beat played on the drum as you listen to the opening choral part of *African Sanctus.* Then tap the following patterns as you listen again. Make a palms-up, silent motion for each quarter rest.

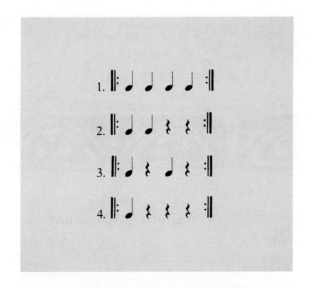

Each quarter note can be divided into two **eighth notes** (♪♪).

- Listen again to the opening choral section of *African Sanctus*, and clap two eighth-note sounds for each beat. As you clap, count aloud from 1 to 8, giving each clap one count.
- Listen to the second and third sections of *African Sanctus*. Clap and count the eighth notes in these sections. Is the new **tempo,** or speed of the beat, faster or slower than that of the first section?
- Listen to the complete *African Sanctus*. Perform these patterns with the choral sections by clapping and counting each line. Make the silent, palms-up motion for the **eighth rest** (ᜪ).

- Select percussion instruments and play the patterns above as an accompaniment to *African Sanctus*.

 CHALLENGE Create your own patterns to accompany *African Sanctus*.

Left, drummers at a festival in Vuaben, Ghana. Above, celebration at a baby-naming ceremony in Accra, Ghana. Below, South African women perform a mine dance.

CALYPSO STYLE

"Run Joe" is a **calypso** song about two brothers who get into trouble. Calypso texts are usually witty, making fun of political and economic issues. The music is rhythmic, danceable, and cheerful. It achieves its unique lilt by stressing melodic notes just ahead of or just behind the steady beat. This type of off-the-beat rhythm is called **syncopation.** Calypso music evolved in Trinidad, in the West Indies, toward the end of the nineteenth century. It also exhibits a strong African influence.

Run Joe

Words and music by Dr. Walt Merrick, Joe Willoughby, and Louis Jordan

2. When you get home, you get to bed
   Call a doctor and tie your head.
   Can't tell Ma to invent a lie.
   Got to have a good alibi.

3. When the Judge ask me how I plea
   Not guilty, sir, most decidedly.
   You can see, judge, at a glance
   I'm the victim of circumstance.

4. If the judge believe what I say
   I'll be home by the break of day.
   If he don't, I'll be looking cute
   Behind the bars in my striped suit.

5. Mother told me not long ago
   Keep away from that worthless Joe.
   If I heard what my mama say
   Wouldn't be in this mess today.

- Perform this pattern during the verses of the song.

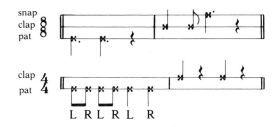

- Perform this pattern during the refrain. Pat your lap with your right and left hands.

You can accompany the refrain of "Run Joe" on guitar or keyboard using two chords built on G, the first (I), and D, the fifth (V), pitches of the **G major scale.**

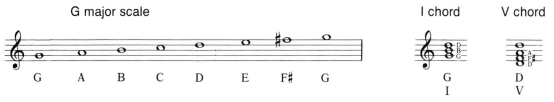

The G or I chord is called the **tonic** chord and is built on the most important pitch or tone of this scale, the **key tone** or home tone. The D or V chord is built on the fifth pitch of this scale and is called the **dominant** chord.

- Listen to the refrain of "Run Joe." Place your palms down on your desk when you hear the I chord. Turn your palms upward when you hear the V chord.

The lowest pitch of each of these chords is called the **root.**

- Give the letter names of the roots of the I and V chords.
- Play the root of each chord on keyboard as you sing the refrain.
- Play the chords (I and V) as you sing the refrain.
- Play this pattern on bells or keyboard as you sing the refrain.

CHALLENGE Create your own melodic pattern on keyboard, bells, or recorder to play on the word *Joe* as you sing the refrain. Use these five pitches. Play your accompaniment as you sing the song.

G A B D E

A STYLE FROM THE FAR EAST

Hiryu Sandan Gaeshi (hē′ rē-yoo̅ sän′ dän gī′ shē) features *taiko*
(tī′ ko̅) ensemble and bamboo flute. Taiko is a large Japanese barrel
drum of ancient origin. In this piece, the drummers express hope for
good fortune, peace, and long life.

• Listen to *Hiryu Sandan Gaeshi*. You will hear several instruments.
  The flute begins the piece alone. In what ways does the mood of
  the piece change after the drums enter?

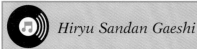 *Hiryu Sandan Gaeshi*

A procession crossing a river at a Japanese festival

In *Hiryu Sandan Gaeshi*, contrast is achieved through the use of different *tone colors*, *tempos*, and *dynamic* changes.

Tone color refers to the sounds of the different instruments.

- Listen again. Name three ways that the drummers create different tone colors.

Dynamics are the levels of loudness and softness in music. They are often shown by the abbreviations of the Italian words *piano* (𝒑) for soft and *forte* (𝒇) for loud. To show gradual changes from one dynamic to another, symbols and words are used.

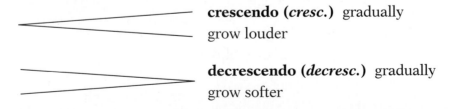

crescendo (*cresc.*) gradually grow louder

decrescendo (*decresc.*) gradually grow softer

- Listen to *Hiryu Sandan Gaeshi* once again for dynamic changes. Do the drums first enter on a crescendo or on a decrescendo? Describe the overall dynamic level of this piece.

13

Create a Sound Composition

Composers often get ideas from other art forms such as theater or poetry. You, too, will have the opportunity to be a composer and create a sound composition based on one of these poems.

- Read the poems aloud. Select one of them and create an original composition that will make a sound picture of the poem. Decide what tone colors, dynamics, and tempo you will use.
- Practice and perform your composition. Have other students guess which poem inspired your composition.

Rainbow Writing

Nasturtiums with
their orange cries
flare like trumpets;
their music dies.

Golden harps
of butterflies;
the strings are mute
in autumn skies.

Vermilion chords,
then silent gray;
the last notes of
the song of day.

Rainbow colors
fade from sight,
come back to me
when I write.

—*Eve Merriam*

Dreams

Hold fast to dreams
For if dreams die
Life is a broken-winged bird
That cannot fly.

Hold fast to dreams
For when dreams go
Life is a barren field
Frozen with snow.

—*Langston Hughes*

Bravado

Have I not walked without an upward look
Of caution under stars that very well
Might not have missed me when they shot and fell?
It was a risk I had to take—and took.

—*Robert Frost*

THE EUROPEAN-WESTERN STYLES

Symphony No. 9 by the German composer Ludwig van Beethoven (lood′ vig vän bā′ tō-ven) contains one of the most famous melodies ever written, the "Ode to Joy."

• Listen to the "Historical Style Montage." It first presents the "Ode to Joy" as Beethoven used it in his Symphony No. 9 and then as it might have sounded if used by composers who lived as much as four hundred years before Beethoven, or as much as one hundred fifty years after.

How is each performance different? Think about tone color, instruments, dynamics, and tempo to help you decide.

 "Historical Style Montage"

• Perform the "Ode to Joy" on keyboard, bells, or recorder as you listen to the "Historical Style Montage." Begin after the Beethoven example.

"Ode to Joy" from Symphony No. 9, Fourth Movement

Ludwig van Beethoven

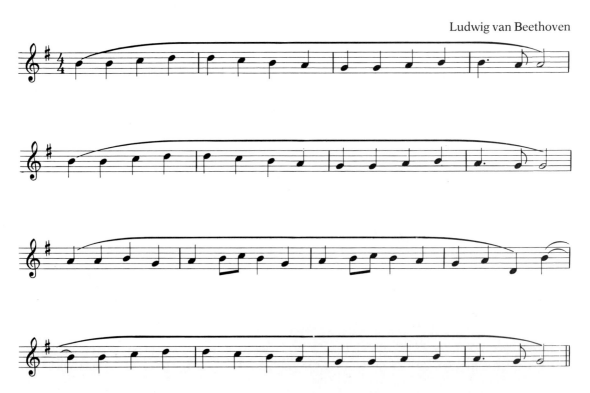

Each time you performed the "Ode to Joy," it was in a different musical style. In European-Western music the terms *Renaissance, baroque, classical, romantic,* and *twentieth century* are used to describe each of the musical styles.

Renaissance   Both religious and secular music, predominantly vocal, instruments used in secular music

Baroque   Steady rhythm, organ used to accompany religious music, secular music written for small groups

Classical   Short, tuneful melodies, gradual dynamic changes, restrained expression of emotions

Romantic   Longer, often complex melodies, more open expression of emotions

Twentieth Century   Unusual rhythms, emphasis on unusual tone colors, great emphasis on experimentation

- Listen to the "Historical Style Montage" again. Identify the order in which the style periods are presented. Use the musical descriptions above to explain your choices.

BAROQUE STYLE

Conducting a Baroque Composition

"Marche" by Jean Baptiste Lully (zhän′ bäp-tēst′ lyo͞o-lē′) has sections in different **meters,** or groupings of beats. Beats grouped in twos are **duple meter.** Beats grouped in threes are in **triple meter.** Groups of beats are shown in **measures** that are separated by **bar lines.**

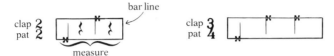

These are the conducting patterns for duple and triple meter. The photographs show the patterns when the conductor faces you.

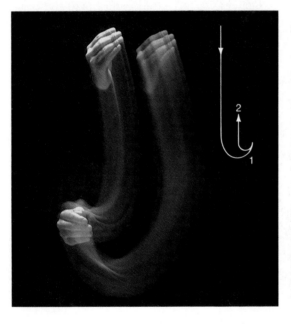

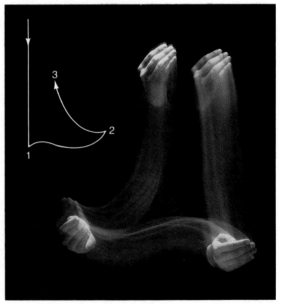

- Listen to the excerpt from Lully's "Marche." It has A and B sections. Tell which conducting pattern to use for each section. Describe the contrast in tempo between the two sections.

  "Marche" (excerpt) by Jean Baptiste Lully

- Listen to the entire "Marche" and conduct showing duple and triple meter.

  "Marche" by Jean Baptiste Lully

18

JEAN BAPTISTE LULLY

Jean Baptiste Lully (1632–1697) became King Louis XIV's most important and influential composer, producing operas and ballets to entertain the French court. For fifteen years Lully controlled much of the music performed in Paris. He was so popular that he was able to persuade King Louis XIV to force other composers to move away from Paris. Thus Lully managed to eliminate most of his competition. He earned enormous sums of money, but no amount ever seemed enough.

An unusual accident caused Lully's death. Instead of using a baton, conductors in those days often kept the steady beat by tapping a large stick on the floor. While conducting this way, Lully struck his own foot. An infection developed, which resulted in his death a month later.

During his career Lully wrote a great deal of dance music. His interest in orchestral tone color can be seen in the wide range of instruments he used in his works.

Jean Baptiste Lully

Analyzing a Baroque Composition

- Listen to Lully's "Marche" again and follow the map by pointing to each measure when the music is provided. When no music is shown, point to the pictures that represent the meter, tone color, dynamics, and form. At call number 4, **ritardando** (ri-tär-dän' dō) means a gradual slowing down of the tempo. At call number 9, the **coda** is the concluding section.

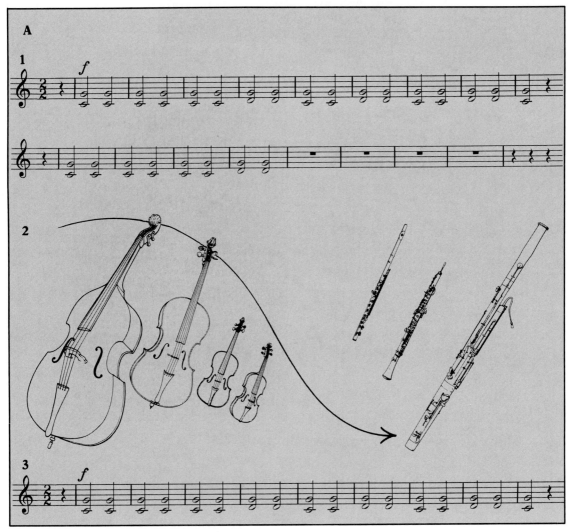

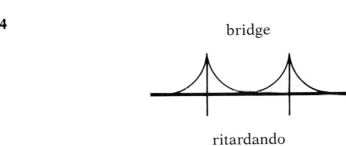

bridge

ritardando

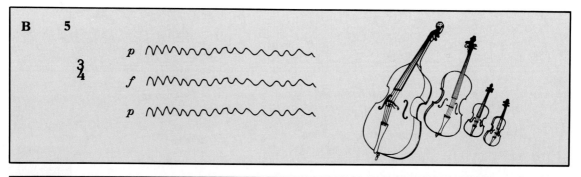

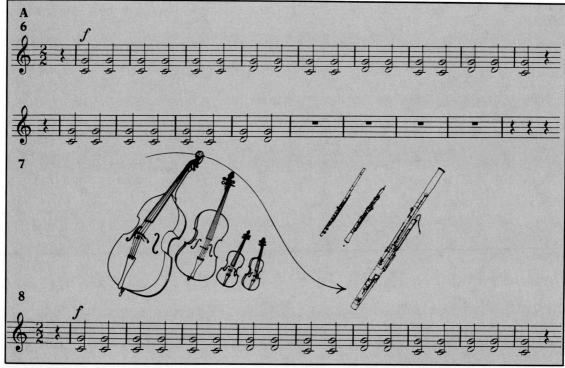

Repetition after a contrasting section creates an ABA, or ternary, form. **Ternary** means having three parts.

• Describe the contrasts between the A and B sections of Lully's "Marche." Identify contrasts in meter, tempo, and tone color.

• Play the A section and the coda of the "Marche" on recorder or keyboard.

The Baroque Period (1600–1750)

Royalty, wealthy families, and large churches hired composers of the baroque period to provide music for special occasions or for entertainment. Operas, ballets, and instrumental compositions were written for the world at large. Large religious choral works— Masses and cantatas—were composed for use in churches. For contrasts in tone color composers used a wide variety of instruments such as the organ, violin, flute, oboe, trumpet, and harpsichord.

Most baroque music has steady, rhythmic patterns. Each section of a larger composition conveys a single mood or emotion. Improvements in instruments made more complex music possible. Two of the most famous composers of all time, Johann Sebastian Bach (yō′ hän se-bäs′ tē-än bäKH′) and George Frederick Handel (hän′ del) lived during this period and produced some of the finest examples of baroque music.

Staircase at the Residenz (with frescos by Tiepolo), Würzburg

During the baroque period, elaborate styles of architecture, art, and clothing were popular. The exterior scene is of a palace in Vienna, Austria. The interior scene is in Würzburg, West Germany. The musicians in the painting are gathered for a formal portrait.

The Concert, Antonio Domenico Gabbiani

The Belvedere, Vienna

Characteristics of Baroque Music

Steady rhythms

Single mood in each section of a musical composition

Wide variety of instruments used for contrasts in tone
   color and dynamics

23

A Romantic Composition

"Farandole" (fä-rän-dôl') is the final selection in the second *L'Arlésienne* (lär-lā-zē-en') Suite by the French romantic composer Georges Bizet (zhorzh' bē-zā'). A **suite** consists of several individual forms linked together. Bizet wrote the suite as background music for a play called *L'Arlésienne,* or "The Woman of Arles." You may recognize the first of the two themes as the Christmas carol "The March of the Three Kings."

- Listen to "Farandole." Each time you hear a number decide whether you are hearing Theme A or Theme B.

 "Farandole" from *L'Arlésienne* Suite No. 2, by Georges Bizet

GEORGES BIZET

Georges Bizet (1838–1875), great opera composer, was born in Paris into a family of professional musicians. His father and uncle were singing teachers, and his mother was an excellent pianist. Bizet showed great promise as a musician at an early age. He entered the Paris Conservatory at nine. At nineteen he had won several prizes for piano, organ, and composition.

Although Bizet was a brilliant pianist, his main interest was composing, especially opera. *Carmen* is his best-known work. His music is very melodic with simple orchestral accompaniments. His music for the play *L'Arlésienne* was ignored by the public when it was first presented in 1872. It was not appreciated until the play was revived after his death.

Theme A of "Farandole" begins with the D minor chord. Theme B begins with the D major chord.

D major chord D minor chord

To play F# (F sharp) on the keyboard, find the black key to the right of F. The symbol ♮ is called a **natural.** It tells you to play F rather than F#. Changing this middle pitch from F# to F changes the D major chord to a D minor chord.

- Play the D minor and D major chords one after the other on keyboard, bells, or guitar to hear the difference between minor and major.

Bizet uses changes between major and minor, and changes in dynamics, to create the romantic style in "Farandole."

- Listen to "Farandole" again. In each section identify the use of major or minor, and changes in dynamics.

Arles, a city in southern France, was founded almost twenty-five hundred years ago. Many of its ancient buildings have been preserved.

The Romantic Period (1830–1900)

Much of the music in movies and on television can be traced back to the kind of music written in the nineteenth-century romantic period. Romantic artists and musicians tried to express their feelings, their outlook, and their hopes and dreams openly. Composers wrote instrumental works that told a story without words. Music became more descriptive, with changes in moods occurring within sections. Long, complex melodies were used to express these moods or emotions. As orchestras became larger and improved instruments were added, tone color became more important than it had been in earlier periods.

Left, the Opéra, Paris, built 1861–75

   Music of the romantic period is very popular today. Many famous romantic works have been used as background music for extremely successful motion pictures. Some of the best known composers of this period were Ludwig van Beethoven (bā′ tō-ven), Franz Schubert (shoo′ bert), Robert Schumann (shoo′ män), Hector Berlioz (ber′ lē-ōz), Frédéric Chopin (shō′ pan), Richard Wagner (väg′ ner), Giuseppe Verdi (ver′ dē), Johannes Brahms (bräms′), Peter Ilyich Tchaikovsky (chī-käv′ skē), and Nicolai Rimsky-Korsakov (rim′ skē kor′ sä-kôv).

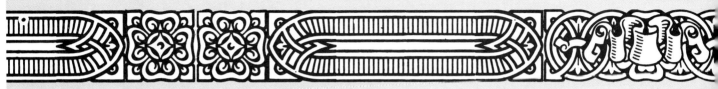

Florentine Story-teller, Vincenzo Cabianca, MUSEO DELL'ARTE MODERNA, Florence

The Ball, James Tissot, MUSÉE D'ORSAY, Paris

Characteristics of Romantic Music

Changes of mood within
sections of a composition
Direct expression of emotions
Long, often complex melodies
Use of large orchestra

Artists of the romantic
period often depicted
scenes of earlier times.
Top, an imaginary scene of
medieval Italy.
Right, women's fashions in
the nineteenth century
often were quite elaborate.

27

A Song in Major and Minor

"Our World" is a twentieth-century song that has sections in both major and minor.

- Listen to the repeated and contrasting sections. You will hear the A section repeat before you hear the B section. Which section is in major and which is in minor?
- Sing the song. Be sure to emphasize the contrasting sections.

Our World

Words by Jane Foster Knox
Music by Lana Walter

Words by Jane Foster Knox
Music by Lana Walter
Copyright © 1985 by Jenson Publications
International Copyright Secured. All Rights Reserved.

ROCK AND ROLL

The term **rock and roll** was invented to describe a new kind of music that captured the energetic spirit of the 1950s. Rock and roll borrowed elements from various styles of music. For example, it took blues scales and blues progressions from rhythm and blues. It took vocal styles from rockabilly, a style of country western music. Its rhythms came from rhythm and blues, rockabilly, and many other styles. The combination of these elements created a unique beat that shook the nation and eventually the world.

Chuck Berry was an early rock and roll innovator. His guitar playing came from the rhythm and blues style. He brought the lead guitar to the forefront of the band, and is remembered as the first great showman of rock and roll. His energetic performances often included his trademark "duck walk" step. Other early rock and rollers were Elvis Presley and Buddy Holly. They became famous stars with their captivating singing, which was influenced by rhythm and blues as well as rockabilly.

Soon after rock and roll became popular in America, its influence spread abroad. In the early 1960s, rock and roll became very popular in Britain. It influenced British groups such as The Rolling Stones and Cream, which featured the guitar playing of Eric Clapton. Another British group influenced by rock and roll was The Beatles, whose impact on popular music has lasted for decades. In the mid-1960s these groups began the "British Rock Invasion," which captured the American rock and roll stage. During the 1970s other English super-groups such as Led Zepplin and The Who added new sounds to rock music.

Left to right:
The Beatles,
Elvis Presley,
Melissa Etheridge,
Sting.

America in the late 1960s was an important place and time for rock and roll. Jimi Hendrix amazed audiences with his electrifying guitar playing. Janis Joplin captivated audiences with her powerful and expressive voice. The group The Doors combined the musical elements of jazz with spoken poetry to create their own unique style. The Grateful Dead began experimenting with long, intricate improvisations at live concerts. These concerts started their reputation as a great live band. All of these artists created innovative music that captured the spirit of their era.

In the early 1990s a new kind of rock music developed called "alternative rock." This music contained elements such as rough and distorted guitars, heavy drum sounds, and emotional singing. It is exemplified by groups such as Pearl Jam and Nirvana. Like the rock groups that preceded them, they added new expressive elements to the music and created their own personal styles.

Rock music is also a reflection of the times. As our culture has changed over the last few decades, rock has also changed and evolved. These changes are easy to hear by contrasting a classic 1950s Chuck Berry song like "Johnny B. Goode" against a 1990s alternative rock song like Pearl Jam's "Even Flow." These and many other artists were honored in the summer of 1995 with the opening of the Rock and Roll Hall of Fame in Cleveland, Ohio. Through its vast collection of memorabilia, the Rock and Roll Hall of Fame pays tribute to the great innovators who have made this music an important part of American culture.

31

Elton John

The pop star Elton John has combined rock and roll with other styles of music to create his own personal style. His well-crafted melodies and unique vocal style have made his ballads and up-tempo rock and roll songs long-lasting favorites.

Elton was born near London, England, in 1947 as Reginald Kenneth Dwight. As a young boy he received recognition for his classical piano playing. Instead of pursuing classical music he joined a rock band in his late teens. He developed a talent for writing catchy pop tunes and eventually changed his name to Elton John.

By the time of his American debut in 1970, he had gone from the shy Reginald to the outrageous Elton John. He is known for popular ballads such as "Daniel" and "Candle in the Wind" (about Marilyn Monroe) as well as rock classics like "Crocodile Rock," "Honky Cat," and "Benny and the Jets." In the 1990s he wrote much of the music for the award-winning Disney film "The Lion King." "Candle in the Wind, 1997," written for the funeral of Diana, Princess of Wales, became the best-selling single of all time.

• Listen to "Believe," composed by Elton John in 1995. How do the singer's vocal style and rhythmic emphasis help to express the lyrics?

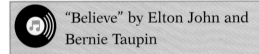

"Believe" by Elton John and Bernie Taupin

• Practice playing these rhythmic patterns. Stress, or emphasize, the accented notes (♩)

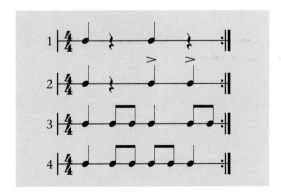

• Play the rhythm accompaniment to "Believe" on page 33 with the recording.

The symbol (|— 4 —|) in the score means you should listen and count
4 measures before beginning to play.

Believe
Rhythm Accompaniment

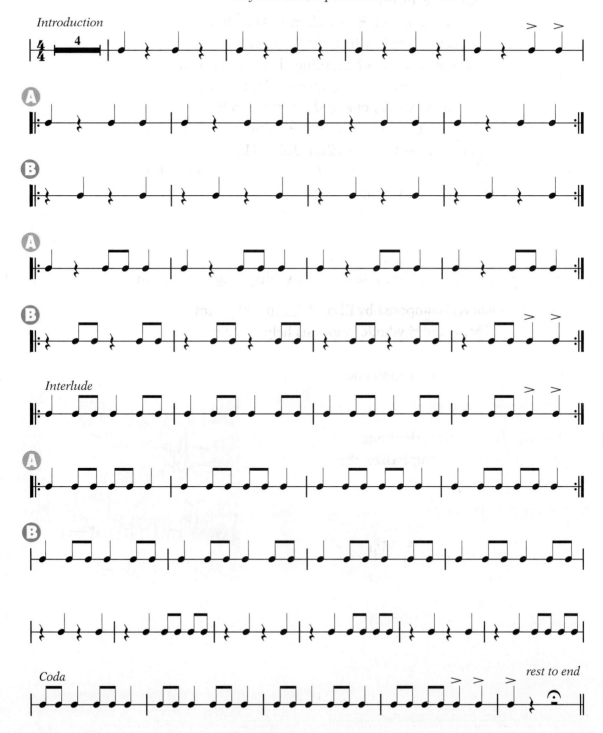

33

- Play this pattern on bells or a keyboard instrument. Find these notes in the melodic accompaniment.

- Play this melodic accompaniment with "Believe."

Believe

Words and music by Elton John
and Bernie Taupin

I believe in love,
it's all we've got.
Love has no boundaries,
costs nothing to touch.
War makes money,
cancer sleeps,
curled up in my father
and that means something to me.
Churches and dictators,
politics and papers,
everything crumbles
sooner or later,
but love.
I believe in love.

I believe in love,
it's all we've got.
Love has no boundaries,
no borders to cross.
Love is simple.
Hate breeds
those who think difference
is the child of disease.
Fathers and sons
make love and guns.
Families together
kill someone
without love.
I believe in love.

Without love
I wouldn't believe
in anything
that lives and breathes.
Without love
I'd have no anger.
I wouldn't believe
in the right to stand here.
Without love
I wouldn't believe.
I couldn't believe in you
and I wouldn't believe in me
without love.
I believe in love.
I believe in love.
I believe in love.

JUST CHECKING

See how much you remember.

1. Listen to the recording of the steady beat and perform these patterns, patting the quarter notes and clapping the eighth notes.

2. Listen to a section of Lully's "Marche" and decide if the meter is duple or triple. Show your answer by conducting. Is the tempo slow, moderate, or fast?

3. Play the "Ode to Joy" on page 16 on keyboard, recorder, or bells as you listen to the "Historical Style Montage." Decide whether the style period of each version of the "Ode to Joy" is Renaissance, baroque, classical, romantic, or twentieth century.

4. Perform this pattern as you listen to the verse of "Run Joe" to experience the syncopated calypso style.

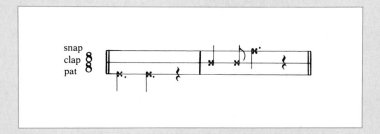

5. Use two movements to show the I and V chords as you listen to the refrain of "Run Joe." Show the chord changes by putting your palms on your desk when you hear the I chord. Put your thumbs up when you hear the V chord.

6. Listen to determine whether the style period of each of these compositions is Renaissance, baroque, classical, romantic, or twentieth century.

7. Listen to a section of Bizet's "Farandole" to determine whether its theme begins in major or minor.

8. Listen to determine whether the style of each example is African, rock and roll, Japanese, calypso, or reggae.

9. Listen and identify the instrument family you hear in these excerpts from Lully's "Marche." Show your answer by pointing to the appropriate picture as each number is called.

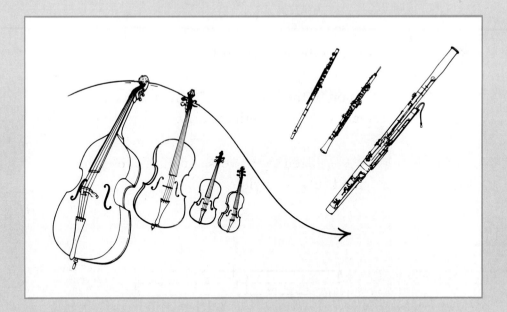

10. Listen to a section of *African Sanctus* and decide if the music sounds more African or more Western.

11. Listen to a section of *Hiryu Sandan Gaeshi* and determine whether you are hearing a crescendo or decrescendo.

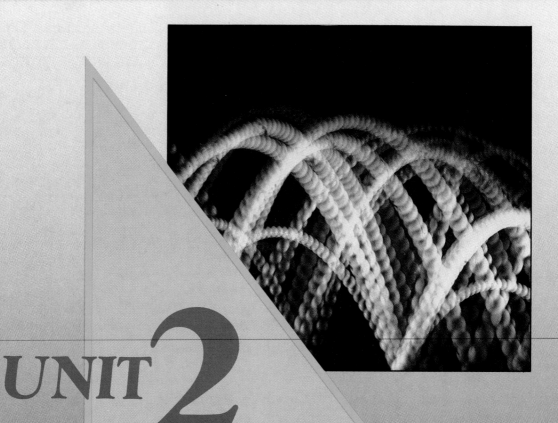

UNIT 2

RHYTHM
PLAYS A ROLE

DUPLE, TRIPLE, AND QUADRUPLE METER

Beats can be grouped in sets. The first beat of each group is emphasized.

- Perform this rhythm in duple meter as you listen to the recording.

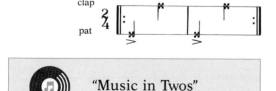

"Music in Twos"

- Listen again, perform the rhythm pattern in duple meter, and play this name game. Each of you, in turn, will say your first name on the accented beat of each measure until everyone has had a turn.

- Perform this rhythm pattern in triple meter as you listen to the recording.

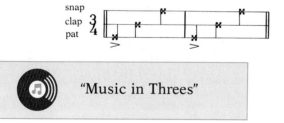

"Music in Threes"

- Listen again, perform the rhythm pattern, and play the name game in triple meter.

- Perform this rhythm pattern in **quadruple meter** as you listen to the recording.

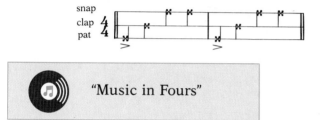

"Music in Fours"

- Listen again, performing the rhythm pattern. Play a variation of the name game in which each of you says your first name on the accented first beat and your last name on the third beat.

- Show duple, triple, and quadruple meter by bouncing a tennis ball on the first beat of each measure. "Change" means to change hands.

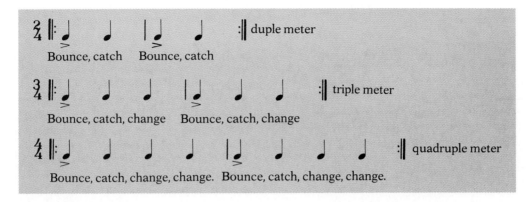

- Show duple, triple, and quadruple by bouncing the ball and then by conducting as you listen to "Meter Identification Montage."

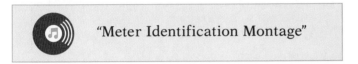

"Meter Identification Montage"

This diagram shows the conducting pattern for quadruple meter. The photograph shows how the pattern looks when the conductor faces you.

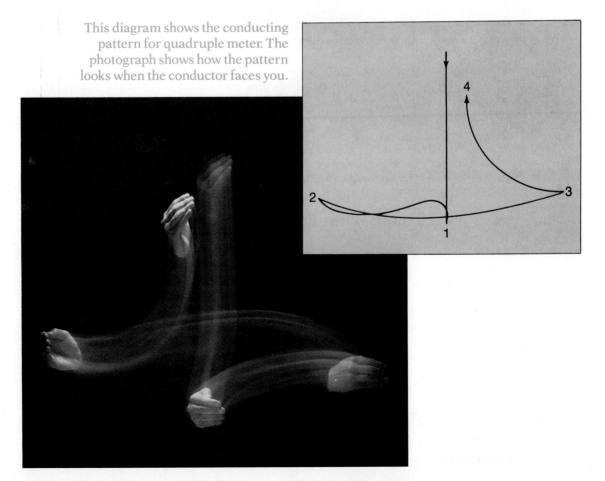

- Listen to "That's What Friends Are For." Decide when the meter changes.
- Sing the song.

That's What Friends Are For

Words and music by Carole Bayer Sager
and Burt Bacharach

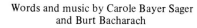

And   I   nev - er thought I'd   feel __ this   way __

__   {1. and as far   as I'm __ con - cerned __ I'm glad   I   got __ the chance __ to   say __
     {2. well you came and o -   pened me __ and now there's so __ much more __ I   see __

A STAGE STYLE

The musical *Pippin* is set in medieval times. However, because it is largely about young people growing up and learning to face the world around them, it has considerable contemporary appeal. Pippin's father, a character based on Charlemagne, wants his son to become a great warrior. Pippin, on the other hand, dreams of magic shows and miracles. Although Pippin never becomes the great warrior his father desired, he does learn to cope with the realities of being heir to the throne.

* Listen to "Love Song," which contains many changes of meter.

 "Love Song" from the musical *Pippin*, by Stephen Schwartz

A scene from the musical *Pippin*.

* Listen to "Mix 'Em Up" and raise your hand when you hear a change from one meter to another.

 "Mix 'Em Up"

- Listen again and show when the composition is in duple, triple, or quadruple meter by conducting the appropriate pattern.

CHALLENGE As you listen to "Mix 'Em Up":

Walk forward and conduct in two when you hear duple meter. Stop and conduct in three when you hear triple meter. Stop and clap four beats in a square formation when you hear quadruple meter.

In "Love Song" Stephen Schwartz used meters of three, four, and six beats. Practice conducting the pattern for six beats in a measure.

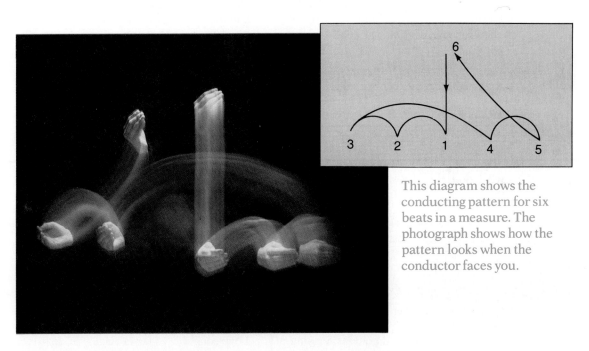

This diagram shows the conducting pattern for six beats in a measure. The photograph shows how the pattern looks when the conductor faces you.

- Look at the first four measures of "Love Song" on page 46 and decide which conducting pattern should be used in each measure.

- Practice conducting the first four measures as you listen to "Love Song."

- Sing "Love Song" (pages 46–47). Play the descant (part tinted in yellow) on recorder, bells, or keyboard.

Love Song

Words and music
by Stephen Schwartz

Rec.

Sit-ting on the floor and talk-ing 'til dawn. Can-dles and con-fi-
Pri-vate lit-tle jokes and sil-ly pet names. Lav-en-der soap and
how can you de-fine a look or a touch? How can you weigh a

- den - ces. Trad-ing old be-liefs and hum-ming old songs and
lo - tions. All of the cli-chés and all of the games and
feel - ing? Ta-ken by them-selves, now they don't mean much. To -

low-er-ing old de-fen-ces. Sing-ing a
all of the strange e-mo-tions. Sing-ing a
-geth-er they send you reel-ing in to a
Love song, la la la__ la la

3rd time cut to Coda ✛

la la la__ la la Love song, la la__ la la la._____

46

IRREGULAR METER

Much of the music you have sung and played moves in either duple, triple, or quadruple meter throughout an entire composition. Sometimes composers use changing meter in a repeating pattern to produce **irregular meter.**

This painting by the American artist Romare Bearden illustrates the spirit of jazz.

One Night Stand, Romare Bearden, CORDIER & ECKSTROM GALLERY, NY

A Little Jazz

- As you listen to the *Take Five* pattern, perform this rhythm pattern, which is a combination of triple and duple meter.

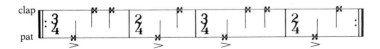

🎵 *Take Five* pattern

This same pattern can be written with five beats in each measure with accents on the first and fourth beats.

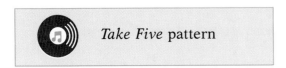

- Listen again. Show this irregular meter by patting your knees on beats 1 and 4 and clapping your hands on beats 2, 3, and 5.
- Continue patting and clapping as you play this variation on the name game. Say your first name on the first beat of your measure and your last name on the fourth beat of your measure.

Traveling in Style

- Perform the pattern in $\frac{5}{4}$ as you recite "Goin' Trav'lin'." Pat the accented beats and make a palms-up motion on each quarter rest.

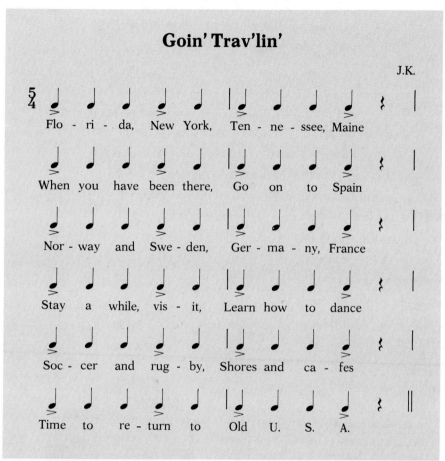

Goin' Trav'lin'

J.K.

Flo - ri - da, New York, Ten - ne - ssee, Maine

When you have been there, Go on to Spain

Nor - way and Swe - den, Ger - ma - ny, France

Stay a while, vis - it, Learn how to dance

Soc - cer and rug - by, Shores and ca - fes

Time to re - turn to Old U. S. A.

- Perform this pattern as you listen to *Take Five*. The composer, saxophonist Paul Desmond, was a member of the Dave Brubeck Quartet.

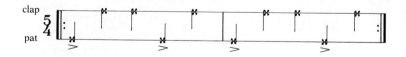

Take Five, by Paul Desmond, performed by the Dave Brubeck Quartet

Changing Meter and a Change in Style

Changing meter and irregular meter are not unique to jazz. About one hundred years before Paul Desmond wrote *Take Five*, a Russian composer was using these same techniques.

The music of Modest Mussorgsky (mo-dest' mōō-sorg' skē) (1839–1881) reflects his great love for his Russian homeland. He often borrowed folk melodies to use as themes for his works. Sometimes he composed original melodies that sounded like Russian folk tunes.

One of his most famous compositions is *Pictures at an Exhibition*, which he composed in memory of an artist friend, Victor Hartmann. Following Hartmann's death, a number of his paintings were exhibited in a gallery. Mussorgsky decided to compose a collection of musical "pictures" inspired by the paintings. Descriptive music of this type is called **program music**.

Mussorgsky named each section after the painting it represented, for example, "The Gnome," "The Old Castle," and "The Great Gate of Kiev." He composed a "Promenade" theme to introduce the work and to lead the listener from "picture" to "picture" as if strolling through an art gallery. This famous "Promenade" theme makes use of changing and irregular meters.

Although Mussorgsky composed *Pictures at an Exhibition* for piano alone, the French composer Maurice Ravel later arranged the work for full orchestra. It is this orchestral version with its beautiful tone colors that most people hear today.

- Listen to "Promenade" and follow the score on page 51 by pointing to the meter signature changes in each measure.

"Promenade" from *Pictures at an Exhibition,*
by Modest Mussorgsky

- Listen again and try to determine which instruments are used to
  create the tone color and dynamics of each section.

Pictures at an Exhibition
Promenade

Modest Mussorgsky

A JAZZ STYLE

Unusual meters, rhythms, harmonies, forms, and tone colors have been used in jazz since 1950. You listened to *Take Five*, a composition in $\frac{5}{4}$ meter.

    Unsquare Dance, composed by Brubeck, is in $\frac{7}{4}$ meter. The composer writes that this unusual meter makes *Unsquare Dance* "a challenge to the foot-tappers, finger-snappers, and hand-clappers. Deceitfully simple, it refuses to be squared."

These photographs show famous jazz musicians. Right, the Dave Brubeck Quartet; below, Marcus Roberts; below right, Lionel Hampton (left) and Stan Getz (right).

Above, Dizzy Gillespie;
left, Thelonius Monk

Meter in Sevens

- Perform this rhythm pattern, which is a combination of duple and triple meter. Step the accented beat.

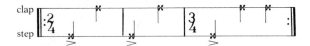

This same pattern can be written with seven beats in each measure, with the first, third, and fifth beat accented.

- Step the accented beats and make a palms-up motion on each quarter rest as you listen to *Unsquare Dance*.

- Listen to *Unsquare Dance* again and perform this **ostinato** (äs-tin-ä′ tō), or repeated pattern, on bells, recorder, or keyboard as an accompaniment.

 Unsquare Dance, by Dave Brubeck

"Samiotissa" means
"girl from Samos."
Samos is a Greek island
in the Aegean
(e-jē′ ən) Sea.

54

Another Meter in Sevens

The Greek song "Samiotissa" (Girl from Samos) is in $\frac{7}{8}$ meter. This meter is similar to the meter of *Unsquare Dance*. It has seven beats to a measure. However, in "Samiotissa" different beats are accented. This shift of accent creates a completely different rhythm.

- Listen to "Samiotissa" and tap the steady beat.
- Sing "Samiotissa."

Samiotissa

English version by Stella Phredopoulos
Music by D.A. Vergoni

Sa - mio - tis - sa, Sa - mio - tis - sa, You will re-turn to Sa - mos. Sa -

- mio - tis - sa, Sa - mio - tis - sa, Is - land of beau-ty and de - light.

You will come home a-gain to me, Sa-mio-tis-sa, There's mu - sic in the sum-mer night.

You will come home a-gain to me, Sa-mio-tis-sa, There's mu-sic in the sum-mer night.

JUST CHECKING

See how much you remember.

1. Listen to the recording and decide if the meter is duple, triple, or quadruple. Show your answers by conducting.

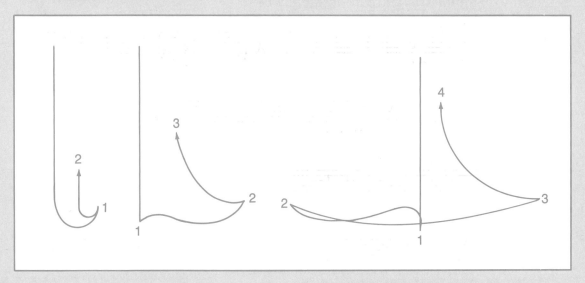

2. Listen to this musical selection, which is an example of changing meters. Identify when the meter changes by conducting the appropriate pattern. The selection begins in duple meter.

3. Perform this pattern in $\frac{5}{4}$ as you listen to "Goin' Trav'lin' " to review irregular meter.

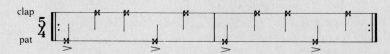

4. Perform this irregular meter pattern as you listen to *Unsquare Dance*.

5. Listen to *Take Five*. Perform a rhythm pattern that shows the meter.

6. Play part of the descant accompaniment to "Love Song" below to review changing meter. The recording has an introduction.

7. Listen to "Love Song" and show the changes of meter by conducting the first four measures as you listen. The recording has an introduction.

8. Clap this pattern as you listen to "Samiotissa" to review irregular meter.

9. Listen to the "Promenade" from *Pictures at an Exhibition* and show the changes of meter by clapping or patting on the first beat of each measure.

Guigass #4, Victor Vasarely,
VASARELY CENTER, NY

UNIT 3

RHYTHM SETS THE BEAT

Peacock's Tail, Arman, MARISA DEL RE GALLERY, NY

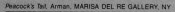

Peacock's Tail, Arman, MARISA DEL RE GALLERY, NY

COMPOUND METER

- Clap the steady beat as you say this chant.

CHEERS

Cheers for soccer, basketball, volleyball,
Track and rugby, too.
We're for swimming, tennis, and racket ball!
Try them all—one's just right for you.

—*Jane Knox*

- As you listen to "Cheers," play the rhythm of the words on sticks or claves.

"Cheers," by Jane Knox

In this chant the **dotted quarter note** (♩.) represents the steady beat. The basic dotted quarter-note beat can be divided into threes. The **dotted quarter rest** (𝄾·) represents one beat of silence and can also be divided into threes.

A meter that uses this steady beat might be represented as $\frac{2}{♩.}$ but is usually represented as $\frac{6}{8}$.

- Use these words to read these rhythms.

- Pat the steady dotted quarter-note beat as you say the poem.

Meter whose basic beat is subdivided into threes and/or sixes is called **compound meter**. Some compound meters are written as $\frac{6}{8}$, $\frac{9}{8}$, or $\frac{12}{8}$.

A SONG IN COMPOUND METER

Oliver! one of the longest running British musicals, is based on Charles Dickens' novel about the adventures of the orphan Oliver Twist. In the song "Consider Yourself," a group of young pickpockets enthusiastically welcomes Oliver.

The dotted quarter note is the basic beat of "Consider Yourself." When dotted quarter notes (♩.) are grouped two to a measure, the meter is represented as $\frac{6}{8}$.

- Listen to "Consider Yourself" as you pat the basic beat. Into how many parts is the basic beat divided?

Is this song in compound meter? Why?

Consider Yourself

from *Oliver!*

Moderate march tempo

Words and Music by Lionel Bart

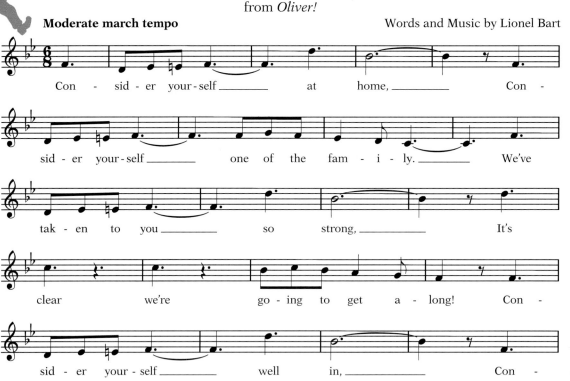

Con - sid - er your-self _____ at home, _____ Con -
sid - er your-self _____ one of the fam - i - ly. _____ We've
tak - en to you _____ so strong, _____ It's
clear we're go - ing to get a - long! Con -
sid - er your-self _____ well in, _____ Con -

sid - er your-self _____ part of the fur - ni - ture. _____ There

is - n't a lot _____ to spare; _____ Who

cares? What — ev - er we've got we share! If it should
No - bod - y

chance to be, we should see some hard - er days, _____ Emp - ty
tries to be lah - di - dah and up - pit - y, _____ There's a

lard - er days, _____ why grouse? _____ Al - ways a
cup o' tea _____ for all. _____ On - ly it's

chance we'll meet some - bod - y to foot the bill, _____ Then the
wise, to be han - dy with a roll - ing pin _____ When the

drinks are on the house! _____ Con -
land - lord comes to call! _____

sid - er your - self _____ our mate, _____ We

don't want to have _____ no fuss, _____ for

af - ter some con - sid - er - a - tion, we can state: Con -

ad lib. ending

sid - er your - self _____ one of us.

63

A Song from *Cats*

Imagine a musical set in a garbage dump. Imagine a musical that has songs based on the poetry of a Nobel Prize winner. Imagine a musical that has no human characters, only cats. Imagine a musical in which Grizabella, an old and tattered alley cat, finds release from her sorrows and rises to heaven on a discarded automobile tire. Imagine a musical in which story, song, and dance are uniquely combined. You have imagined *Cats*, one of the most successful musicals of the past two decades.

In the song "Memory," Grizabella wishes her youth and beauty could return. It is probably the most familiar song from *Cats*.

- As you listen to "Memory," pat the basic beat. Is the song in compound meter? Why?

 "Memory," from the musical *Cats*, by Andrew Lloyd Webber, Trevor Nunn, and T.S. Eliot

Left, Grizabella, who sings "Memory" in the musical *Cats*. Below, the entire cast of *Cats*. Grizabella is at the far right. This musical has been performed around the world in many languages.

Sometimes dotted quarter notes are grouped four to a measure. This meter is represented as **12/8**.

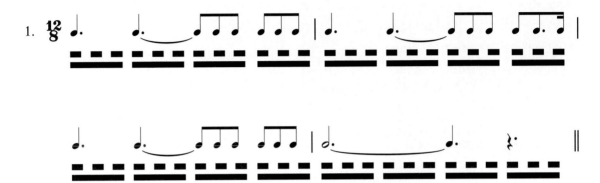

- Listen to "Memory" again. Listen for this rhythm in the voice.

- Now listen to "Memory" once more. Listen for a phrase that begins like this.

Below, a scene from *Cats*

CONDUCTING IN COMPOUND METER

"Joyfully Sing" is a folk song about the joy of singing in harmony.

- Listen to Version 1 of "Joyfully Sing." Conduct in a slow six-beat pattern.

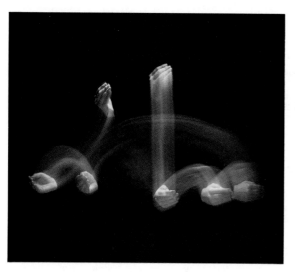

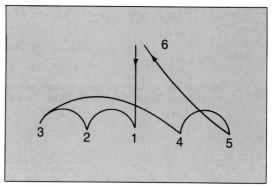

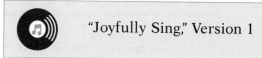

"Joyfully Sing," Version 1

- Listen to Version 2 of "Joyfully Sing," which is performed at a different tempo. Decide which conducting pattern best fits the music.

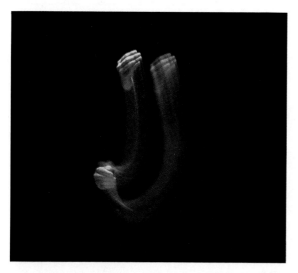

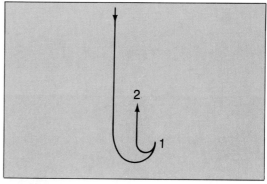

"Joyfully Sing," Version 2

When compound meter is performed at a slow tempo, it is usually conducted in the six-beat pattern. When compound meter is performed at a fast tempo, it is usually conducted in the two-beat pattern.

Joyfully Sing

Traditional German round
Arr. M.J.

Fields surround the village of Kaub, West Germany.

- Listen to "Joyfully Sing" (Version 2) again and identify the changes in meter.

- Perform these rhythm patterns as you listen to "Joyfully Sing" one more time.

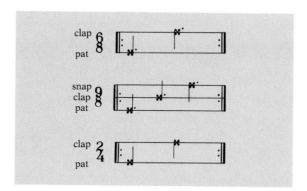

- Sing "Joyfully Sing." Look for the meter changes as you sing.

- Listen to "Compound Meter Montage" and decide which conducting pattern best fits each composition.

 "Compound Meter Montage"

CLAUDE BOLLING

Claude Bolling was born in Cannes, France, in 1930. He was a child piano prodigy and was studying harmony by the age of twelve. Bolling's interest in jazz also began at an early age. By age fifteen, he was making professional appearances throughout France as a jazz pianist. By the time he was in his mid-twenties, he had become one of the most popular jazz musicians in Europe. He has won several recording industry awards.

Bolling has also received international acclaim as an accompanist-composer. He has worked with such performers as Liza Minnelli, Jerry Lewis, Duke Ellington, and Jean-Pierre Rampal. Bolling has also written scores for dozens of French and American films.

Bolling's Suite for Violin and Jazz Piano is a unique combination of jazz and classical styles. "Caprice," a section of this suite, contains both compound and quadruple meter.

- Listen to this section of "Caprice" and raise your hand when you hear changes in meter.

 "Caprice," from Suite for Violin and Jazz Piano, by Claude Bolling

PERFORMING POLYRHYTHMS

Polyrhythm is the simultaneous combination of two or more contrasting rhythmic patterns.

"*Hay Que Trabajar*" (ī kā trä-bä-här´) contains *polyrhythms*. The style of "*Hay Que Trabajar*" is known as *salsa*. This style was born in New York City when Cuban and Puerto Rican music met big band jazz. Salsa is dance music that combines the rhythms and harmonies of Latin America and Africa with those of blues, jazz, and rock.

- Listen to "*Hay Que Trabajar*" to hear polyrhythms and the sound of salsa. In addition to the very active rhythm section, the large band you will hear includes saxophones, trombones, and trumpets, which give it a bright sound. Salsa vocals typically feature a soloist and the *coro*, or chorus, which is usually the band members themselves.

 "*Hay Que Trabajar*" by Angel Santiago

You can accompany the A sections of "*Hay Que Trabajar*" with many different rhythm patterns.

- Practice each of the rhythms on page 71.

- Follow the listening map and perform with the recording.

Tito Puente, whose band is heard in this recording, is a very popular Latin music performer, with more than a hundred albums.

Hay Que Trabajar
Listening Map

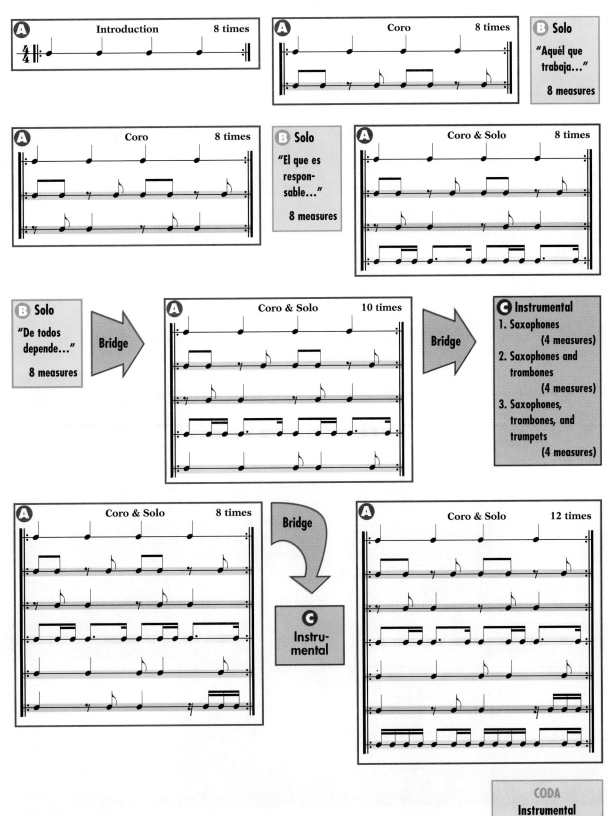

Listening to Polyrhythms

Polyrhythms are found in many different styles of music. Match the picture with the music you are hearing as you listen to "Polyrhythm Montage."

 "Polyrhythm Montage"

Above, a scene from *The Rite of Spring* in the Joffrey Ballet's re-creation of the original 1913 version

Above, a scene from *Cats*. The "garbage" on the stage is the same size it would appear to a real cat.

Above, a steel band from Trinidad. Left, the Ladzekpo Brothers, an African music and dance ensemble

Creating Polyrhythms

You can combine words to create different rhythm patterns.

- Read and perform each of the five rhythms in "Weather."
- Perform "Weather" to create polyrhythms.

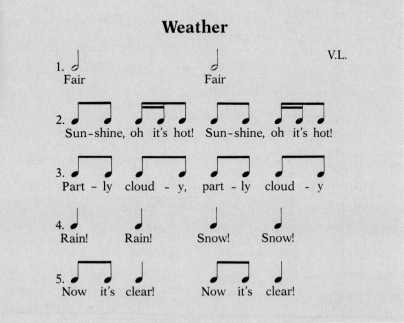

Weather

V.L.

1. Fair   Fair

2. Sun-shine, oh it's hot! Sun-shine, oh it's hot!

3. Part – ly cloud – y, part – ly cloud – y

4. Rain!   Rain!   Snow!   Snow!

5. Now it's clear! Now it's clear!

- Use other words to create compositions with polyrhythms. Here are two examples.

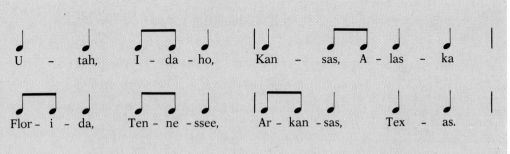

U – tah,   I – da – ho,   Kan – sas,   A – las – ka

Flor – i – da,   Ten – ne – ssee,   Ar – kan – sas,   Tex – as.

- Choose names of states, classmates, or automobiles to create your own rhythm patterns. Perform the compositions you created for your classmates. Learn and perform the polyrhythms created by your classmates. Mix and match rhythms from different compositions to create additional polyrhythms.

JUST CHECKING

See how much you remember. Listen to the recording.

1. Listen to the steady beat and perform these rhythm patterns individually and then together.

2. Listen to the steady beat and perform these rhythm patterns in $\frac{6}{8}$ meter by clapping as you say the words.

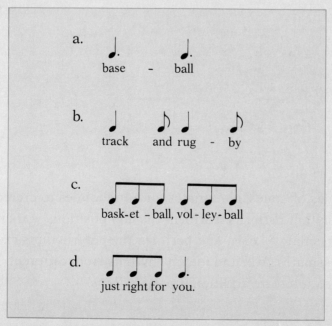

3. Listen to these recordings and decide if the style of each example is salsa, jazz, or Broadway musical.

4. Listen to this excerpt from "Caprice" from Claude Bolling's Suite for Violin and Jazz Piano. Determine if this section is in compound or quadruple meter. Demonstrate your answer by conducting the appropriate pattern.

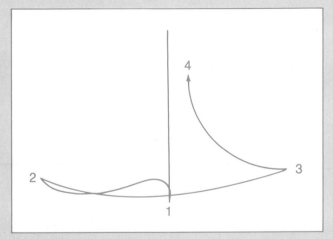 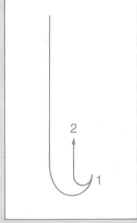

5. Listen to two contrasting selections in compound meter. In which selection does the six-beat conducting pattern fit? In which selection does the two-beat conducting pattern fit? Describe the tempo of each selection.

6. Listen to the following musical selections and decide which ones contain polyrhythms.

7. Listen to the following musical selections and decide if they are examples of simple or compound meter.

UNIT 4
MELODY

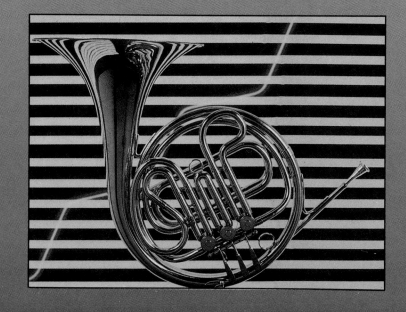

77

MELODY AND HARMONY

A Song in D Major

- Listen to "River" and decide how many singers and which instruments you hear.

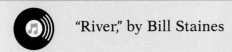

"River," by Bill Staines

Words and music by Bill Staines

Riv - er, take me a - long, In your sun - shine

sing me your song. Ev - er mov - ing and wind - ing and___

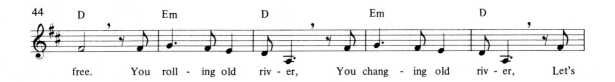

free. You roll - ing old riv - er, You chang - ing old riv - er, Let's

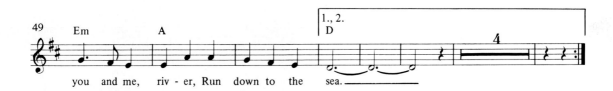

you and me, riv - er, Run down to the sea.___

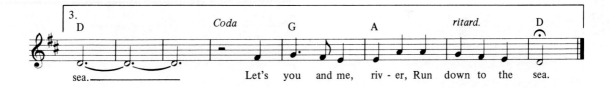

sea.___ Let's you and me, riv - er, Run down to the sea.

2. I've been to the city and back again;
   I've been touched by some things that I've learned,
   Met a lot of good people, and I've called them friends,
   Felt the change when the seasons turned.
   I've heard all the songs that the children sing
   And I've listened to love's melodies;
   I've felt my own music within me rise
   Like the wind in the autumn trees.

   Refrain

3. Someday when the flowers are blooming still,
   Someday when the grass is still green,
   My rolling river will round the bend
   And flow into the open sea.
   So here's to the rainbow that's followed me here,
   And here's to the friends that I know,
   And here's to the song that's within me now;
   I will sing it where'er I go.

   Refrain

The melody of "River" contains the pitches of the **D major scale.**

D	E	F♯	G	A	B	C♯	D	D	C♯	B	A	G	F♯	E	D
1	2	3	4	5	6	7	8	8	7	6	5	4	3	2	1

- Give the letter names of the pitches that begin and end the song.
- Which measures contain the chord symbol D?

The **home tone** D is the focus or **tone center** for "River." When music has a strong tonal center or pitch focus, it is called **tonal music.** It is said to have **tonality.**

When you play or sing two or more pitches together, you are creating **harmony.** Harmonic **consonance** results when the combination of pitches blends.

Right, the North Platte River, Nebraska. Below, the Firth River, Yukon Territory, Canada

Play this melodic accompaniment on keyboard or bells with "River." Since it is based on the D major scale, this folklike harmonic accompaniment is **consonant**.

Melodic Accompaniment to "River"

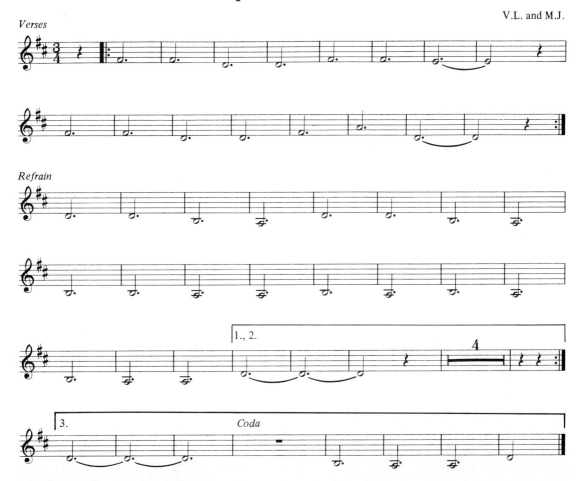

V.L. and M.J.

A Melody in D Major

Johann Pachelbel (yō′ hän päKH′ əl-bel) used pitches from the D major scale in his Canon. You may have heard it in commercials and films. The melodies follow one another and, when combined, create harmony.

● Listen to the Canon to hear how Pachelbel used a major scale as a basis for the melodies.

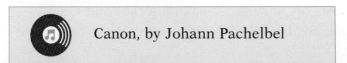

Canon, by Johann Pachelbel

TEXTURE IN MUSIC

Performing a Canon

A **canon** is a musical composition in two or more voice parts.
A musical phrase is started by one voice and repeated exactly by
successive voices, which begin before the first voice has ended. The
combination of voices produces harmony.

"Ahrirang" is a Korean folk song about the Ahrirang Pass in the
mountains near the city of Seoul.

• Learn to sing "Ahrirang" as a canon.

Ahrirang

Korean folk song
English words by M.S.

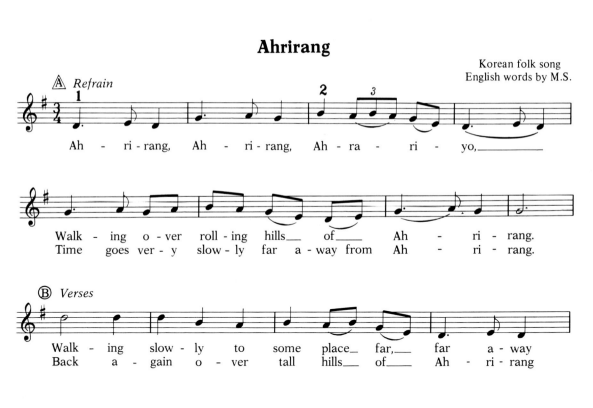

 Try to perform "Ahrirang" as a canon by clapping the rhythm of
the melody without singing it.

Musical Texture

Texture in music refers to the way layers of sound are combined. When you sang "Ahrirang" the first time without accompaniment, you sang in unison. Unison singing creates a texture known as **monophonic**, meaning one sound.

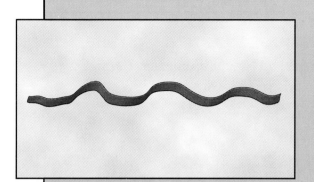

When you sang "Ahrirang" as a canon, you created a texture know as **polyphonic** (po-lē-fo′nik), meaning many voices sounding together.

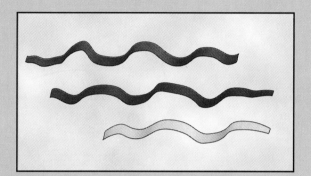

When you sang "River," the melody was in the foreground with accompaniment in the background. This texture is called **homophonic**.

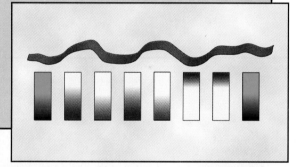

An **oratorio** is a large musical work for solo voices, chorus, and orchestra performed without special costumes or scenery. The "Hallelujah" Chorus from George Frederick Handel's oratorio *Messiah* is one of the most famous choral works in the English language. Handel creates harmonic interest by setting the text in monophonic, polyphonic, and homophonic textures.

The word *hallelujah* is stated and restated by different sections of the chorus almost like a cheering section. Other lines of the text are sung solemnly to emphasize their serious message, and for contrast. The festive quality of the piece is made even more brilliant by the trumpets and timpani. The story is told that at one of the first performances, the English king, George II, was so moved by the music that he stood up to show his approval.

- Identify the texture you hear when a number is called. The four main themes are shown.

 "Hallelujah" Chorus from *Messiah*, by George Frederick Handel

Versailles (vair-sĭ') Cathedral, France, is in the baroque style.

1. Introduction

2. Theme A

Hal - le - lu - jah, Hal - le - lu - jah, Hal - le - lu - jah, Hal - le - lu - jah, Hal -

- le - lu - jah,

3. Theme B

for the Lord God Om - nip - o - tent reign - eth. Hal - le -

- lu - jah, Hal - le - lu - jah, Hal - le - lu - jah, Hal - le - lu - jah,

4. Theme B repeated higher

for the Lord God Om - ni - po - tent reign - eth. Hal - le -

lu - jah! Hal - le - lu - jah! Hal - le - lu - jah! Hal - le - lu - jah!

5. Theme C

The king - dom of this world is be - come

6. Theme D

And He shall reign for ev - er and ev - er

7. "King of Kings and Lord of Lords" is heard in long note values; "forever and ever" is added in shorter note values. Gradually, this moves higher and higher.

8. Theme D repeated

And He shall reign for ev - er and ev - er,

9. "King of Kings and Lord of Lords" is heard in long note values; "forever and ever" is added in shorter note values.

10. The coda ends with four "hallelujahs" followed by a dramatic pause and a final "hallelujah" in very long note values.

George Frederick Handel, Thomas Hudson, By courtesy of the
NATIONAL PORTRAIT GALLERY, London

GEORGE FREDERICK HANDEL

George Frederick Handel (1685–1759) is one of the two most respected and revered musicians of the baroque period. He and Johann Sebastian Bach created musical compositions that brought the baroque period to its peak.

Handel was born in Germany in 1685, and began his formal musical training at the age of eight. In his early twenties he visited Italy and was impressed and influenced by the Italian baroque musical style. After leaving Italy, he went to England and became a favorite of the royal family. He became a British citizen in 1726.

Handel is remembered today for the English oratorios he wrote later in his life. However, he was probably more well known in his day for the fine Italian-style operas he wrote and produced. His most famous oratorio, *Messiah*, was composed in 1741 in less than three weeks and was an immediate success. On April 6, 1759, when completely blind, Handel conducted a performance of *Messiah* in London. Eight days later he died and was buried in Westminster Abbey.

A NEW WAY TO ORGANIZE A MELODY

Composers use different techniques to create and develop melodies.

- Read "Backward Bill." What repeated word in the poem suggests how a composer might work with a melody?

Backward Bill

Backward Bill, Backward Bill,
He lives way up on Backward Hill,
Which is really a hole in the sandy ground
(But that's a hill turned upside down).

Backward Bill's got a backward shack
With a big front porch that's built out back.
You walk through the window and look out the door
And the cellar is up on the very top floor.

Backward Bill he rides like the wind
Don't know where he's going but sees where he's been.
His spurs they go "neigh" and his horse it goes "clang."
And his six-gun goes "gnab," it never goes "bang."

Backward Bill's got a backward pup,
They eat their supper when the sun comes up,
And he's got a wife named Backward Lil,
"She's my own true hate," says Backward Bill.

Backward Bill wears his hat on his toes
And puts on his underwear over his clothes.
And come every payday he pays his boss,
And rides off a-smilin' a-carryin' his hoss.

—*Shel Silverstein*

Day and Night is by the Dutch artist M. C. Escher. Each side of this
woodcut is the reverse of the other.

• Perform "Retrograde in D Major" on keyboard, recorder, or
  bells. The melody in measures 9–16 is a backward version of
  measures 1–8. The last tone in measure 8 becomes the first tone
  in measure 9. When a melodic pattern is reversed so that its
  beginning becomes its end, it is called a *retrograde*.

Retrograde in D major

- Compare the pitches of the melody in measures 1–8 with measures 9–16. Are the phrases of equal length? Are the same pitches used in both sections?

- Perform "Rhythms in Retrograde."

Rhythms in Retrograde

V.L. and M.J.

- Choose percussion instruments and perform "Rhythms in Retrograde."
- Perform "Sounds in Retrograde."

Sounds in Retrograde

V.L.

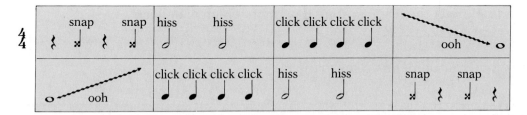

- Perform "Rhythms in Retrograde" and "Sounds in Retrograde" in combination.

 CHALLENGE Create, notate, and perform your own retrograde sound piece.

A NEW KIND OF PITCH ORGANIZATION

Twelve-Tone Music

- Count all the black and white keys to determine the number of different pitches from C to B on the keyboard.

One kind of twentieth-century music is **twelve-tone,** or **serial,** music. In this musical style, the composer organizes all twelve tones in a **row.**

The song "The Web" is based on a twelve-tone row. It also makes use of retrograde. Here is the original tone row upon which "The Web" is based.

- Play this tone row on bells or keyboard.

- Play the retrograde on bells or keyboard.

- Follow the score as you listen to "The Web." Identify the words where the retrograde begins.

90

The Web

Words by Susan Lucas
Music by David Ward-Steinman

- Sing "The Web" or play it on bells or keyboard with the instrumental parts.

In twelve-tone music, all twelve tones are played in the order the composer has chosen until each tone has been used once. The row is deliberately organized so that the melody has no tonal center. When a melody has no tonal center or tonic pitch to which all other tones relate, it is called **atonal.**

- The composer of "The Web" decided to use a tone row to organize the pitches of this song. He also chose to use retrograde. Suggest a reason why he might have done it.
- Create your own atonal composition by:

  1. Choosing an order in which to play each of the twelve tones without repetition of any tone to create an atonal melody
  2. Deciding on a meter and a rhythmic pattern for your melody
  3. Reversing the order of the melody, playing it backward, in retrograde

 CHALLENGE Add an instrumental steady beat, a rhythmic ostinato, or a body percussion accompaniment to your melody. Find a way to notate your composition.

Wassily Kandinsky painted *Improvisation XIV* in 1910, about ten years before Arnold Schoenberg introduced twelve-tone music.

Expressionism in Music

Arnold Schoenberg (shən′ berg) (1874–1951) is known as one of the leaders of *expressionism* in music. The **expressionist** movement became popular in the early twentieth century. It was a movement in which artists—painters, composers, or authors—tried to produce works that expressed their own feelings about an object or event, rather than depicting the object itself in a realistic manner.

In music this type of creative activity required some new method of dealing with notes, chords, tone colors, and rhythms. Schoenberg first introduced twelve-tone, or serial, music around 1920. His new approach to composing often shocked people. He took away things they expected to hear. Melodies did not always sound "pretty." There were no major or minor harmonies.

- Listen to this example of Schoenberg's work.

 Begleitungsmusik zu einer Lichtspielscene (excerpt), Op. 34, by Arnold Schoenberg

Expressionist styles developed in art as well as in music. The painting on the right is a portrait of Arnold Schoenberg, done in 1917. Below, an expressionist painting by the Norwegian artist Edvard Munch.

Girls on the Bridge. Edvard Munch. NATIONAL GALLERY, Oslo

Portrait of Arnold Schoenberg. Egon Schiele

93

JUST CHECKING

See how much you remember. Listen to the recording.

1. Listen to the recording and perform these melodies by singing or playing the bells or keyboard. The recording has a four-measure introduction.

a.

b.

2. The harmony you just performed could best be described as:
   atonal and dissonant   tonal and consonant

3. Perform or listen to "Ahrirang" as a canon.

4. Listen to the last part of "River" and identify the home tone by humming it or playing it on keyboard, recorder, or bells.

94

5. Listen to a portion of the "Hallelujah" Chorus and determine whether the texture is monophonic, polyphonic, or homophonic. Show your answer by pointing to the diagram that shows the texture as each number is called.

monophonic   polyphonic   homophonic

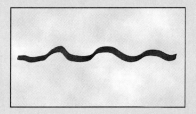 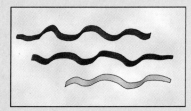 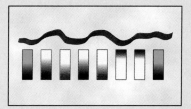

6. Perform the following body percussion to review *retrograde*.

Rhythms in Retrograde

V.L. and M.J.

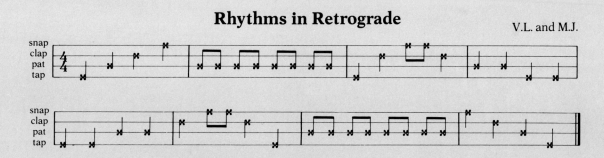

7. Listen to "The Web" to review melodic retrograde. In which measures is the melodic pattern reversed so that its end becomes its beginning?

8. On keyboard or bells play the following pitches that make up the twelve-tone row on which the melody of "The Web" is based.

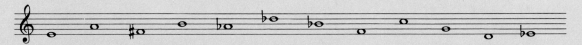

9. Play the retrograde of this tone row on keyboard or bells.

UNIT 5

HARMONY

Pictures Through Music

The music of the gospel song "Climbing Up to Zion" reflects the meaning of the words.

- Follow the different ways the melody is presented as you listen to the song. Decide whether the melody sounds higher or lower each time it repeats.

 "Climbing Up to Zion," by Wintley Phipps

- Sing the melody.

Climbing Up to Zion

Words and music by Wintley Phipps

WINTLEY PHIPPS

Wintley Phipps has traveled an unusual path to his career in religious music. He was born in Trinidad, West Indies, but raised in Montréal, Canada. Although familiar with hymns and church music from his early childhood, he did not come into contact with African American gospel music until his college days in Alabama. It was there that he started composing.

After earning a master's degree in divinity, Reverend Phipps knew that he would be devoting his life to church work. His love of music, however, continued. Today, Reverend Phipps both composes and performs his unique multicultural music.

Gospel Music

Gospel music is a type of religious music that originated in the South. It developed in African American Baptist churches during the 1930s, and quickly became more widely known. By the 1940s and 1950s radio stations all over the country played songs by such gospel singers as Rosetta Tharpe and Mahalia Jackson.

Gospel is different from other forms of African American religious music. The composer is usually known. The songs have instrumental accompaniments with complex harmonies, and the melodies are often quite elaborate. Gospel music, like jazz, has many polyrhythms. Early lyrics were based on the gospels but later became expressions of personal experience as well. In the 1990s, Kirk Franklin had an enormous impact on gospel music.

Gospel music has influenced rhythm and blues and soul music. The foot-stomping frenzy of gospel blended naturally into the intensely expressive soul music of James Brown, Otis Redding, and Ray Charles. A great number of rhythm and blues singers got their start by singing gospel music in church, including Aretha Franklin and Dionne Warwick.

Changing the Key for Effect

"Mi Caballo Blanco" is a popular song by Francisco Flores del Campo (frän-sēs′ kō flô′ res del käm′ pō) that describes the devotion of the South American ranchers for their horses. As in "Climbing Up to Zion," the composer moves the melody into different scales, or **keys**, to create an effect.

- Listen and decide if the song moves to higher or lower keys.

 "Mi Caballo Blanco," by Francisco Flores del Campo

Mi Caballo Blanco

Words and music by
Francisco Flores del Campo

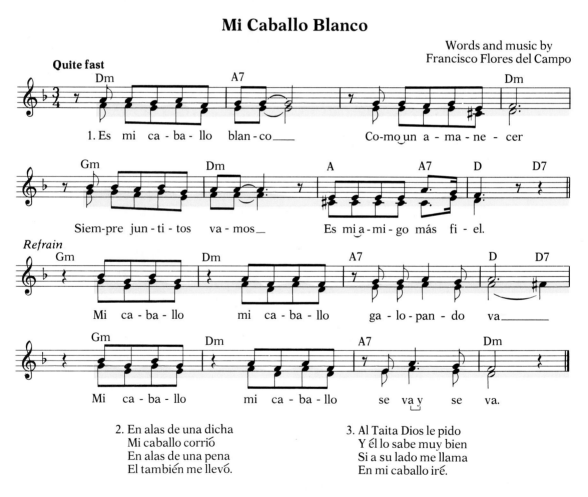

2. En alas de una dicha
   Mi caballo corrió
   En alas de una pena
   El también me llevó.

3. Al Taita Dios le pido
   Y él lo sabe muy bien
   Si a su lado me llama
   En mi caballo iré.

Each section of "Mi Caballo Blanco" is based in a minor key and starts on a different pitch. The change from a section of music based on one scale to a section of music based on another scale is called **modulation.**

100

- Perform these three melodic accompaniments to "Mi Caballo Blanco." They are based on the D minor, E minor, and F minor scales.

Melodic Accompaniment to "Mi Caballo Blanco"

- Sing the song and perform the accompaniments.

Creating Variety in Music

Composers use modulation to create interest and variety in their compositions.

- Follow the chart as you listen to the opening section of Concertino for Flute and Orchestra by Cécile Chaminade (se-sēl′ sha-mē-näd′). The theme is stated several times.

 Concertino for Flute and Orchestra, by Cécile Chaminade

1. Statement of theme (key of D major)

2. Statement of theme (key of A major)

3. Statement of theme (key of B♭ major)

4. Statement of theme (key of D major)

- Listen again and decide how the composer uses dynamics and **register,** the high to low range of a voice or instrument, to create interest and variety.

CÉCILE CHAMINADE

Cécile Chaminade (1857–1944) made her first appearance as a concert pianist at the age of eighteen in her native Paris. She was an illustrious piano soloist and conductor, and traveled widely in France, England, and the United States from 1892 until well into the twentieth century. An active composer as well as performer, Cécile Chaminade is remembered mainly for her elegant piano compositions, many of which she performed in concert.

THE BLUES—AN AMERICAN STYLE

Playing the Twelve-Bar Blues

The **blues** is a style of music that was created by African Americans around the turn of the century. The words to blues songs are usually about loneliness, sadness, or lost love. The blues has its own scale and chord pattern called the **twelve-bar blues.**

- Listen to early blues singer Gertrude "Ma" Rainey sing "Hear Me Talking to You." Identify the instruments that accompany the performance.

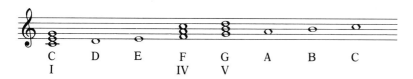

"Hear Me Talking to You," by Gertrude "Ma" Rainey

Blues harmony is based on three chords of the major scale: the tonic (I) chord, the dominant (V) chord, and the chord based on the fourth pitch of the scale called the **subdominant** or **IV chord.** You can play an accompaniment for all traditional blues songs once you learn these three chords.

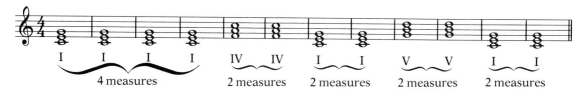

This twelve-bar accompaniment to "Hear Me Talking to You" shows a twelve-bar blues pattern.

- Learn to play the chords in the twelve-bar blues. Then play them with the song.
- Create your own melody and words to go with the twelve-bar blues.

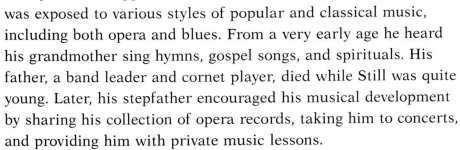

WILLIAM GRANT STILL

William Grant Still (1895–1978) is often referred to as the dean of African American composers. Best known for his music using African American and other American folk songs, he received many awards and honors as the result of his outstanding work.

Still grew up in a middle-class family in Mississippi and Arkansas and was exposed to various styles of popular and classical music, including both opera and blues. From a very early age he heard his grandmother sing hymns, gospel songs, and spirituals. His father, a band leader and cornet player, died while Still was quite young. Later, his stepfather encouraged his musical development by sharing his collection of opera records, taking him to concerts, and providing him with private music lessons.

Still arranged and composed music and directed the band at his college. In 1916 he studied with the French composer Edgar Varèse, further developing his composing skills.

The 1931 premiere of Still's *Afro-American Symphony* by the Rochester Symphony under Howard Hanson was the first performance by a major symphony orchestra of a symphonic work by an African American composer. Later, Still became the first African American to conduct a major American orchestra, the Los Angeles Philharmonic. In 1949 his opera *Troubled Island* was the first composed by an African American to be performed by a major opera company, the New York City Opera. He was also one of the first African American composers to write music for radio, films, and television.

The Blues in a Symphony

Theme A of the first movement of William Grant Still's *Afro-American Symphony* is based on the twelve-bar blues. The overall mood of the music is one of longing, and is related to this verse of Paul Laurence Dunbar that was later applied to the music.

> All my life long twell de night has pas'
> Let de wo'k come es it will,
> So dat I fin' you, my honey, at last,
> Somewaih des ovah de hill.

- Follow the map as you listen to the first movement of *Afro-American Symphony*. The term **pizzicato** (pit-zi-kä′ tō) in boxes 2 and 9 tells the string players to pluck the strings instead of using the bow.

 Afro-American Symphony, First Movement, by William Grant Still

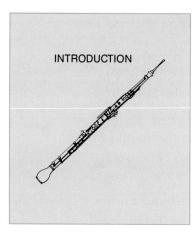

INTRODUCTION

1 THEME A

SOLO

2 THEME A

SOLO

PIZZICATO

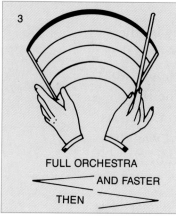

3

FULL ORCHESTRA

AND FASTER

THEN

4 THEME B

SOLO

WITH OTHER STRINGS

5 THEME B

WITH OTHER STRINGS

6 THEME B (IN MINOR)

7 THEME A TRANSFORMED

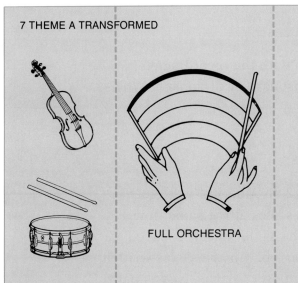

FULL ORCHESTRA

WOODWINDS

8 THEME B (IN MINOR)

9 THEME A

PIZZICATO

WITH WOODWINDS

10 CODA

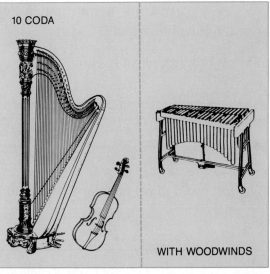

WITH WOODWINDS

107

Consonance and Dissonance

Tones that do not seem to sound as though they go together are
called **dissonant**.

- Play the first part of "America" on bells or keyboard with this
  recording. Does the music sound consonant or dissonant? Why?

"America," Version 1

- Play the first part of "America" again with the recording of
  Version 2. Does the music sound consonant or dissonant? Why?

"America," Version 2

The dissonance in harmony in Version 2 of "America" was created
by using two different tonal centers or scales at the same time.
When music has two tonal centers at the same time, it is called
bitonal. The bitonal harmony in Version 2 of "America" was written
by the twentieth-century American composer Charles Ives as part
of a set of variations on the song "America." The variations were
written for pipe organ.

The right hand plays harmony based on the F major scale.

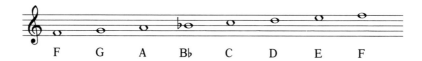

F G A Bb C D E F

The left hand plays harmony based on the Db major scale.

Db Eb F Gb Ab Bb C Db

- Listen to *Variations on "America"* to determine how the composer used different types of harmony, dynamics, and rhythm to create interest and variety.

 Variations on "America," by Charles Ives

1. Introduction: Based on the beginning of the song; phrase "My country, 'tis of thee" most prominent; *ff*

2. "America": Presented in a traditional style; harmony consonant; *pp*

3. First Variation: Melody in bass with continually moving sixteenth notes above melody; *pp*

4. Second Variation: New harmonization of the theme much like the close harmony of a barbershop quartet

5. Interlude: Theme played as a canon; in bitonal harmony

6. Third Variation: Change of rhythm, which produces an effect similar to a calliope; *f*

7. Fourth Variation: Rhythm for theme based in the style of a polonaise, a dance of Poland; now based on a minor scale

8. Interlude: Again uses dissonant bitonal harmony

9. Fifth Variation: Melody played on the keyboard; contrasting line in the pedal part (the lowest part); directions to organists say to play the pedal part as fast as the feet can go

10. Coda: Described by Ives as "in a way a kind of take-off on the Bunker Hill fight."

This work is typical of Ives's strongly original style of music. He takes a recognized melody and treats it in a very creative way.

 CHALLENGE Create your own variations on "America." Change the rhythm, the tempo, or the style.

CHARLES IVES

Charles Ives (1874–1954) grew up in a small town in Connecticut where his father was the local bandmaster. He received his early musical training from his father, who encouraged him to experiment with all sorts of sound combinations to "stretch his ears." Ives liked the harsh dissonance created by playing "America" in one key with the right hand at the keyboard and in another key with the left. Doing this at the same time created bitonality.

As a teenager Ives became a church organist, and one can imagine that he enjoyed shocking the congregation by changing the harmonies of familiar songs like "America."

Because he thought his unconventional music was not going to be popular, Ives went into the insurance business. Eventually he founded a successful insurance agency and became very wealthy. However, music remained his first love, and he continued to compose evenings and weekends.

Ives found ideas for his music in the folk and popular music he knew as a boy: hymns, ragtime, village band concerts, church choir music, patriotic songs, and dances. Perhaps it was these sounds that gave him the idea for his *Variations on "America,"* written for pipe organ.

TELLING A STORY
THROUGH MELODY AND HARMONY

Franz Schubert's "The Erlking" is one of the finest examples of *art song* romanticism. An **art song** is a composition for solo voice and instrumental accompaniment, usually keyboard. The term *art song* is used to distinguish such songs from folk songs and popular songs. In the text to "The Erlking" the German poet Johann Wolfgang von Goethe (gə(r)′ tə) tells of a father riding on horseback through a storm with his child in his arms. The boy, who is very sick with a high fever, remembers the legend that whoever is touched by the king of the elves, the Erlking, must die.

"The Erlking" has four separate characters. Usually all are sung by one person. Schubert uses a wide range of pitches and contrasts in vocal registers to depict each of the four characters. Contrasts of major and minor tonality also help to identify the characters.

- Listen to the beginning of "The Erlking," and choose one word to describe the mood. Which of these musical characteristics do you think help to express that mood?

  major/minor   soft/loud   fast/slow

 "The Erlking," by Franz Schubert

- Listen to "The Erlking" and follow the translation of the German text.

The Erlking

Narrator

1. Who is that riding like the wind through the night?
   It is a father, holding his child.
   He holds him safely in his arms,
   He holds him tightly and keeps him warm.

Father

2. "My son, why do you hide your face so anxiously?"

Son

3. "Father, don't you see the Erlking?
   The Erlking with his crown and his train?"

Father

4. "My son, it is a streak of mist."

Erlking

5. "Ah, small boy, come away with me.
   We'll play the greatest games with you.
   We'll walk by the river, see beautiful flowers.
   My mother has fantastic clothes for you."

Son

6. "My father, my father, don't you hear
   the Erlking whispering promises to me?"

Father

7. "Be quiet, stay quiet, my child;
   the wind is rustling in the dead leaves."

Erlking

8. "Ah, fine boy, are you sure you won't come with me?
My daughters will take good care of you.
There'll be parties every night—singing, dancing.
They'll cradle and dance you, and sing you a lullaby."

Son

9. "My father, my father, and don't you see there
the Erlking's daughters in the shadows?"

Father

10. "My son, my son, I see it clearly;
the old willows look so gray."

Erlking

11. "I must have you with me.
If you won't come, then I will use force!"

Son

12. "My father, my father, now he is taking hold of me!
The Erlking has hurt me!"

Narrator

13. The father shudders, he rides swiftly on,
he holds in his arms the groaning child,
he reaches the courtyard weary and anxious;
in his arms the child was dead.

- Listen again to "The Erlking," and answer these questions.

How do dynamics create the mood?
How does the piano accompaniment set the mood of the story?
Which character sings in major?
Why is the remainder of the song in minor?

 "The Erlking," by Franz Schubert

 CHALLENGE Think of your favorite songs. Which song seems to use dynamics, accompaniment, and major or minor most effectively to set a mood? Compare this to how Schubert set the mood in "The Erlking." Share your song with your classmates.

Schubert Playing the Piano, Gustav Klimt

Schubert Playing the Piano is by the Austrian artist Gustav Klimt (1872–1918). Klimt chose to paint the scene in a romantic style.

114

A view of Vienna in Schubert's time

FRANZ SCHUBERT

Franz Schubert, drawing after a water-color by W.A. Rieder

The music of every important composer has something special to offer. In the case of Franz Schubert (1797–1828), it is outstanding melodies, easily remembered for their beauty and simplicity.

Growing up in Austria as the son of a schoolmaster, Schubert received his musical training as a choirboy in the Royal Chapel. Schubert also began a teaching career, but soon abandoned this to devote himself entirely to music.

Schubert composed over six hundred songs for voice and piano, and once composed eight songs in one day. Besides songs, he composed instrumental music including symphonies, chamber music, and solo piano music. Schubert's world-famous "Unfinished" Symphony (so called because it has only two movements instead of the usual four) contains many beautiful melodies. Occasionally Schubert used melodies from his own songs as themes for his instrumental pieces as in the "Trout" Quintet for Piano and Strings and the String Quartet No. 14 in D Minor, known as the "Death and the Maiden" Quartet. Schubert's music also is important in that his style bridges the classical and romantic periods.

JUST CHECKING

See how much you remember.

1. Perform this melodic pattern on recorder, bells, or keyboard.

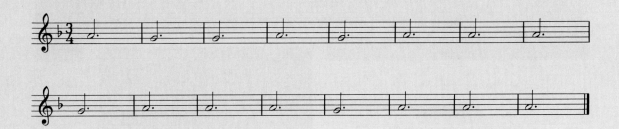

2. Perform this twelve bar blues harmonic progression on bells or
   keyboard.

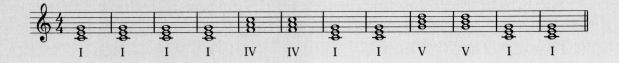

3. Listen to part of "Climbing Up to Zion" to review modulation.
   Decide if the melody sounds higher or lower each time it repeats.

4. Listen to a section of the Concertino for Flute and Orchestra and
   decide how the composer uses dynamics and register to create
   interest and variety.

5. Listen and determine whether the style period for each of these
   examples is romantic, twentieth century, blues, or gospel.

6. Listen and determine whether the harmony in each example
   sounds more consonant or dissonant.

7. Listen to a section of "Mi Caballo Blanco" and raise your hand when you hear the music modulate.

8. Listen to a section of "Mi Caballo Blanco" and decide if the music modulates to a higher or lower key.

9. As you listen to these examples from "The Erlking," decide which character is singing, based on whether you hear major or minor and the register of the melody.

10. Listen to Theme A of the *Afro-American Symphony*. Identify the instrumental tone color by naming the picture that best describes what you are hearing.

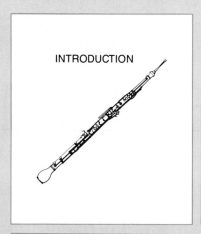

INTRODUCTION

1 THEME A

SOLO

2 THEME A

SOLO

PIZZICATO

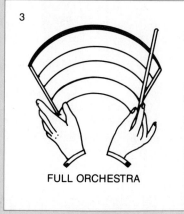

3

FULL ORCHESTRA

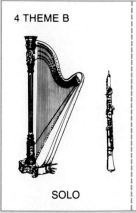

4 THEME B

SOLO

WITH OTHER STRINGS

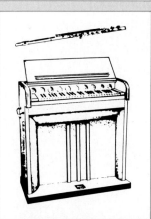

Dolmen in the Snow, Johann Christian Clausen Dahl,
MUSEUM DER BILDENDEN KÜNSTE, Leipzig

UNIT 6

FORM
AND
STYLE

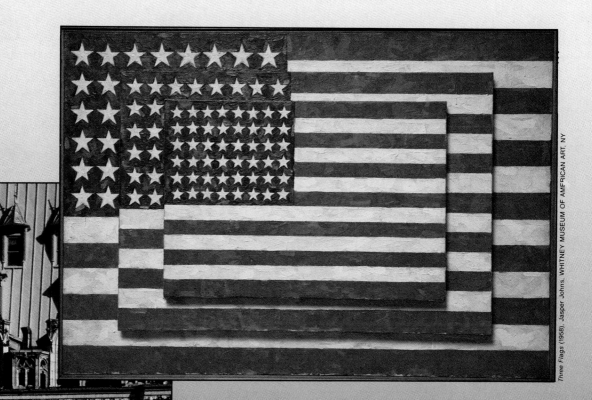

Three Flags (1958), Jasper Johns, WHITNEY MUSEUM OF AMERICAN ART, NY

Birds of Paradise, Arman, MARISA DEL RE GALLERY, NY

BUILDING BLOCKS OF FORM

When you create a story, you put words and thoughts into sentences. When you create music, you put musical thoughts into musical sentences called phrases. A **phrase** expresses a complete musical idea. Phrases of equal length contain the same number of beats. Phrases can be described as the building blocks of form.

As you listen to "Magenta":

- Clap the beat to show the length of the first phrase.
- Snap the beat to show the length of the next phrase.
- Move your hands in an arc to show the lengths of the phrases.

clap   snap

 "Magenta" by Greg Hansen

As you listen to "Magenta" again:

- Step the beat to show the length of the first phrase.
- Stand still and move your hands in an arc to show the length of the next phrase.

 "Patterns" by Greg Hansen

- Listen to "Patterns," and change your movement patterns as you step each phrase.

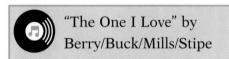 "The One I Love" by Berry/Buck/Mills/Stipe

- Listen to "The One I Love" by R.E.M. How many beats are in each phrase? How many different melodies do you hear?

Play this melodic accompaniment on bells or a keyboard instrument with "The One I Love."

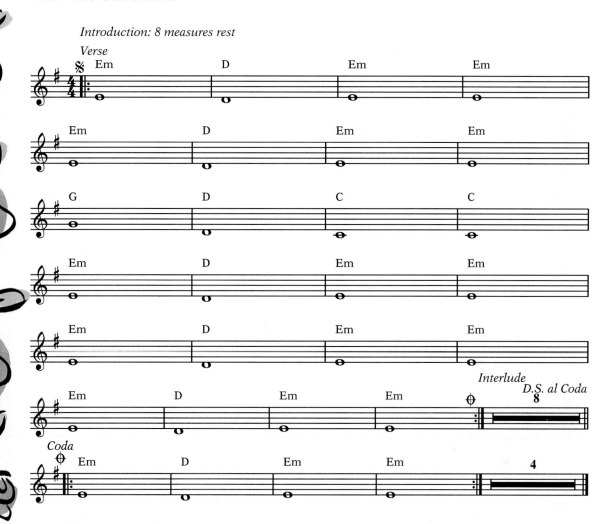

Practice this chord progression on a keyboard.

Then, as you listen again, play the chordal accompaniment shown by the chord symbols on a keyboard instrument.

R.E.M

In the early 1980s a movement called alternative rock began in the world of popular music. Reacting to the glossy, synthesized style of American and British popular music of the time, alternative rock bands returned to the roots of American rock in search for a less contrived sound. R.E.M., a four-man band out of Athens, Georgia, represents one of these alternative bands.

The original band members—Michael Stipe, Peter Buck, Mike Mills, and Bill Berry—formed the band R.E.M. in 1980. They combined elements from American folk, British punk, and rock and roll to create their own unique sound. R.E.M. was one of the first alternative bands to achieve a large national following. They helped pave the way for a number of other alternative rock bands. R.E.M.'s innovative albums incorporate a variety of styles. Examples include "Out of Time," which uses folk instruments such as the mandolin, and "Monster," which has a rougher, more punk-influenced rock and roll sound. R.E.M. is known for having melodies that are well crafted and lyrics that are thought provoking. "The One I Love," released in 1987, was R.E.M.'s first Top-Forty hit single.

PHRASES OF DIFFERENT LENGTHS

Composers can organize their phrases in many ways. Each phrase in "The One I Love" is four measures long. The melodic accompaniment on page 121 follows this four-measure-phrase structure. In "(Life Is a) Celebration," Rick Springfield uses another technique with phrases to create interest and variety.

- As you listen to "(Life Is a) Celebration," decide if the phrases are all the same length.

 "(Life Is a) Celebration" by Rick Springfield

- Listen again and move your hand in an arc on each phrase.

- Sing the song.

"(Life Is a) Celebration"

Words and music by
Rick Springfield

Lord, I'm gon - na cel - e - brate.   Life is a cel - e - bra - tion,

Life is a cel - e - bra - tion,

come on now_ and cel - e - brate, cel - e - brate.

look it's a rev - e - la - tion. So   cel - e - brate now, cel - e - brate life.

Cel - e - brate now, cel - e - brate life.

To Coda ⊕

Cel - e-brate now, cel - e - brate life.   Cel-e-brate now, cel - e - brate life.

Cel - e-brate now, cel - e - brate life.   Cel-e-brate now, cel - e - brate life.

D.S. al Coda ⊕ *Coda*

Cel - e-brate now, cel-e -

Cel-e-brate now, cel-e -

-brate life.   Cel - e - brate, cel - e - brate,   cel - e - brate, cel - e - brate,

-brate life.   Cel - e - brate, cel - e - brate,   cel - e - brate, cel - e - brate,

cel - e - brate, cel - e - brate,   cel - e - brate, cel - e - brate   life!

cel - e - brate, cel - e - brate,   cel - e - brate, cel - e - brate   life!

125

REPETITION: THE BASIS OF FORM

Motives in Architecture

When architects design buildings they often repeat small units or shapes such as squares, rectangles, circles, or triangles to create a much larger form. Identify some of the small units used to create the buildings pictured here.

Below, the chapel at the Air Force Academy in Colorado Springs. Right, the Flatiron Building in New York City. Bottom, Habitat, in Montréal, Canada.

Motives in Music

Composers often use repetitions of short musical ideas to develop the form of a composition. These ideas are called *motives*. **A motive** is a short, easily recognized musical unit that keeps its basic identity through many repetitions.

In "Floe" from *Glassworks* by Philip Glass, different motives are used to create a larger form.

- Perform these motives from "Floe" on keyboard, recorder, bells, or guitar.

Motives from "Floe"

- Listen to "Floe" and identify the order in which you hear each motive.

 "Floe" from *Glassworks*, by Philip Glass

- Listen again and perform each motive, with the recording, on keyboard, recorder, bells, or guitar.

127

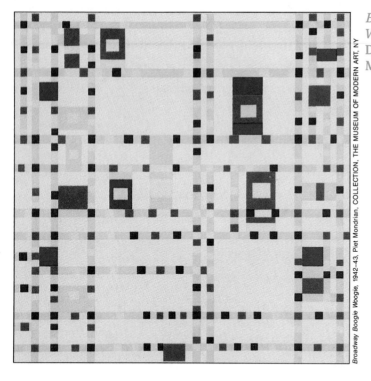

Broadway Boogie Woogie is by the Dutch artist Piet Mondrian.

Motives in Art

The use of motives is found in many art forms. The two works shown on this page both use repetition of small forms to create a much larger form. The first, *Broadway Boogie Woogie*, by Piet Mondrian, was inspired by the artist's viewing of the traffic on Broadway from his studio in a nearby skyscraper. He compared the cars and trucks to the rhythms of boogie-woogie. The second work is a piece of computer art. What shape or form serves as a motive for this work?

Philip Glass and Minimalism

The contemporary composer Philip Glass was born in Baltimore in 1937. Like many composers, he had a traditional musical education. However, he is most noted for his music in the twentieth-century style called **minimalism.**

While studying music in Europe, Glass met the great Indian sitar player Ravi Shankar, who introduced him to Indian classical music. Later, Glass traveled to Morocco and India to study Eastern music first hand. The influence of Eastern music ultimately was reflected in his own music. While he worked to perfect his style back in the United States, Glass took a variety of jobs, including moving furniture, doing carpentry, and driving a cab. About the same time, he met several painters and sculptors who influenced his work. Their method was to emphasize one aspect of visual art (for example, color or texture) to create the greatest possible effect with the least possible means. Glass adapted this method to his music, in combination with characteristics of the Eastern music he had studied.

Minimalist music does not imitate the sound of Eastern music. However, it does contain some of the same techniques, such as repetition of short rhythmic and melodic patterns. This emphasis on repetition is the basis of all minimalist music. In contrast, other Western musical styles emphasize melody or harmony. Young audiences in particular have found Glass's blend of rock realism and Eastern mysticism appealing.

"Floe" is a typical example of the minimalist style. In it, Glass achieves his effects with only a few repeated rhythmic and melodic ideas. By using orchestral instruments—especially the brasses—in unusual ways, Glass creates the tone qualities that are characteristic of minimalist music.

STORY TELLING THROUGH SONG

The Ballad

A **ballad** is a narrative poem or song. The ballad is one of the oldest forms of poetry and one of the oldest kinds of music. Its beginnings are almost impossible to trace, partly because the earliest composers of ballads probably could not read or write. The ballad form apparently was established by 1400. Ballads were passed down by word of mouth from generation to generation. European settlers brought their ballads to the New World, besides composing new ones. Some surviving ballads from the 1500s and 1600s were sung in much the same way as we sing them now.

In the ballad "The Golden Vanity," we learn the story of a captain and his clever cabin boy. Eight different verses, all set to repetitions of the same melody and harmony, describe an adventure of trickery and wit.

"The Golden Vanity" is a folk song ballad set in strophic form. **Strophic form** repeats the same melody or section of music with each new verse or stanza of text.

- Listen to "The Golden Vanity" and follow the story.

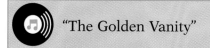 "The Golden Vanity"

- Perform the melodic accompaniment to "The Golden Vanity" on keyboard, recorder, or bells.

The Golden Vanity

English Folk Song

131

3. 〜

The captain was pond'ring the course he would pursue,
When up spoke the cabin boy, the youngest of the crew.
"Pray, sir, what will you give me to rout the foe for you
As they sail upon the Low Lands Low?" *(two times)*

4. 〜

The captain was amazed and a little bit annoyed
To think he must depend on a lowly cabin boy,
But he said he'd give his daughter, his very pride and joy,
If he'd sink them in the Low Lands Low. *(two times)*

5. 〜

The boy spread his arms and into the sea he dived.
He swam and he swam, it's a wonder he survived!
He bored some tiny holes in the other vessel's side
And he sank it in the Low Lands Low. *(two times)*

6. 〜

Then back once again to the Vanity he sped.
He thought as he swam of the pretty girl he'd wed,
For, "You shall have my daughter," the captain'd plainly said,
"And you'll sail upon the Low Lands Low. *(two times)*

7. 〜

And when he reached the ship and was safely at her side,
"Good captain, help me come aboard!" the cabin boy did cry.
The captain, though ignored him, and merely breathed a sigh
As he sailed upon the Low Lands Low. *(two times)*

8. 〜

"Good captain, help me up," cried the cabin boy once more,
"Or else I'll bore your ship and send it to the ocean floor."
The captain then moved quickly and pulled the lad aboard
And they sailed upon the Low Lands Low. *(two times)*

Both England and the United States sailed
ships such as this during the 1700s and 1800s.

132

- After you have become familiar with the rhythm of the song, learn this melodic accompaniment.

The Golden Vanity
Challenge Melodic Accompaniment

An Art Song

The art song was one of the most important forms of the romantic period. These songs usually combine a solo voice with piano accompaniment. Through poetry and music, art songs express a particular mood or idea, often with deep emotion. Like "The Golden Vanity," "*Schwanenlied*" (shvän´ en lēd) is in strophic form. "*Schwanenlied*" was composed by Fanny Mendelssohn Hensel. The text was written by Heinrich Heine (hīn´ riKH hī´nə) (1797–1856), one of the greatest German poets.

- Listen to "*Schwanenlied*," and read the English translation of the German text on page 135. Decide on a word to describe the mood of the text.

 "*Schwanenlied*," by Fanny Mendelssohn Hensel

FANNY MENDELSSOHN HENSEL

Fanny Mendelssohn Hensel

Fanny Mendelssohn Hensel (1805–1847), German composer and pianist, was the oldest of four children in an extremely talented family. Her grandfather was a well-known philosopher, and her brother Felix also became a renowned composer and pianist. Fanny displayed great musical talent at an early age. Felix often remarked that she was a better pianist than he was. He always asked her advice on his musical ideas before writing them down.

Fanny published only five collections of songs and a piano trio during her lifetime. In fact, her early works were published under Felix's name. Queen Victoria's favorite Mendelssohn song, "*Italien*," actually was written by Fanny. Her art songs, such as "*Schwanenlied*," reveal many characteristics of the romantic period, such as direct expression of emotions and long, complex melodies.

Schwanenlied (Swan's Song)

Verse 1

Es fällt ein Stern herunter aus seiner funkelnden Höh,
A star falls down from its sparkling heights.

das ist der Stern der Liebe, den ich dort fallen seh.
That is the star of love that I see falling.

Es fallen von Apfelbaume, der weissen Blätter so viel,
So many white leaves fall from the apple tree

es kommen die neckenden Lüfte, und treiben damit ihr spiel.
The teasing breezes come and playfully use them for their games.

Verse 2

Es singt der Schwan im Weiher, und rudert auf und ab,
The swan sings in the pond and glides back and forth,

und immer leiser singend, taucht er ins Fluthengrab.
And ever so softly singing he dips into the deep watery grave.

Es ist so still und dunkel, verweht ist Blatt und Blüth,
It is so still and dark, leaves and blossoms have disappeared.

der Stern ist knisternd zerstoben, Verklungen das Schwanenlied.
The star's brilliance is gone. The swan's song has died away.

Which of these musical characteristics express the mood of *"Schwanenlied"*?

slow or fast   major or minor   mostly loud or mostly soft

JUST CHECKING

See how much you remember. Listen to the recording.

1. Listen to the steady beat and perform these motives on keyboard, recorder, bells, or guitar.

2. Perform this melodic accompaniment on bells, recorder or keyboard.

3. Perform this melodic accompaniment on keyboard, bells, or recorder with the first 8 measures after the introduction of "The One I Love."

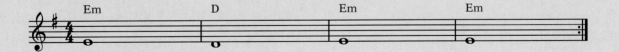

4. Listen to a portion of "The Golden Vanity" and determine if the form is strophic or ternary.

5. Listen to a portion of "(Life Is a) Celebration" and show the regular and irregular phrase structure by moving your hand in an arc.

6. Listen to *Schwanenlied* and decide whether the composition is in major or minor.

7. Perform a body percussion movement to show the equal eight-beat phrase lengths in "The One I Love."

8. Name some musical characteristics that express the mood of "*Schwanenlied.*"

UNIT 7

ELEMENTS
OF FORM

Still Life with Fruit Bowls, Carafe, and Fruit, Paul Cézanne, LOUVRE, Paris

View from Wind River Mountains, Wyoming, Albert Bierstadt, THE MUSEUM OF FINE ARTS, Boston

REPETITION IN MUSIC

Identifying Motives

The second movement of Ludwig van Beethoven's Symphony No. 7 is based on repetition of rhythmic and melodic motives.

- Perform these rhythmic motives by patting the quarter notes, pat-sliding the tied notes, clapping the eighth notes, and snapping the triplets with alternating hands.

Each of the following melodies uses one of the rhythmic motives you have performed.

- Identify the melody that uses rhythmic motive 1, motive 2, and motive 3.

- Listen and match the rhythmic motives 1, 2, or 3 with recorded examples a, b, and c from the second movement of the Seventh Symphony.

 Beethoven Seventh Motive Montage

Which of the melodies in the Beethoven Seventh Motive Montage sounded smooth and connected?

Which of the melodies sounded detached and crisp?

Music that sounds smooth is said to be performed **legato** (le-gä′ tō). Music that sounds detached and crisp is said to be performed **staccato** (stä-kä′ tō). Notes to be played or sung staccato are written this way: ♩ or ♩ .

Symphony orchestras often consist of over a hundred musicians. These two photos show the Boston Symphony Orchestra in performance.

Identifying Motives in a Listening Map

- Listen to the first portion of the second movement of Beethoven's Symphony No. 7. When you hear rhythmic motive 1 (♩ ♪♫ | ♩ ♩), find it on the map.

 Symphony No. 7, Second Movement, by Ludwig van Beethoven

- Examine the map. Find rhythmic motive 2 (𝄽 ♩ | ♩ ♩) and rhythmic motive 3 (♫♫ ♫♫).
- Follow the map as you listen to the second movement of Beethoven's Symphony No. 7.

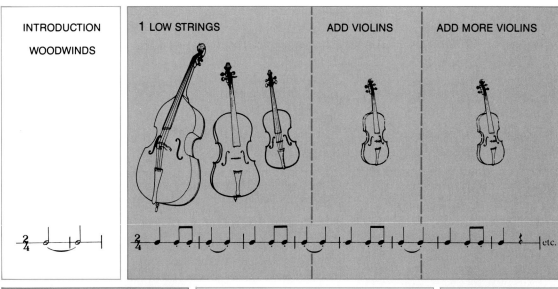

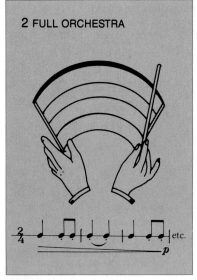

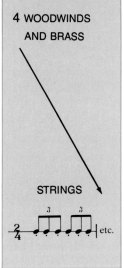

5 STRING BASSES: MELODY (PIZZICATO)

WOODWINDS
AND STRINGS:
ACCOMPANIMENT

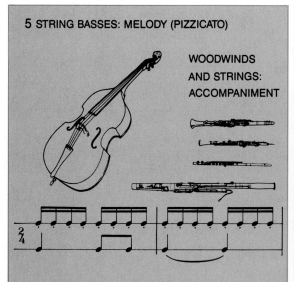

6 POLYPHONY

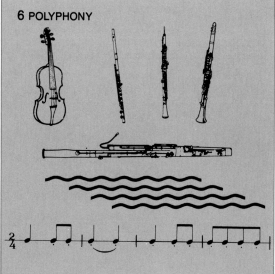

7 FULL ORCHESTRA

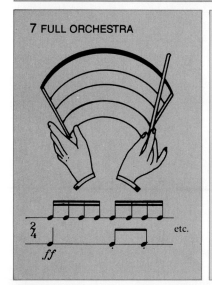

8 WOODWINDS: MELODY

STRINGS: ACCOMPANIMENT

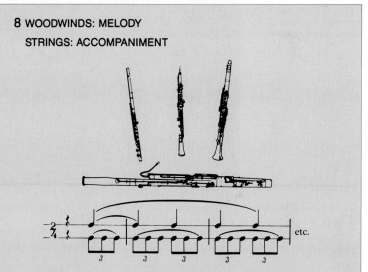

9 CODA

STRINGS (PIZZICATO) AND

WOODWINDS   WITH

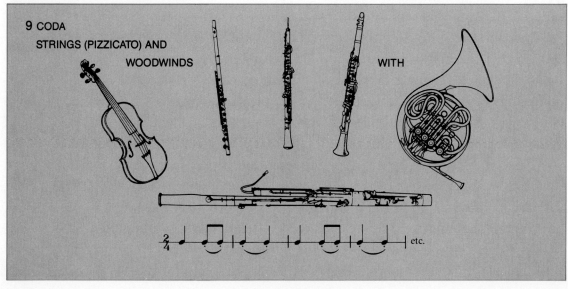

Artists of the classical period often depicted scenes of ancient Greece and Rome.

Countryside of Arcadia, Nicolas Poussin, LOUVRE, Paris

The Classical Period (1750-1830)

The characteristics of music from the classical period are charm, delicacy, and gracefulness. Melodies generally are short and tuneful. Beneath this seeming simplicity there are often deeper feelings; however, these feelings are usually understated. A single section of a classical work can have contrasting moods, and dynamic changes include crescendo and decrescendo. Classical composers wrote operas and concertos, as did the earlier baroque composers. They also established some new musical forms, the symphony and the string quartet.

The orchestra of today developed during this period in musical history. Great composers of the classical period include Haydn (hī′ dən) and Mozart (mōt′ särt). Early works of Beethoven are often considered to be classical in style. However, Beethoven is credited by most musicians with ushering in the next great period in musical history, the romantic period.

Characteristics of Classical Period Music

Changes of mood within sections of a composition
Dynamic changes including crescendo and decrescendo
Short, tuneful melodies
Controlled feelings or emotions
Emphasis on unity and balance

The Pantheon, Paris

Hippocrates Refusing the Presents of Artaxerxes, Anne-Louis Girodet-Trioson, FACULTÉ DE MEDECINE, Paris

Above, architects of the classical period often were influenced by Greek and Roman styles. Left, this painting illustrates a scene from the life of Hippocrates, the ancient Greek "father of medicine."

145

Repetition in Art

Arthur Dove's painting *Clouds and Water* is made up of simple curved shapes that are repeated and contrasted. The waves in the water are repeated in the shapes of the mountains and clouds. Contrast is provided by the different colors of the water, land, and sky. The sails on the three boats provide additional contrasts of color and movement. Each area of the painting is an adaptation, expansion, contraction, alteration, or elaboration of a basic curved shape.

• Compare the different shapes and forms in the painting.

Clouds and Water, Arthur G. Dove. THE METROPOLITAN MUSEUM OF ART, NY

Transforming a Musical Idea

Like the artist who painted *Clouds and Water,* a composer may decide to adapt, expand, contract, alter, or elaborate a musical idea. This transformation of a musical idea is known as **development.**

Because the melody of "America" is well known, you can probably remember how different parts of the song sound. This should enable you to explore some of the techniques composers use to develop a musical idea.

- Sing through one verse of "America." Use the lyrics to help you keep track of each measure while you are singing.

America

Words by Samuel F. Smith
Music by Henry Carey

How many times does the rhythmic pattern ♩ ♩ ♩ | ♩. ♪ ♩ appear in the song?

The rhythmic pattern you just identified is called a **rhythmic motive.**

- Perform the beginning of "America."

- Create your own rhythmic motives by changing the rhythm of one measure.

You have just altered the rhythm of the melody.

- Perform "America" on keyboard, recorder, or bells.
- Perform measure 1 and then measure 11.

My coun-try from ev - 'ry___

You have just created a **melodic motive** from portions of "America."

- Create your own melodic motives by combining other measures of the song.
- Perform measures 7 and 8, then perform measures 9 and 10.

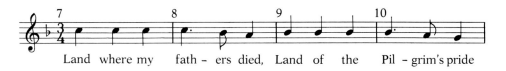

Land where my fath – ers died, Land of the Pil – grim's pride

Do measures 9 and 10 sound higher or lower than measures 7 and 8?

Do they have the same or different rhythm patterns?

Although the diamond shapes in this computer art are turned at different angles, you can still recognize their basic form.

You can use any of these techniques, along with many others, to develop a musical idea:

        Altering rhythms

        Altering melodies

        Creating rhythmic and melodic motives

Organization in the First Movement of a Symphony

The symphony as a musical art form emerged during the classical period. A **symphony** is a long orchestral work organized into four movements. The first movement is almost always in what is called *sonata allegro form*. **Sonata allegro form** consists of three sections much like ABA form.

The A section sometimes begins with a foreshadowing of the musical ideas to come. This is called the *introduction* and is followed by the presentation of two or more musical ideas or themes. These themes are often contrasting in nature. The presentation of the themes is called the *exposition*. The B section is developmental. Here the themes presented in the exposition are adapted, expanded, contracted, altered, and elaborated. The composer uses a variety of techniques to transform the original musical ideas. The last section of sonata allegro form is the *recapitulation* in which the composer restates each of the themes. This section sometimes ends with a summary called the *coda*.

The following diagram depicts sonata allegro form graphically.

A	B	A
Exposition	Development	Recapitulation
(Ideas stated)	(Ideas transformed)	(Ideas restated)
Themes A and B introduced	Themes A and B developed	Themes A and B restated

Twentieth-century composer Sergei Prokofiev (ser-gā′ prō-kof′ yəf) (1891–1953) wrote his first symphony in the style of the classical period. The symphony is referred to as **neoclassical** since it exhibits all the characteristics of a classical symphony but was written almost a century after the close of that musical period.

The first movement of Prokofiev's Symphony No. 1 in D Major, or *Classical Symphony,* is an excellent example of sonata allegro form.

- Follow the listening map of the first movement of Prokofiev's *Classical Symphony,* as you listen to the music.

 Classical Symphony, First Movement, by Sergei Prokofiev

EXPOSITION

1 THEME A

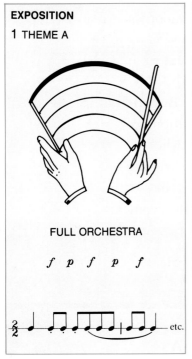

FULL ORCHESTRA

f p f p f

2 TRANSITION

WOODWINDS AND STRINGS

p f p f

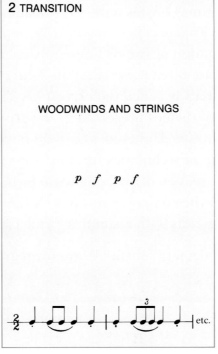

3 INTRODUCTION TO THEME B

WOODWINDS AND STRINGS

4 THEME B

VIOLINS: MELODY
BASSOONS: ACCOMPANIMENT

MOSTLY *pp*

5 CONCLUSION OF EXPOSITION

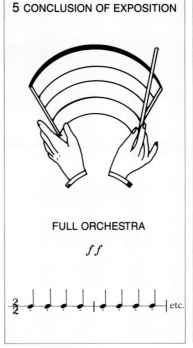

FULL ORCHESTRA

ff

6 PAUSE

DEVELOPMENT
7 DEVELOPMENT OF
THEME A IN MINOR

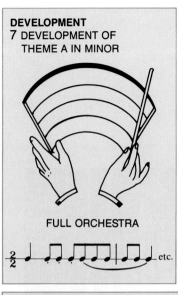

FULL ORCHESTRA

8 DEVELOPMENT OF TRANSITION

WOODWINDS AND STRINGS

f p f

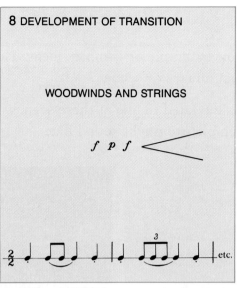

9 DEVELOPMENT
OF THEME B

LOW STRINGS, THEN
FULL ORCHESTRA

ff

10 CONCLUSION
OF DEVELOPMENT

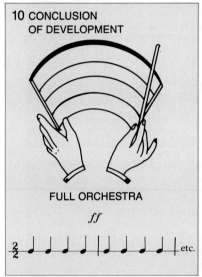

FULL ORCHESTRA

ff

RECAPITULATION
11 THEME A

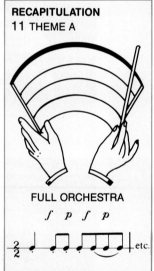

FULL ORCHESTRA

f p f p

12 TRANSITION

WOODWINDS
AND STRINGS

f p f p

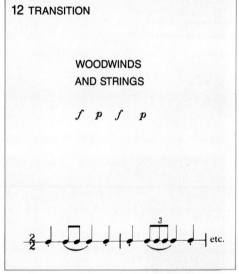

13 INTRODUCTION
TO THEME B

WOODWINDS
AND STRINGS

14 THEME B

VIOLINS: MELODY
BASSOONS: ACCOMPANIMENT

MOSTLY *pp*

15 CONCLUSION OF
RECAPITULATION

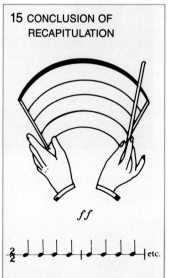

ff

PROGRAM MUSIC

Sounds can be used to convey simple or complex ideas. They can also be organized to depict images or scenes.

- Before listening to music related to one of these scenes, imagine what the music for each picture might sound like.

- Listen to the music and select the scene that is most like the music.

 Program Music Example

The terms below describe some of the musical characteristics of pitch, rhythm, and tone color that helped you select the scene. Which characteristics helped you make your choice?

fast	melody	no steady beat	common tone colors
slow	no melody	steady beat	unusual tone colors
loud		strong beat	repeated patterns
soft		weak beat	no repeated patterns

The term *program music* is often used to describe musical works that tell a story, describe an action or event, paint a picture, or create an impression. The term is used in contrast to **absolute music**, music which attempts to do none of those things.

Program music was a popular style of the nineteenth century. People were interested in poetry, prose, mythology, history, and current events. They especially enjoyed hearing musical interpretations of those interests. Composers often used literature or history as a guide for developing their music.

Wellington's Victory by Ludwig van Beethoven is an example of program music that depicts a dramatic battle in 1813 between the French and British armies.

You may recognize three of the main themes in *Wellington's Victory*. The first theme, representing the British army, is "Rule Britannia." This theme is often used in films or on television to represent the British people. The second theme, "Marlborough," represents the French army and is best known to small children as "The Bear Went Over the Mountain." The last popular theme heard is "God Save the King," which uses the same melody as our own patriotic song "America."

- Listen to the three main themes used by Beethoven in *Wellington's Victory*.

 Wellington's Victory Theme Montage

- As you listen to *Wellington's Victory,* follow the listening map. You can determine the losers because the theme representing the defeated army is played in minor and at a soft dynamic level.

 Wellington's Victory, by Ludwig van Beethoven

Listening Map to *Wellington's Victory*

1
TRUMPETS

DRUM

2

3
TRUMPETS

DRUM

4

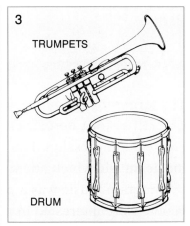

5

TRUMPETS

SOLO

6

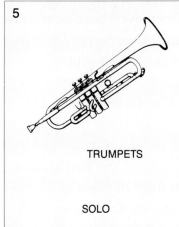

FULL ORCHESTRA

7

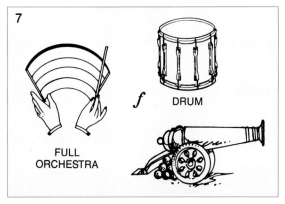

FULL ORCHESTRA

f DRUM

8

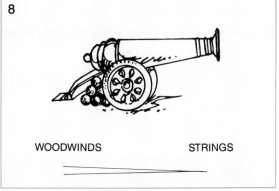

WOODWINDS   STRINGS

9

WOODWINDS   STRINGS

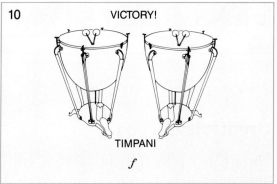

10   VICTORY!

TIMPANI

f

11

"GOD SAVE THE KING"

p

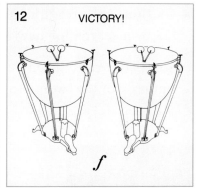

12   VICTORY!

f

13

"GOD SAVE THE KING"

p f p f p f p f p f

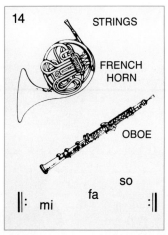

14   STRINGS

FRENCH HORN

OBOE

so

||: mi   fa   :||

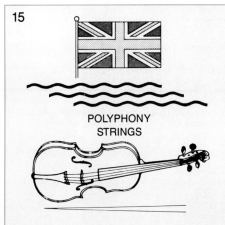

15

POLYPHONY
STRINGS

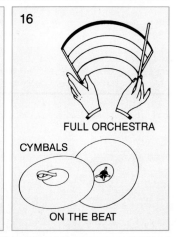

16

FULL ORCHESTRA

CYMBALS

ON THE BEAT

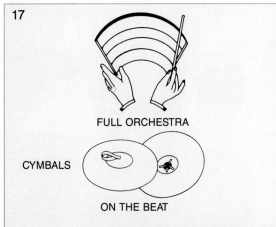

17

FULL ORCHESTRA

CYMBALS

ON THE BEAT

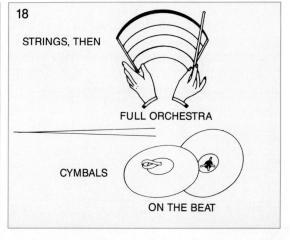

18

STRINGS, THEN

FULL ORCHESTRA

CYMBALS

ON THE BEAT

155

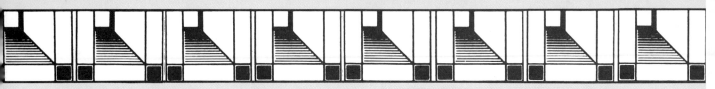

CREATIVITY IN THE TWENTIETH CENTURY

Creativity in Art

The creative principles of balance, unity, control, and variety were extremely important during the baroque, classical, and romantic periods. Some artists of the twentieth century have continued the traditions of the past. To others creativity has been characterized by a search for new ideas and new sounds.

- Examine the contemporary works of art pictured on these pages. Which works illustrate the experimentation of the twentieth century? Which works illustrate the principles emphasized during earlier style periods?

Street View, James Valerio, FRUMKIN/ADAMS GALLERY, NY, Collection of Dr. Larry and Marlene Milner

Artists of the twentieth century have created art in many styles. The painting above is by the American artist James Valerio. The sculpture at right is by the English artist Henry Moore.

Family Group, Henry Moore, THE TATE GALLERY, London

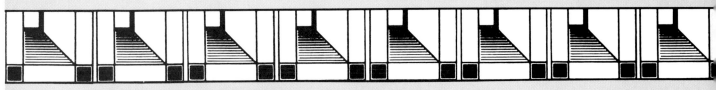

Three Musicians, Pablo Picasso, PHILADELPHIA MUSEUM OF ART

Pablo Picasso painted
Three Musicians (left)
in 1921. Joseph Cornell
created his "pantry ballet"
just for fun.

A Pantry Ballet (for Jacques Offenbach), Joseph Cornell, THE NELSON-ATKINS MUSEUM OF ART, Kansas City, MO

A Composition in Free Form

"A Marvelous Place" is a composition for speaking chorus. The score for this composition looks unusual because it is in *free form*. A composition is in **free form** when the order of the individual sections of the piece can change from one performance to the next. "A Marvelous Place" contains six events that can be performed in any order.

- Examine the score and identify the six events which can change.
- Listen to the recording and follow the score to get ready to perform this composition.

"A Marvelous Place"

A Marvelous Place

Traditional verse
Music by M.J.

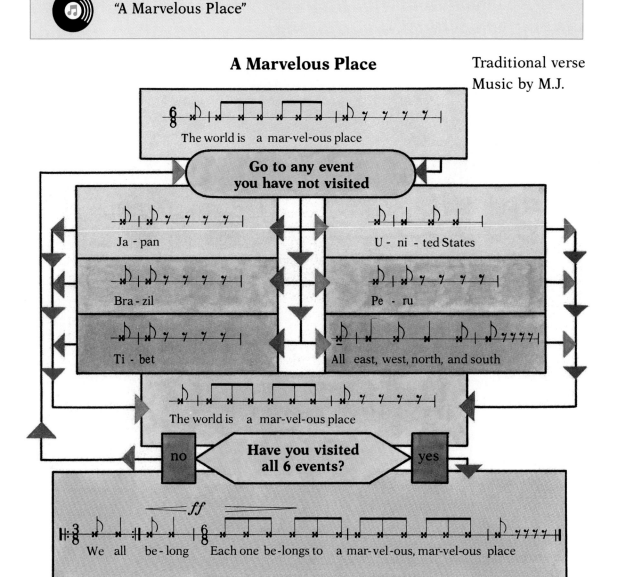

repeat gradually louder until all parts are performing

Creating Free Compositions

Free composition is not new. Composers in different style periods have experimented with giving up their power to make decisions about melody, harmony, tone color, and form. In 1751, William Hayes, an English composer, wrote *The Art of Composing Music by a Method Entirely New, Suited to the Meanest Capacity*. He described a method in which a small paint brush is dipped in ink. The brush then is shaken over music paper so that the ink falls on the staff lines. The ink splatterings then become the note heads. The classical composer Wolfgang Amadeus Mozart created music in which melodies were to be played in an order determined by a spinning dial, such as you see at carnivals.

Here are several suggestions to help you create free compositions. What is free about each of these compositional techniques?

Stick Melody
1. Choose eight pitches.
2. Assign each pitch a number.
3. Number eight sticks.
4. Drop the sticks and read from left to right to determine the order of pitches to be performed.

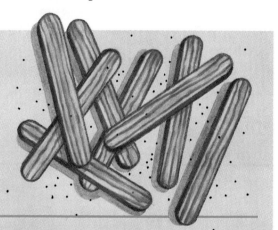

A	0
B	1
C	2
	:
B′	8.
C′	9

Telephone Harmony
1. Choose ten pitches
2. Assign each pitch a number. (0–9)
3. Select 3 ten-digit phone numbers.
4. Write each as a pitch pattern.
   2 1 2-7 0 2-7 8 9 6
   CBC-A′AC-A′B′C′G
5. Perform the three patterns at the same time to produce harmony.

- Combine aspects of both of these free compositional techniques to create music with melody and harmony. Think of other free techniques that can be used to create music.

JUST CHECKING

See how much you remember. Listen to the recording.

1. Listen to the steady beat and perform these rhythm motives by patting the quarter notes, pat-sliding the tied notes, clapping the eighth notes, and snapping the triplets with alternating hands.

2. Identify the melody below that uses rhythm motive 1, motive 2, or motive 3 above.

3. Listen to this section of the second movement of Beethoven's Symphony No. 7 and decide whether the articulation is legato or staccato.

4. Which of the following defines legato? Which defines staccato?

   a. detached and crisp
   b. smooth and connected

5. Listen to this section of the *Classical Symphony,* by **Sergei Prokofiev.**
   Identify the different parts of the exposition section by
   pointing to the descriptions on the listening map.

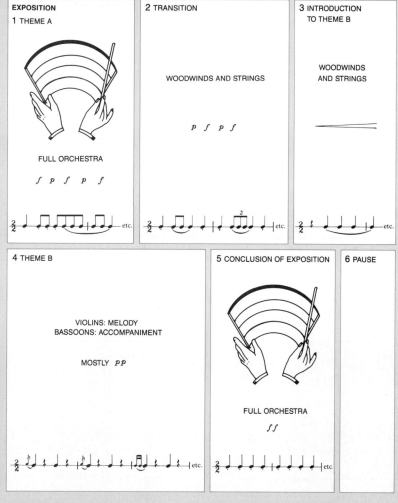

6. Listen to this version of the "America" melody. It is an example of:

   alteration of rhythm   creating a motive

7. Which of the following describes free form?

   a. order of sections can change b. order stays the same

UNIT 8

TONE COLOR IN DIFFERENT STYLES

Guitar, Paris (1912, early), Pablo Picasso, COLLECTION, THE MUSEUM OF MODERN ART, NY

163

Creating Sounds

Musicians have often explored new ways to create sound. Twentieth-century musicians have continued to experiment with tone color. They have developed new instruments. They have also experimented with unusual ways to play traditional instruments. The musicians in these pictures are creating new tone colors.

- Listen to these examples of traditional instruments producing musical sounds in new ways.

"Tone Color Montage"

Percussion Instruments

Percussion instruments are among the oldest musical instruments in the world. Ancient writings, drawings, carvings, and sculptures show percussion instruments in a variety of settings.

Percussion instruments are generally used to establish or maintain the beat. Many musical compositions feature strong, repeated rhythms on percussion instruments.

- Read and practice each pattern with your drumsticks using the matched grip. Use your right hand (R) and left hand (L) as indicated.

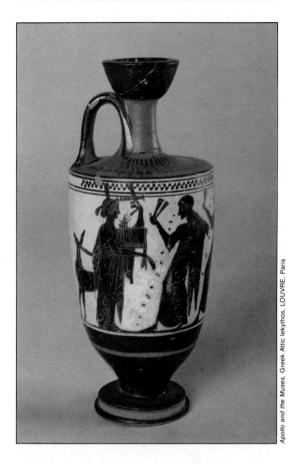

This Greek vase is about twenty-five hundred years old. The god of music, Apollo, is shown at left. The woman at right is playing an ancient percussion instrument.

Apollo and the Muses, Greek Attic lekythos. LOUVRE, Paris

A $\frac{4}{4}$ R L R L R R L R R L R L R L R R L R

B $\frac{4}{4}$ R R L R R L R R L R R L

C $\frac{4}{4}$ RLRLRLRLR L RLRLRLRLR L RLRLRLRLR L RLRLRLRLR

D $\frac{4}{4}$ RLRLRLRLR R L RLRLRLRLR R L RLRLRLRLR R L RLRLRLRLR

Performing a Rhythmic Accompaniment

Vangelis (van-je′ lis), a Greek composer, created the theme music for the Academy Award-winning film *Chariots of Fire*. The rhythms you have performed can be played as an accompaniment to *Heaven and Hell*, Part 2, another of his compositions.

- Listen to the recording of *Heaven and Hell*, Part 2. Read and perform the rhythmic accompaniment with your drumsticks using the matched grip.

 Heaven and Hell, Part 2 by Vangelis

Accompaniment to *Heaven and Hell*, Part 2

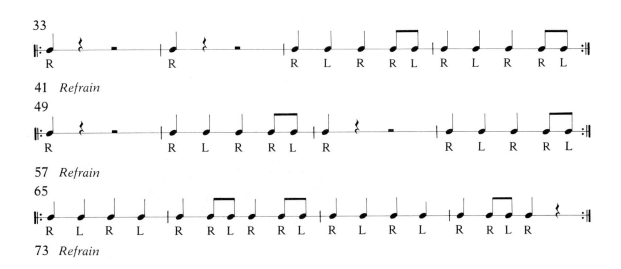

33
R   R   R L R R L R L R L

41 *Refrain*

49
R   R L R R L R   R L R R L

57 *Refrain*

65
R L R L R R L R R L R L R L R R L R

73 *Refrain*

VANGELIS

The Greek composer Vangelis was born in Athens in 1943. He is basically a self-taught musician. As a child he studied the piano and later the pipe organ. His interest in the variety of sounds that could be produced by the pipe organ led Vangelis to its modern equivalent, the synthesizer. The possibilities of producing both traditional and non-traditional sounds attracted him.

Vangelis performed with the Greek rock band Formynx. Political pressures led him to leave Greece and settle in Paris. He composed soundtracks for many European films and television documentaries.

The synthesizer has enabled Vangelis to use many new sounds. He finds this instrument the best means of expressing his musical ideas. He has composed, produced, and performed on over forty record albums.

New Percussion Sounds

Sometimes percussionists use their instruments in new or different ways. In this example, the drumsticks are used in different ways to create new tone colors. The symbol ✗ means "hold the drumsticks in the air and tap them lightly together." The symbol ✗→ means "hold the drumsticks in the air, tap them together, then slide one over the other as shown in this photograph."

• Read and practice these patterns with your drumsticks.

• Perform these patterns as you listen to *Heaven and Hell*, Part 2 again. Use this order:

A–B–C–D–E–D–E–D–C–D

PERFORM WITH NEW TONE COLORS

Notation

The tone colors of "Misty, Moisty Morning" are produced by using traditional instruments in new ways. The composer used some special notation to indicate these new sounds.

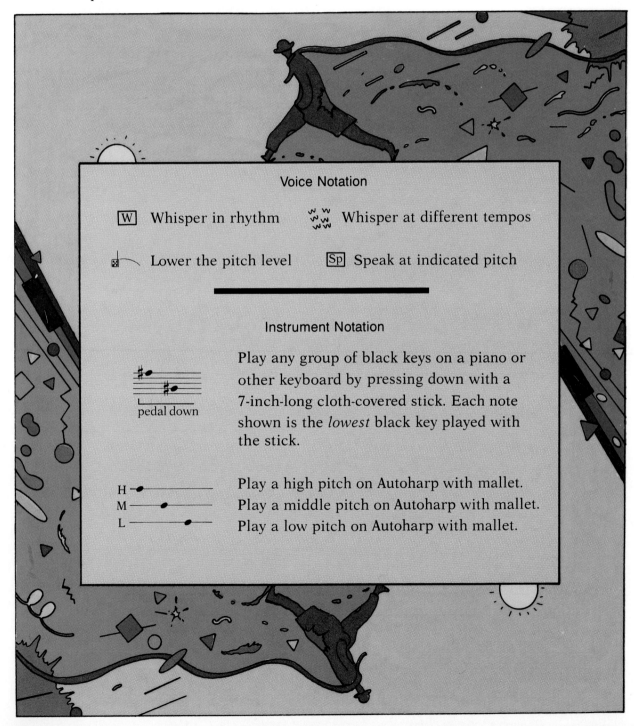

Voice Notation

W	Whisper in rhythm		Whisper at different tempos
	Lower the pitch level	Sp	Speak at indicated pitch

Instrument Notation

pedal down

Play any group of black keys on a piano or other keyboard by pressing down with a 7-inch-long cloth-covered stick. Each note shown is the *lowest* black key played with the stick.

H — Play a high pitch on Autoharp with mallet.
M — Play a middle pitch on Autoharp with mallet.
L — Play a low pitch on Autoharp with mallet.

- Perform "Misty, Moisty Morning" to experience music with new tone colors.

Misty, Moisty Morning

Traditional text
Music by M.J.

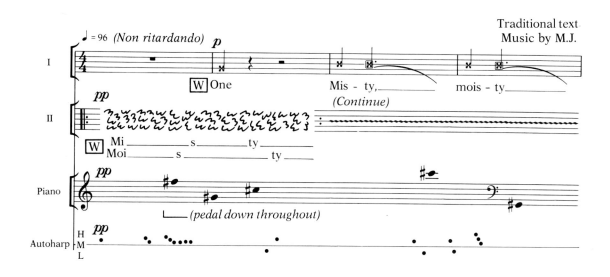

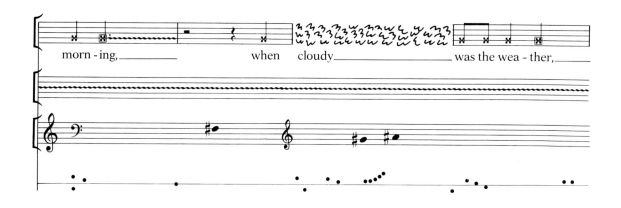

Other New Tone Colors

Krzysztof Penderecki (kris' tof pen-de-re' skē) is a contemporary Polish composer who draws novel sounds from voices and traditional instruments. He also was one of the first composers to experiment with sounds such as saws cutting wood and paper rustling, as well as unusual vocal effects. His *Saint Luke Passion* was an immediate success after its premiere in 1966.

- Listen to part of the *Saint Luke Passion*. Listen for singers hissing, shouting, and whispering, and for percussive effects produced by voices in the chorus.

 Saint Luke Passion by Krzysztof Penderecki

FROM PIPE ORGAN TO SYNTHESIZER

Pipe Organ

During the baroque period (1600–1750) the pipe organ was a popular instrument. It could produce a wide variety of sounds.

- Listen for the sound of the pipe organ.

 Toccata and Fugue in D Minor, by Johann Sebastian Bach

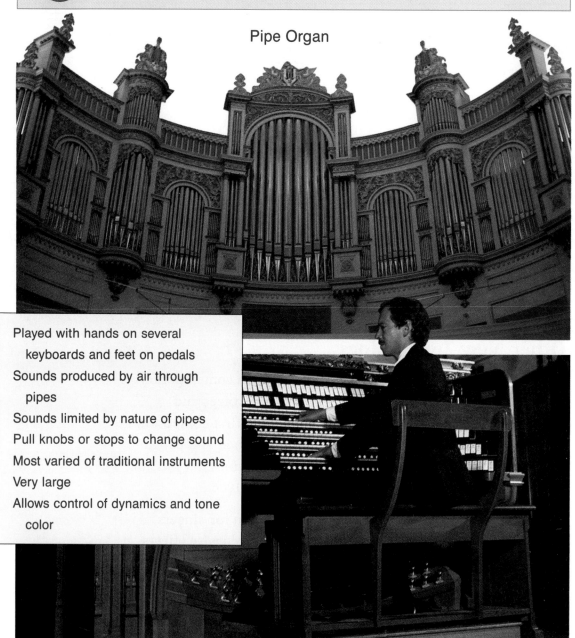

Pipe Organ

Played with hands on several
  keyboards and feet on pedals
Sounds produced by air through
  pipes
Sounds limited by nature of pipes
Pull knobs or stops to change sound
Most varied of traditional instruments
Very large
Allows control of dynamics and tone
  color

Synthesizer

The Greek composer Vangelis first composed for the pipe organ. He later became interested in the synthesizer because of its even greater tone color possibilities. He composed "Alpha," from his *Albedo 39,* for the synthesizer.

- Listen and describe the traditional and nontraditional sounds.

 "Alpha," from *Albedo 39,* by Vangelis

Ensembles for Synthesizer takes advantage of other tone color possibilities.

- Listen for the many sounds of the synthesizer.

 Ensembles for Synthesizer by Milton Babbitt

Usually played with hands on one or more keyboards

Sounds produced by electronic components

Sound limited only by composer's imagination

Buttons and knobs change sounds

Most flexible of nontraditional instruments

Generally small and compact

Allows almost total control of tone color, pitch, rhythm, and dynamics.

Moving to Sounds of the Twentieth Century

These pictures show contemporary dance movements.

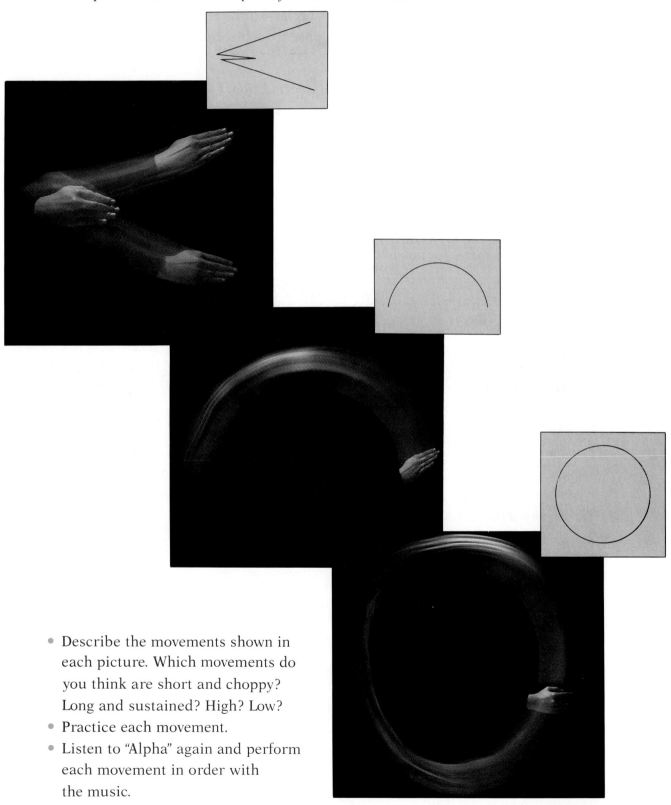

- Describe the movements shown in each picture. Which movements do you think are short and choppy? Long and sustained? High? Low?
- Practice each movement.
- Listen to "Alpha" again and perform each movement in order with the music.

NEW SOUNDS FROM A FAMILIAR INSTRUMENT

What Is It?

Sometimes familiar instruments can produce new or different tone colors.

* Listen to this music. Try to identify the instrument or instruments you hear.

 The Perilous Night, by John Cage

The instrument you heard is a **prepared piano.** Pianos can be prepared in several ways. Items made of wood, metal, or rubber can be placed on or between the strings of the piano. Other piano sounds are produced when the performer strums the strings inside the piano or uses a mallet to hit the wood of the piano. It all depends what sounds the composer wants produced.

John Cage, an American composer, developed the idea of the prepared piano and used it in his compositions to produce different tone colors.

Inside the Piano

A piano has many parts: keyboard, pedals, hammers, strings.
You can look inside a piano to see how the parts work together.

- Observe the hammers. What do they do?

- Place your hand across a group of strings. Play the keys for these strings. What happens to the tone?

- The thickness of the strings and the number of strings related to each key affect the sound produced by the key. Locate the thickest strings. What kind of tone do their keys produce?

- Locate the keys that use three strings; two strings; one string. What kind of tones do these keys produce?

- Find the pedals. What is the purpose of each?

Performing on a Prepared Piano

"Eraser Piano Tees" is a prepared piano composition written for eight prepared notes.

- Prepare four low notes on the piano by using two large rubber erasers. Place each eraser between two sets of low strings.

- Prepare four middle range notes (near middle C) by using four golf tees. Place each tee between the two strings for each middle range note.

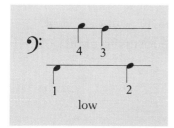

- Use your prepared piano notes to play this composition. The pitches are numbered from the lowest to highest.

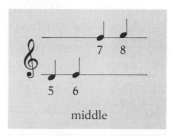

Eraser Piano Tees

Dorothy Gail Elliott

177

THE ELECTRONIC REVOLUTION

Electronic musical instruments were developed in the twentieth century. These instruments produce new sounds that were not possible on acoustic instruments such as the piano. In 1927 Leon Theremin (ther´ə min), a Russian scientist and musician, invented the first electronic musical instrument, the Theremin. To control the volume and the pitch of its eerie sound, the player moves his or her hands toward or away from the instrument's antennas. The Theremin detects these physical motions through disruptions of a magnetic field.

Maurice Martenot (mär te nô´), a French musician, invented the earliest form of the synthesizer in 1928. The invention of the synthesizer further expanded the range of musical sounds. The synthesizer combines different electronic wave forms to create (or synthesize) complex sounds.

With the invention of the transistor and then the integrated circuit, the technology to create and manipulate electronic sound became easier and less expensive to use.

The electronic revolution moved quickly in music. By the late 1950s many studios for electronic music were in operation. They increased the availability of new electronic sounds. The Moog and Bulcha synthesizers of the 1960s allowed musicians to create a diverse range of sounds. Sometimes these sounds are designed to imitate acoustic instruments such as a violin. Other times they create unusual and totally unique sounds.

Today personal computers are often used to create and manipulate complex sounds. Some allow you to record and play back any sound you choose. Many computers contain soundcards and options that allow you to access a variety of tone colors through **FM** or **wave synthesis**, **compact disc** (CD), and **General MIDI** technology. With the addition of a simple **tone generator** a computer will allow you to manipulate an even greater variety of interesting tone colors.

One Composition—Several Styles

Isao Tomita

Pictures at an Exhibition by Modest Mussorgsky was composed for the piano alone. The French composer Maurice Ravel arranged the work for full orchestra. In 1975 the Japanese composer Isao Tomita created an electronic version.

- Listen to "Promenade" from *Pictures at an Exhibition* in piano, orchestral, and electronic versions. Compare them. In which version is the contrast of dynamics and tone color most obvious? Which version do you find most interesting? Why?

 "Promenade Montage"

More Electronic Music

Milton Babbitt has long been a composer of electronic music. His control of sound is evident in *Composition for Synthesizer*, composed in 1960–1961. The synthesizer produces pitches and rhythms from directions provided by the composer. This work presents sounds with an evenness and a speed only possible through electronics.

 Composition for Synthesizer, by Milton Babbitt

As you listen to this composition follow this description:
1. Two gonglike sustained chords. A staccato melody.
2. Two sustained chords. Two staccato melodies.
3. One sustained chord. Two high staccato melodies with a low, legato melody.

MILTON BABBITT

Milton Babbitt, distinguished contemporary American composer, was born in Philadelphia in 1916. He received his early musical training in Jackson, Mississippi, and went on to study at New York University and Princeton University. He later became a professor of music at Princeton, where he also taught mathematics.

Babbitt began a program of electronic music at Princeton and Columbia universities, working with the newly developed synthesizer. He helped create the Columbia–Princeton Electronic Music Center, which became a haven for experiments in electronic music. Babbitt has also written many books and articles on music and musicians. His theories about mathematics and music and his innovations with the synthesizer have influenced the musical thinking of many young American composers.

RECYCLING FOR SOUND

Found Objects

Composers sometimes search for new sound sources when
traditional musical instruments are not able to produce all the
sounds that they want. *Suite for Percussion*, by Lou Harrison, uses
both traditional percussion instruments and new sound sources.
His new sources include **found objects**, or everyday objects.

- Listen for both traditional instruments and found objects you
  think were used.

Suite for Percussion, by Lou Harrison

Your Own Recycled Sound Composition

You and your classmates can create your own compositions using new sources for sound. It is more fun to work in small groups.

1. Work with your group to identify classroom objects (found objects) that would be good sound sources.
2. Experiment with your new instruments. Discover one short sound and one sustained sound.
3. To create unity, play one instrument continuously throughout the composition.
4. Plan a definite beginning and a definite ending.
5. Plan a definite order for different players.
6. To create variety, use three or four different instruments for contrast. Use silence, different dynamics, different tempos, and different pitches. Try different combinations.
7. Perform your composition several different ways.
8. Tape-record different performances of your composition.
9. Decide which of your performances demonstrates the most contrast. Which one is the most interesting?

Unusual Instruments

After World War II, the United States Navy left many large, empty oil containers in the West Indies. These fifty-gallon steel containers inspired the people of the West Indies to create their own special instruments. The oil containers were cut and hammered into steel drums. Groups of steel drum players formed bands with their own unique tone color.

- Listen for the tone color of the steel drums as you pat or clap the steady beat.

Steel Band Music

Creating New Instruments

Harry Partch (1901-1973), an American experimental composer, inspired others with his creative ideas. He also invented original instruments for special effects.

- Listen to learn about his composition *Spoils of War* and the unique instruments used in it.

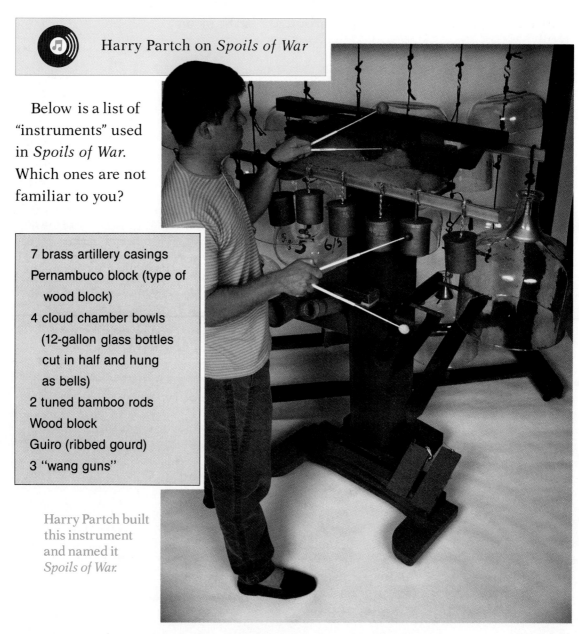

🎵 Harry Partch on *Spoils of War*

Below is a list of "instruments" used in *Spoils of War*. Which ones are not familiar to you?

7 brass artillery casings
Pernambuco block (type of wood block)
4 cloud chamber bowls (12-gallon glass bottles cut in half and hung as bells)
2 tuned bamboo rods
Wood block
Guiro (ribbed gourd)
3 "wang guns"

Harry Partch built this instrument and named it *Spoils of War.*

Many modern composers feel free to use any sounds that have the qualities they like. What found instruments might you use to improvise music?

REVIEW

JUST CHECKING

See how much you remember. Listen to the recording.

1. Listen to the steady beat and perform these rhythms on drumsticks using the matched grip.

2. Listen to a portion of the *Saint Luke Passion* and identify the unusual vocal effects.

3. Listen to excerpts of three versions of "Promenade" and describe the contrasts of dynamics and tone color.

4. The unique tone color of this ensemble is produced on homemade instruments. Name the instrument.

5. Perform these vocal sounds with the recording of "Misty, Moisty Morning."

6. Listen to this selection and tell whether the tone color is created by a pipe organ or a synthesizer.

7. Listen to "Alpha" from *Albedo 39* by Vangelis. Use appropriate contemporary dance movements with this piece.

8. Name and describe two unusual instruments or familiar instruments used in unusual ways.

9. Listen and identify the selection you hear. Choose from the titles below.
   a. Toccata and Fugue in D minor
   b. "Alpha" from *Albedo 39*
   c. *Heaven and Hell,* Part 2
   d. "Promenade" from *Pictures at an Exhibition*
   e. *The Perilous Night*

10. Listen to a portion of *The Perilous Night* and describe how the composer used a traditional instrument to produce different tone colors.

11. Listen to a portion of *Spoils of War* and describe several of the original instruments Harry Partch invented.

YEAR-END REVIEW

1. Listen to determine whether the style of each example is African, rock and roll, Japanese, calypso, or reggae.

2. Listen to Bizet's "Farandole" and determine whether the form of the selection is AB or ABA.

3. Listen to this musical selection, which is an example of changing meters. Identify when the meter changes by conducting the appropriate pattern. The selection begins in duple meter.

4. Listen to this excerpt from "Caprice" from Claude Bolling's Suite for Violin and Jazz Piano. Determine if this section is in compound or quadruple meter. Demonstrate your answer by conducting the appropriate pattern.

5a. Play the following pitches on keyboard or bells that make up the twelve-tone row on which the melody of "The Web" is based.

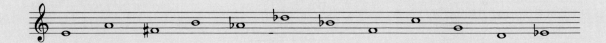

5b. Play the retrograde of this tone row on keyboard or bells.

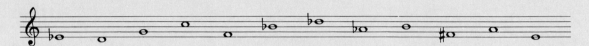

6. Perform this twelve-bar blues harmonic progression on bells or keyboard.

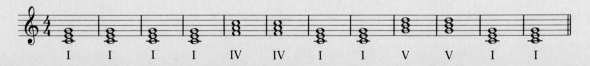

7a. Listen to a section of "Mi Caballo Blanco" and raise your hand when you hear the music modulate.

b. Listen to a section of "Mi Caballo Blanco" and decide if the music modulates to a higher or lower key.

8. Listen to *"Schwanenlied"* and decide whether the composition is in major or minor.

9. Listen to this section of Symphony No. 1 by Sergei Prokofiev. Identify the different parts of the exposition section by pointing to the descriptions on the listening map.

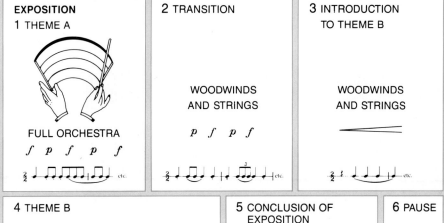

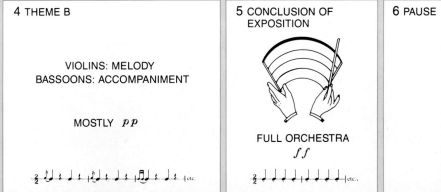

10. Listen and identify the selection you hear. Choose from the titles below.

    a. Toccata and Fugue in D minor

    b. "Alpha"

    c. *Heaven and Hell,* Part 2

    d. "Promenade" *(Pictures at an Exhibition)*

    e. *The Perilous Night*

WESTERN MUSICAL STYLES

Francesco Veracini

Chopin Playing the Piano in Prince Anton Radziwill's Salon at Berlin. Siemiradski

O Care, thou wilt despatch me, by Thomas Weelkes

One of the most popular forms of vocal music in the Renaissance was the **madrigal** (mad′ ri-gəl). Madrigals were written in polyphonic style, usually for five singers. They generally were short works, simple in structure. The lyrics were taken from both great literature and popular poetry. Like the popular songs of today, most madrigals were about love, happy or unhappy. Other topics included politics and issues of the day. Most madrigals were in **strophic** form, with each verse being sung to essentially the same music. This made madrigals easy to learn.

Vocal music was especially popular in the Renaissance, which is often called the "Golden Age of Singing." Church music was sung by professional, all-male choirs, but madrigals were sung by both men and women. Madrigals were performed at social gatherings and as home entertainment. Usually one performer sang each part, sometimes accompanied by recorders, lutes, or viols playing the same music.

In *O Care, thou wilt despatch me*, the English composer Thomas Weelkes looks to music to cheer him up.

> O Care, thou wilt despatch me,
> If music do not match thee.
> Fa la la la la la la.
> So deadly dost thou sting me,
> Mirth only help can bring me.
> Fa la la la la la,
> Fa la la la la la.

- Listen for the two moods the composer portrays. How does the music depict his unhappiness? How does it depict the joy he hopes to find in music?

 O Care, thou wilt despatch me, by Thomas Weelkes

- Compare madrigals with today's pop music. What do both have in common?

During the Renaissance, people enjoyed singing and playing music together. The instruments shown in these paintings include viols (early members of the violin family), lutes, recorder, and a type of portable harpsichord.

Hearing, Abraham Bosse

Group with Lute Player and Three Musicians on the Terrace of a House, unknown 16th-century artist

BAROQUE

"Spring" (First Movement) from *The Four Seasons,* by Antonio Vivaldi

The **concerto** (kôn-cher′tō) was one of the most important instrumental forms used in the baroque period. The term *concerto* comes from the Italian word *concertare* (kôn-cher-tä′ re), which suggests a friendly argument or contrasting forces. In a concerto, one instrument or group of instruments is set against the orchestra.

The Four Seasons is a group of violin concertos written around 1725 by the Italian baroque composer Antonio Vivaldi (än-tō′ nē-ō vi-väl′ dē) (1675-1741). Each concerto is accompanied by a poem, also written by Vivaldi, describing that season. This is a very early example of **program music,** music that tells a story or describes a scene.

One of the musical characteristics emphasized in the baroque concerto was *contrast.* In a style typical of the baroque, Vivaldi used two contrasting groups of instruments, contrasting melodies, and abrupt contrasts of loud and soft.

Rialto Bridge. Canaletto. GALLERIA CORSINI, Rome

Vivaldi was born in Venice and lived most of his life there. This painting by the Italian artist Canaletto (1697–1768) shows Venice as it looked during Vivaldi's lifetime.

"Spring" begins with the main theme played by everyone. Sections of a concerto played by everyone are called **ritornello** (ri-tôr-ne′ lō). The contrasting sections, called **episodes,** are played by the solo players. The music played suggests musical descriptions of spring, such as birds singing, murmuring waters, lightning and thunder.

Each picture represents musical sounds. The term *concertino* (kôn-cher-tē′ no) refers to the solo instrument or instruments. *Tutti* (tōō′ tē) refers to all the instruments together.

- Which pictures are similar? Which are different?

- Listen to "Spring" and notice the contrasts in tone color, themes, and dynamics. Follow the map as you listen.
- Describe the sound of the baroque orchestra. What instruments are used? What keyboard instrument can you hear throughout the concerto?

 "Spring" (First Movement), from *The Four Seasons*, by Antonio Vivaldi

Listening Map of "Spring" (First Movement) from *The Four Seasons*

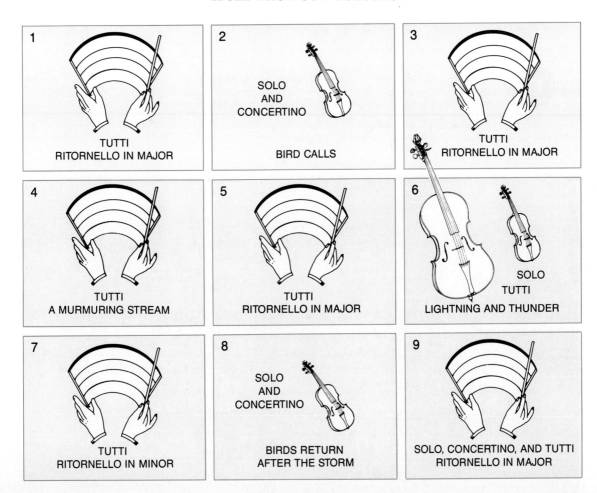

1 TUTTI RITORNELLO IN MAJOR	**2** SOLO AND CONCERTINO — BIRD CALLS	**3** TUTTI RITORNELLO IN MAJOR
4 TUTTI A MURMURING STREAM	**5** TUTTI RITORNELLO IN MAJOR	**6** SOLO TUTTI LIGHTNING AND THUNDER
7 TUTTI RITORNELLO IN MINOR	**8** SOLO AND CONCERTINO BIRDS RETURN AFTER THE STORM	**9** SOLO, CONCERTINO, AND TUTTI RITORNELLO IN MAJOR

Quintet for Clarinet and Strings in A Major, K. 581, Fourth Movement, by Wolfgang Amadeus Mozart

Compositions for small groups of instruments are called **chamber music** because they are designed to be performed in rooms (chambers) rather than concert halls. Like **symphonies** (works for full orchestra), chamber works are in several movements.

For the fourth and final movement of his Clarinet Quintet, Wolfgang Amadeus Mozart (volf′ gäng ä-mä-dä′ ōōs mōt′ särt) decided to write a theme with six variations and a **coda,** or conclusion. The theme itself is a very simple one, which Mozart varies in several ways. For example, he shows off the instruments' abilities to change from major to minor, or to play **legato** (lā-gä′ tō, smoothly) or **staccato** (stä-kä′ tō, detached). For contrasting tone color, Mozart even leaves out the clarinet entirely in one variation.

- Listen to the music and read the description on page 195. Notice the contrast between staccato and legato sections.

 Quintet for Clarinet and Strings in A Major, K. 581, Fourth Movement, by Wolfgang Amadeus Mozart

1. *Theme:* Cheerful, staccato theme is played and immediately repeated. The second part of the theme, momentarily legato, leads right back to the first (staccato) part, and this is repeated.

2. *Variation 1:* Clarinet, legato, has a new tune as strings play the staccato basic theme. This continues into Part 2 of the theme.

3. *Variation 2:* Strings agitated, but melody soars when clarinet enters. In Part 2 the agitation continues.

4. *Variation 3:* A change to minor gives a melancholy quality to the theme. This entire variation is played by strings only.

5. *Variation 4:* Rapid passages in clarinet accompany a return to the jolly mood of the theme in the strings.

6. *Adagio (Variation 5):* Change to a slow tempo is introduced by a series of chords and descending passages on the clarinet. Strings play yet another variation on the theme, joined by a wistful song on the clarinet, and this segment is repeated. The second part of the theme has the clarinet dominating, then giving in to the strings, and this segment also is repeated. A short, legato passage leads to:

7. *Allegro (Variation 6):* Another treatment of the basic theme. A coda of four chords brings this music to a strong conclusion.

Below, a typical chamber music concert during Mozart's time. Right, the child Mozart (at the keyboard) with his father and sister.

Mozart as a Child, with his Father and Sister, Carmontelle, MUSÉE CONDE Chantilly

The Concert, Augustin de Saint Aubin

"Un bel dì vedremo," from Madama Butterfly, by Giacomo Puccini

Opera is one of the most exciting of all musical forms, for it offers not only music, but also dramatic action, scenery, costumes, interesting stories and, often, unusual lighting effects. An opera performance, therefore, is a special event.

Madama Butterfly, by the Italian composer Giacomo Puccini, is one of the most popular operas ever written. Puccini's characters are understandable and human.

Madama Butterfly is another name for Cio-Cio-San (chō′ chō-sän), a young Japanese woman who marries an American naval officer, Lieutenant Pinkerton. She plans to devote her life to this marriage, but to Pinkerton, it is just a temporary fling until he meets and marries the American woman of his dreams. Butterfly remains true, but Pinkerton, while in America, marries someone else. When Butterfly realizes that Pinkerton has deserted her, she kills herself.

Butterfly sings the famous **aria** (ä′ rē-ä, solo song) *"Un bel dì vedremo,"* while she still believes Pinkerton will come back to her. She tells her servant, Suzuki, that one beautiful day Pinkerton will return, and she describes everything she thinks will happen.

The powerful opening melody of this aria occurs again near the end of the song, making a kind of ABA form. Butterfly's belief that Pinkerton will return to her is reflected in the straightforward melody. Near the end of her song, the music becomes more insistent as she talks herself and her servant into believing that what she says actually will come to pass.

As you listen to this selection, you will notice that the composer has provided several changes of mood and tempo to illustrate the situations Butterfly describes. Puccini's melody is strong at the beginning when Pinkerton's return is described, but becomes gentler as Butterfly tells of her own reactions to the situation. She will stay where she is, waiting anxiously for Pinkerton to find her, almost unable to control her emotions. The first melody returns as she describes their first meeting. The aria reaches its peak near the end as Butterfly tries to assure Suzuki that Pinkerton will, indeed, return.

Right, poster advertising a 1906 production of *Madama Butterfly*. Below and page 198, Renata Scotto in the Metropolitan Opera production. Below is the wedding scene; on page 198, *"Un bel dì vedremo."*

197

- Follow the Italian words and their translation as you hear them. Notice how Puccini's music reflects the hopes and feelings to which Butterfly refers.

Un bel dì, vedremo
Levarsi un fil di fumo
Sull'estremo confin del mare.
E poi la nave appare.
Poi la nave bianca
Entra nel porto,
Romba il suo saluto.
Vedi? È venuto!
Io non gli scendo incontro. Io no. Mi
  metto là sul ciglio del colle e aspetto,
  e aspetto gran tempo e non mi pesa la
  lunga attesa.
E uscito dalla folla cittadina un uomo,
  un picciol punto s'avvia per la collina.

Chi sarà? Chi sarà? E come sarà giunto
  che dirà? Che dirà? Chiamerà
  Butterfly dalla lontana. Io, senza dar
  risposta me ne starò nascosta un po'
  per celia, e un po' per non morire al
  primo incontro, ed egli alquanto in
  pena chiamerà, chiamerà: "Piccina
  mogliettina olezzo di verbena" i nomi
  che mi dava al suo venire.

Tutto questo avverrà, te lo prometto.

Tienti la tua paura, io con sicura fede
  l'aspetto.

One fine day, we shall see
A thread of smoke rising
Over the horizon
And then the ship will appear.
Then the white ship
Enters the harbor.
Her salute thunders out.
You see? He has come!
I don't go down to meet him. Not I.
  I stand on the brow of the hill and wait,
  and wait a long time and do not weary
  of the long watch.
Out of the city crowds there comes a
  man—a tiny speck—who makes his way
  toward the hill.
Who can it be? Who can it be?
  And when he arrives what will he say?
  What will he say? He will call
  Butterfly from the distance. I, without
  answering, will stay hidden partly for
  fun, and partly so as not to die at the
  first meeting. And he, a little troubled,
  will call, he will call: "My little wife,
  my sweet-scented flower"—the names
  he used to call me when he came.
All this will come to pass, I promise you.

Keep your fears: I, with unshakeable
  faith, will await him.

 "Un bel dì vedremo," from *Madama Butterfly,* by Giacomo Puccini

Étude in E Minor, Opus 25, No. 5, by Frédéric Chopin

Polish composer Frédéric Chopin specialized in writing music for the piano. Among his finest works, which include waltzes, sonatas, and many other pieces, are his **études**. *Étude* means "study," and an étude's purpose is to help students with technical playing problems. Chopin's études are more than just studies, however, because they are important musical selections in their own right. Chopin played several of them in his concerts, and many pianists do so today.

Of the more than two dozen études that Chopin composed, the Étude in E Minor, Opus 25, No. 5, is particularly impressive. Its opening section (A) is mainly staccato and is played at a fast tempo. The middle section (B) offers an expressive legato, in a slower tempo. When the A section returns, its staccato idea brings to mind the strong contrast that exists between the three sections of this work. Chopin includes a coda (ending section) with chords and a melodic trill at the close.

• Listen to the Étude in E Minor and raise your hand when you hear the contrasting B section.

• How does the étude show unity and variety?

 Étude in E Minor, Opus 25, No. 5, by Frédéric Chopin

Chopin Playing the Piano in Prince Anton Radziwill's Salon at Berlin, Siemiradski

Chopin often played private concerts in the homes of the nobility.

Frédéric Chopin, Eugène Delacroix, LOUVRE, Paris

199

Infernal Dance, from *The Firebird*, by Igor Stravinsky

Through movement, ballet can express feelings that would be difficult or impossible to say in words. Some ballets are story ballets. Stravinsky's *The Firebird* is one of the finest story ballets of the twentieth century. Based on a Russian folk legend, it tells of Prince Ivan. He discovers a magic garden whose inhabitants are under the spell of an evil king named Kastchei (käs-chā′ ē). With the help of the enchanted firebird, Ivan breaks the spell. This releases, among the others, the girl he marries, and all ends happily.

In the Infernal Dance, Stravinsky describes the King Kastchei's evil power through ominous-sounding themes, abrupt changes of instruments and dynamics, and strong rhythms. One can imagine, just by listening to this music, Kastchei's menacing gestures and his domination of the scene, even without seeing his actions on stage.

- Listen to the music and read the description below.

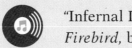 "Infernal Dance" from *The Firebird,* by Igor Stravinsky

1. Loud chord—brasses and bassoons present ominous theme; theme is repeated.
2. Xylophone joins the proceedings.
3. A flowing melody in the strings.
4. Xylophone alternates with other instruments.
5. Smoother melodic ideas in strings and other instruments, soft and loud.
6. Entire orchestra plays the smoother idea at a loud dynamic level.
7. Suddenly soft, though the scary mood continues.
8. Theme (soft) punctuated by xylophone.
9. Crescendo built with shorter, faster notes.
10. Brasses alternate with other instruments.
11. Faster tempo builds a peak; music ends with one loud chord, then a soft chord.

"Tonight," from *West Side Story*, by Leonard Bernstein and Stephen Sondheim

When *West Side Story* opened on Broadway in 1957, it was quite different from other musical plays of the time. In it, the story of Romeo and Juliet was transplanted to New York's West Side and given a contemporary flavor by the use of popular music styles.

The plot of *West Side Story* concerns two street gangs, the Jets and the Sharks, each of which wants to rule the neighborhood. At the beginning of the story Tony, formerly a member of the Jets, has quit the gang and taken a job in hopes of bettering his life. One night at a dance Tony meets Maria, a Puerto Rican girl. They fall in love. But Maria and Tony's romance is doomed from the start. Maria is the sister of Bernardo, the leader of the Sharks, and is engaged to Bernardo's friend Chino. Despite this the two lovers meet secretly. In a scene reminiscent of the famous balcony scene in *Romeo and Juliet* they sing the beautiful duet "Tonight" on the fire escape outside Maria's apartment.

The two rival gangs plan a rumble (fight) to determine who will rule the neighborhood. Tony tries unsuccessfully to stop the fight and make peace between the two gangs. Bernardo and Tony's best friend Riff fight as everyone else watches. The rules for the fight specify no weapons, but knives are drawn and Bernardo kills Riff. In a grief-stricken rage, Tony takes Riff's knife and kills Bernardo. The gang members scatter as the police arrive.

Anita, Bernardo's girlfriend, learns the outcome of the rumble and goes to Maria to break the news about Bernardo to her. Maria is only concerned about Tony. Angrily, Anita tells her that Tony killed Bernardo. Maria is sorrowful, but is determined to forgive Tony.

Tony and Maria make plans to go away together. When Maria is delayed she sends Anita with a message for Tony. Anita goes to the store where Tony works and encounters some of the Jets. They know she is Bernardo's girlfriend and taunt her. Enraged, Anita gives them a different message for Tony: Chino found out about Tony and Maria, and killed her.

Tony, numb with grief, goes looking for Chino. But Chino finds Tony first, and shoots him in revenge for Bernardo. Maria finds Tony lying in the street. She cradles him in her arms as he dies. United by tragedy, the rival gangs finally make an effort at peace and jointly carry Tony's body away as Maria follows.

West Side Story contains solos, duets, instrumental sections, and ensembles (music in which several people sing at the same time). If several actors were to talk at the same time, the audience would not be able to understand them. However, in music, two or more things can happen at once, and the results will still be understandable. This ensemble, entitled "Tonight," has several different ideas going on at the same time: Maria and Tony express their love for each other; Anita looks forward to an evening of fun; and the opposing gangs plot the rumble that is about to take place.

- Follow the story line in "Tonight" by reading the descriptions.

1. *Jets*: "The Jets are gonna have their day tonight."
   Sharks: "We're gonna hand them a surprise tonight."
   Brief, jazzy introduction, Jets and Sharks in a fast tempo, with a strong rhythmic accompaniment.

2. *Anita*: "Anita's gonna get her kicks tonight."
   Introduced by brief, jazzlike pattern; same melody that was sung by Jets and Sharks, but sung as a solo.

3. *Tony*: " Tonight, tonight."
   A new melody is introduced; rhythmic accompaniment here is more subdued for this soaring, smoother tune, which depicts Tony and Maria's love for each other.

4. *Maria* continues Tony's melody of "Tonight."

5. Comments from gang members.
   Strong accompaniment returns, illustrating the warlike mentality of the gangs.

6. *Maria* sings "Tonight" with short comments in the background by the *Jets*, the *Sharks*, *Tony*, and *Anita*. Each melody is different from the others, even though they are all sung at the same time. The quintet reaches an exciting conclusion.

- Decide how the composer provides different music for each character or group.

These scenes are from the film of *West Side Story*. Above, the rumble. Tony (Richard Beymer) is facing forward. Left, Anita (Rita Moreno) and some friends on the roof of their apartment building.

"Tonight," quintet from *West Side Story*, by Leonard Bernstein and Stephen Sondheim

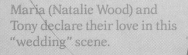

Maria (Natalie Wood) and Tony declare their love in this "wedding" scene.

Lieutenant Kijé Suite, by Sergei Prokofiev

Lieutenant Kijé (kē′ jā) was a Russian film for which Sergei Prokofiev (ser′ gā prō-kō′ fē-ev) composed the score. The story of *Lieutenant Kijé* is a humorous one, set in the nineteenth century. One day the czar of Russia is looking at military reports and misreads the name *Kijé* in an account of a heroic deed. When the czar asks questions about Lieutenant Kijé, his advisors are afraid to tell him that he has made a mistake. Consequently they proceed to make up a life story for the imaginary Lieutenant Kijé.

In the first movement of the suite, "The Birth of Kijé," a solo cornet theme decribes Kijé's birth and some of his supposed military exploits. A separate theme is used to represent Kijé himself. This theme reappears in later movements of the suite whenever Kijé is present.

- Listen to the first movement of this suite and identify the instruments that Prokofiev uses to convey the idea of Kijé's military service.

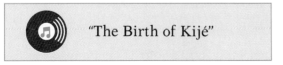

"The Birth of Kijé"

The advisors continue their story, and in the second movement of the suite, "Romance," Kijé falls in love. A "love song" theme is played by string bass, cello, and tenor saxophone. This is followed by themes from Kijé's wedding and the celebration afterward.

A scene from
the 1934 film
Lieutenant Kijé

Prokofiev uses these two themes in the third movement, "The Wedding of Kijé," to describe the relationship between the stately ceremony (Theme 2) and the celebration (Theme 3). Kijé's theme (Theme 1) also is heard throughout.

• Listen and identify which theme you hear for each number.

 "The Wedding of Kijé"

The advisors describe more of Kijé's deeds to the czar. Their plan backfires when the czar is so interested that he asks to meet Kijé! The advisors must do something quickly. They tell the czar that Kijé has died and has been buried with full military honors.

In the fifth and last movement, "The Burial of Kijé," Prokofiev uses many of the themes from the earlier movements to remind the audience of Kijé's life. Then the solo cornet returns with the opening theme as the hero is laid to rest.

An Arrangement by William Dawson

Some musicians arrange rather than compose music. In arranging, a musician takes an existing composition and resets it for a different combination of musical resources. For example, a work for two voices may be arranged for two clarinets.

One of the challenges an arranger faces is to keep the arrangement from overpowering the unique qualities of the original music. William Dawson illustrated his sensitivity and skill in preserving the characteristics of spirituals in his choral arrangement of "Ev'ry Time I Feel the Spirit."

William Dawson was born at the turn of the century. He arranged many African American spirituals. By creating arrangements, he

William Dawson, composer, arranger, and conductor

made it possible for choirs to perform this exciting and expressive music. As choir director at Tuskeegee Institute in Alabama, Dawson shared his arrangements with people throughout the United States and Europe.

"Ev'ry Time I Feel the Spirit" is one of William Dawson's best-known choral arrangements. He used strongly syncopated rhythms, contrasts between group and solo singing, and the improvised quality of the choral parts to create an exciting musical setting.

Learn the melody before you listen to a performance of "Ev'ry Time I Feel the Spirit" by the Brazeal Dennard Chorale.

- Perform the melody by singing it or playing it on keyboard or bells.

Ev'ry Time I Feel the Spirit

African American Spiritual

Ev - 'ry time I feel the spi - rit Mov - in' in my heart. I will pray; Yes; ev'ry

time I feel the spi - rit Mov - in' in my heart I will pray.

- Listen to the Brazeal Dennard Chorale perform "Ev'ry Time I Feel the Spirit."

 "Ev'ry Time I Feel the Spirit"

The Brazeal Dennard Chorale of Detroit, Michigan, specializes in performing music by African American composers and arrangers. Named after its conductor, the group has performed many concerts in the Detroit area as well as in Michigan and Ohio.

The Brazeal Dennard Chorale. Mr. Dennard is at the lower right.

MUSIC OF THE WORLD'S CULTURES

209

THE INFLUENCE OF WORLD CULTURES

Musicians, dancers, authors, architects, and sculptors get their ideas from many different sources. They are often influenced by the cultural traditions of other countries.

Sometimes the characteristics of other cultures are obvious. At other times cultural influences may be more difficult to identify. The College Life Insurance headquarters buildings have characteristics of contemporary styles and the styles of ancient Egypt.

- Identify the contemporary characteristics of these buildings.
- Identify the ancient Egyptian characteristics.

Left, the pyramids at Giza, Egypt. Below, the College Life Insurance Headquarters, Indianapolis, Indiana.

Mixing Musical Cultures

In this first section you will listen to music that mixes the characteristics of music of the United States with characteristics of the music of another culture. Some ways musicians do this are to combine instruments, rhythm, melodies, or harmonies of both cultures.

Kogoklaras (kō-gō-klä′ räs) is one example of this mix. It combines characteristics of Indonesian music and music of the United States.

Right and below, dancers from the island of Bali, Indonesia. The dancers must practice for years to master these difficult techniques.

- Listen and identify musical characteristics of Indonesia and the United States.

 Kogoklaras, by Vincent McDermott

American and Indian Cultures Interact

Other cultures, including that of India, have influenced the music of the United States. Shakti, a musical group from the United States, combines Indian traditional music and instruments with rock style instruments of the United States in "Come On Baby Dance With Me."

- Listen for characteristics of Indian music and music of the United States.

 "Come On Baby Dance With Me," performed by Shakti

You can learn these instrumental parts to perform accompaniments to "Come On Baby Dance With Me."

- Practice each part before performing with the recording.

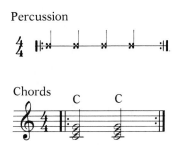

- Form groups. One group should play the percussion part with drumsticks or other percussion instruments. The other group should play the chords on guitar or keyboard.

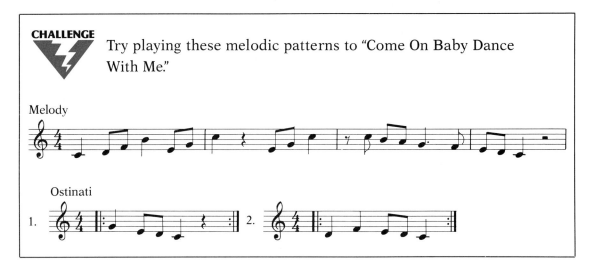

CHALLENGE Try playing these melodic patterns to "Come On Baby Dance With Me."

Melody

Ostinati

1.   2.

THE MUSIC OF INDIA

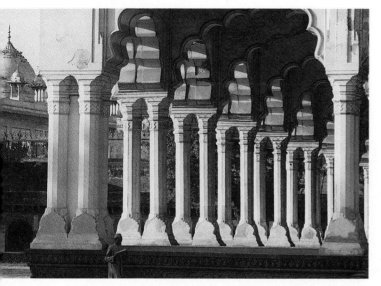

The Hall of Public Audience, Agra, India

"Come On Baby Dance With Me" is a combination of Indian music and music of the United States. Next you will hear Indian concert music. Like Western jazz, Indian concert music is improvised. In some Indian music, one pitch, called a *drone*, is repeated in such a way that it is sounding continuously. This drone pitch provides a background for the creation and performance of rhythmic and melodic patterns. In *Madhu Kauns*, (mä' doō käns), the pitch D-flat (the black key to the left of D on the keyboard) is repeated as the drone.

• Listen for the D-flat drone in *Madhu Kauns.*

 Madhu Kauns

• Play D-flat at the proper time on keyboard or bells as you listen again.

Rhythm patterns in Indian music usually are longer than those in Western music. Instead of two, three, or four beats to a group, Indian rhythm patterns can have ten, twelve, fourteen, or sixteen beats. These patterns are repeated and used as a basis for improvisation.

• Perform the steady beat on percussion instruments with *Madhu Kauns.*
• Next play the D-flat drone and the steady beat with the recording.

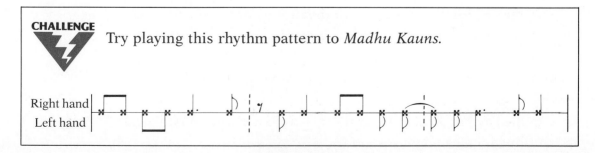

CHALLENGE Try playing this rhythm pattern to *Madhu Kauns.*

213

Tone Colors in the Music of India

The melody of *Madhu Kauns* is performed on a *sitar* (si' tär). The sitar is a twenty-six-stringed instrument somewhat like a lute. The performer uses six of these strings to play a melody. The rest of the strings vibrate when the melody is played, resulting in a continuous layer of sound.

Top, girls from northern India. Above, Ravi Shankar (center), a world-famous sitar player. The other performers in his ensemble play the tambura (right), a stringed instrument that produces the drone pitches, and the tabla (left), drums.

- Listen again to *Madhu Kauns* and focus on the sound of the sitar.

 Madhu Kauns (excerpt)

The sitar melodies combine with the drone pitch and repeated rhythms played on hand drums to give Indian music its distinctive sound.

The traditional music of India is performed in concert settings. Members of an Indian audience are familiar with the repeated rhythms. As they listen they frequently move their hands silently in time to the rhythm. How is this different from the way an audience in the United States might respond?

Xylophone ensembles are popular in many parts of Africa. These performers are members of the Senufo tribe from the Ivory Coast.

MUSIC OF MALI

In the African nation of Mali, *xylophone ensembles* frequently perform complex rhythmic and melodic patterns. Xylophones in an ensemble can vary. Sometimes other instruments perform with the xylophones, for example, guitar, metal clappers, drums, or voice.

Musicians in a xylophone ensemble perform rhythms in several different ways. They can repeat just one rhythm pattern or alternate between patterns. They can echo a pattern that another musician has just played or create new patterns.

- Listen to *Kondawele,* a piece from Mali.

 Kondawele (excerpt)

You can use these rhythms to create a percussion ensemble in the style of those found in Mali.

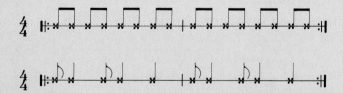

- Perform both lines of rhythm. Use different melodic and percussion instruments for each line.
- Notice how the sound of your ensemble changes when you use different instruments. Try other combinations of instruments.

215

The Sounds of Gambia

Rhythmic variety is characteristic of traditional music from the African country of Gambia. *Kelefa ba* (ke-le′ fä bä) is an example of this style of music. Each of its rhythm parts is different from the others. When they are performed together, the result is a rhythmically complex and constantly changing musical sound.

- Listen to *Kelefa ba* to hear this rhythmic variety.

Kelefa ba

- Practice each of these rhythm patterns on unpitched percussion instruments.

- Compare the rhythm patterns. Which has mostly short note values? Mostly long note values?
- Form three groups. Listen to the changing rhythmic sound as two groups perform two of the rhythm patterns at the same time. Have the third group add the third part.
- Perform the rhythm patterns with the recording of *Kelefa ba*. Listen for the changes in rhythm.
- Practice this melodic pattern on keyboard or bells. Play it with *Kelefa ba.*

- Form four groups to perform the three rhythm patterns and the melodic pattern with *Kelefa ba.*

216

Instrumental and Vocal Sounds of Gambia

Some Gambian music is performed by a solo voice and a stringed instrument called a *kora* (kô' rä). The kora, a kind of harp-lute, comes in several sizes with from five to twenty-one strings. A small metal disk with metal rings attached produces a rasping sound when the performer plucks or strums the strings.

Throughout West Africa, professional musicians are called *griots* (grē' ō). In Gambia, griots are very important, because one of their roles is to record the history of the Gambian people. They pass this history on through their music. In contrast, people of Western cultures write books to record their history. The griots compose songs to comment on historical events.

Listen to *Cedo* (kā' dō), a Gambian history, to hear the tone color of the kora.

🎵 *Cedo*

Koras are made in many sizes, from small (left) to large (below). *Cedo* is played on a large kora.

217

A singer performs the melody in *Cedo*.

• Listen to *Cedo* again. Choose the words that best describe the quality of the voice: light or heavy, rough or smooth, strong or weak.

In this Ivory Coast village, boys of the Yaou tribe listen as a storyteller recounts a tribal legend.

Instrumental and Vocal Sounds of Zimbabwe

Zimbabwe, also an African country, is about thirty-five hundred miles southwest of Gambia. In music from Gambia, stringed instruments are used, while in Zimbabwe, the *mbira* (m-bē′ rä), or thumb piano, is important.

The woman who sings the piece you are about to hear is named Stella Rambisai Chiweshe (stel′ lä räm-bē-sä′ ē chē′wä-shä). She is known as the "Queen of Mbira." Like *Cedo*, *Chigamba* (chē-gäm′ bä) has the feeling of improvisation, however, the tone colors of the instrumental accompaniments are very different.

• Listen to *Chigamba* and choose the words that best describe the quality of the voice: light or heavy, rough or smooth, strong or weak.

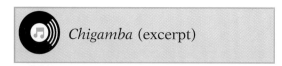

Chigamba (excerpt)

218

The mbira is a melodic instrument. It has a wooden frame with metal tongs attached. The performer plays the mbira by pulling down or plucking each tong, causing it to vibrate. A dried gourd serves to amplify the sound, much like the body of a guitar. In other African cultures, the mbira is called the *sansa, likembe, budongo,* or *kalimba*.

In Zimbabwe, the mbira is used in many different musical ways. It can be used as a solo instrument to express personal feelings. Frequently it is used in religious settings. At other times it accompanies songs of love or politics.

Chigamba features the mbira and voice. Both perform variations of the same melody.

The mbira is found in many African cultures. Recently, it has become popular in Western musical styles.

- Practice playing or singing this variation of the melody heard in *Chigamba*, then listen to the recording again and listen for it in its many forms.

- Practice this rhythm accompaniment to *Chigamba*, then play it with the recording.

The mbira also has been used in American music. Both jazz and popular music groups have included its traditional sounds in a new context. With the MIDI, the sound of the mbira is readily available for use as a tone color in modern composition.

THE MUSIC OF TURKEY

The *ney* (nā) is a flutelike wind instrument used in the music of Turkey and other countries of the Middle East. It is a hollow cane tube with six finger holes in front and one in back. Unlike the flute, which is held horizontally, the ney is held at an angle when it is played.

The classical music of Turkey is performed on the ney. In this music the performer frequently performs long solos. Sometimes a ney performance includes drums and stringed instruments. The ney is associated with a religious sect, and is played during certain religious services.

The ney is popular throughout the Middle East.

- Play this Turkish scale on keyboard, recorder, or bells. (B-sharp and C are the same key on a keyboard.)

- Listen to *Taksim* (täk′ sim), or improvisation, *in Mode Segah*. It is performed on the ney. This piece is based on the scale you just played, which is called mode *segah* (sā′ gä).

 Taksim in Mode Segah

The ney performer plays along melodic lines that are frequently improvised, or made up on the spot. Single tones of the scale are used as centers around which melodies are developed. In this example, each white note is the center of a melody, or tonal center.

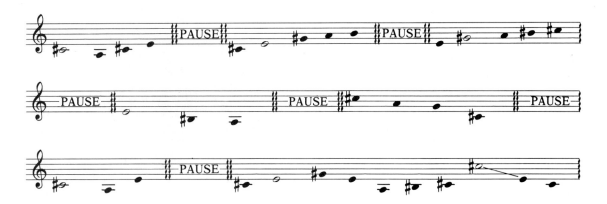

Many times a performer uses *ornaments* with a melody. **Ornaments** are added notes that decorate a basic melody.

- Listen to *Taksim in Mode Segah* again. Try to hear each melodic line and its tonal center. Notice the ornaments the performer adds to the melody, and the long pauses.

Turkey has long been a meeting place between Europe and Asia. These ruins of a fortification are on the Mediterranean coast at Üçagiz near Kale.

THE MUSIC OF JAPAN

In Japan the *nagauta* (nä′ gä-ōō-tä) ensemble is used to accompany a popular form of operalike drama called *kabuki* (kä′ bōō-kē). The nagauta ensemble is similar to the xylophone ensemble of Mali in that it contains percussion instruments as well as pitched instruments. However, the nagauta ensemble performs only in very formal concert settings to accompany the kabuki plays.

The nagauta ensemble contains three different drums: the *o-tsuzumi* (ō′ tsōō-zōō-mē), the *ko-tsuzumi* (kō′ tsōō-zōō-mē), and the *taiko* (tī′ kō). The o-tsuzumi and ko-tsuzumi are doubleheaded laced drums. The player holds the drum on the shoulder and plays it with the other hand. The performer can make the pitch of the ko-tsuzumi high or lower by squeezing the laces while striking the head of the drum. The taiko also is double headed and laced, but is hung from a frame and played with sticks.

The nagauta ensemble also includes two pitched instruments. One is a stringed instrument, the *shamisen* (shä′ mē-sen), and the other, the *bue* (bōō′ ā), is a wind instrument.

Above, the nagauta To-On-Kai in performance. In the front row are one bue, three o-tsuzumi or ko-tsuzumi, and one taiko. The shamisen players in the upper row are awaiting their turn.

- Listen to *Sambaso* (säm′ bä-sō). Follow the description of the music.

 Sambaso

1. Ko-tsuzumi and taiko are heard; voice; drum calls; music becomes faster.
2. Vocal solo; drum calls are heard.
3. The bue is heard, along with the shamisen.
4. The shamisen presents an ascending pattern, then a melodic pattern.
5. Shamisen and bue continue melody; music gradually becomes faster.
6. Bue and drum calls are heard.

Some scenes of Japan. Opposite page, umbrellas drying after painting at a factory. This page, top, a shamisen player. Above, Himeji Castle, near Osaka, the most famous medieval Japanese castle. Left, a festival scene at Sapporo, on Hokkaido island.

The Sound of the Gamelan

You heard a combination of Indonesian music and the music of the United States in *Kogoklaras* on page 211. This section concentrates on Indonesian sound alone.

The *gamelan* (gä' me-län) is the traditional instrumental ensemble of Indonesia. The ensemble consists of gongs and metallophones, rhythmic drums, flute, and stringed instruments. Some of the gongs play melodies, and others set the meter of the music.

A gamelan from Bali, Indonesia, with gongs, metallophones, and drums. The flute player is near the upper right-hand corner.

In Indonesia, the gamelan accompanies dance, drama, and puppet theatre. Although other types of musical ensembles are common in Indonesia, the gamelan is the most important. There are many different kinds of gamelans, and each kind uses a slightly different set of pitches. Some ensembles perform with five pitches and some use seven. Others use as few as four.

The sound of each instrument in the gamelan has a distinctive quality. As performers repeat rhythmic patterns, the sound joins with others to create layers of sound.

Perform in Gamelan Style

One type of gamelan rhythm develops when the musicians read the same line of rhythm. Instead of performing all of the notes, however, they alternate with other ensemble members to share the notes of the rhythm pattern. The interlocking sounds of their instruments creates an interesting rhythmic and melodic quality.

• Clap this gamelan rhythm.

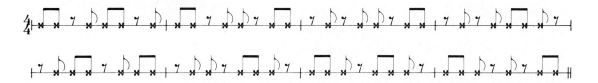

• Perform in gamelan style with a partner:

1. Each of you should clap or pat every *other* note of the rhythm pattern. Listen closely to the change in the sound of the rhythm as you alternate.
2. You and your partner should each choose an unpitched percussion instrument.
3. Perform the rhythm pattern on percussion instruments. Alternate the notes.

Melodic patterns on pitched instruments also are part of gamelan music. Some patterns are based on a four-pitch scale:

• Perform a two-pitch gamelan-style melodic pattern with a partner:

1. Each of you should choose one pitch on a bell set, handbell set, xylophone, keyboard, or any pitched object.
2. With your partner, decide which pitch will be played first.
3. Perform the rhythm pattern at the top of the page. Alternate with your partner so that you each play every other note. Listen closely to the change in the sounds as you alternate the two pitches.

BORROWING MUSICAL IDEAS

One composer who was deeply influenced by music of another culture was Claude Debussy (klôd də-byu-see). One of the aspects of Indonesian music that interested Debussy was the layering of sound. Stratification occurs when layers of melody or sound are heard.

Stratification occurs not only in music but also in nature. These layered rice terraces are on Luzon, in the Philippines.

- Practice this melody on keyboard or bells.

- Form several groups and perform the melody in stratification. All start at the same time, but each group performs the melody at a different tempo and in different octaves. This creates different layers of sound.

The melody you just performed is similar to part of the melody found in *Gêndhing KÊMBANG MARA* (gen-ding´ kem-bang´ mä´ rä), gamelan music from the city of Solo on the island of Java, Indonesia.

- Listen to *Gêndhing KÊMBANG MARA*.

Gêndhing KÊMBANG MARA (excerpt)

CLAUDE DEBUSSY

Claude Debussy (1862–1918) was one of the greatest French composers. Debussy was born in a suburb of Paris and was encouraged to play the piano at an early age. He entered the Paris Conservatory when he was eleven and studied there for eleven years. Debussy created a musical style known as *impressionism*. During his years in Paris he became acquainted with impressionist painters such as Claude Monet, whose works brought out the effects of light and color on nature. He created a style of music that used different harmonies and exotic rhythms to evoke delicate and mysterious moods.

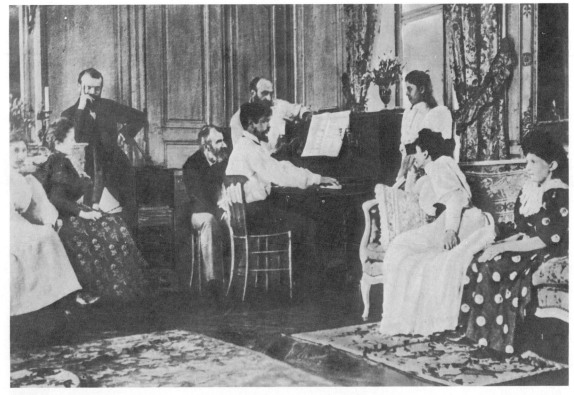

This photo shows the young Debussy playing the piano in a private home in Paris.

227

Debussy's *"Pagodes"*

At the international Paris Exposition in 1889, Debussy had the opportunity to hear a gamelan ensemble from Java, one of the Indonesian islands. He was fascinated by the sounds of this exotic music. A different gamelan ensemble performed at the 1900 Paris Exposition. Again Debussy was intrigued by the music. The rhythms and melodies he heard challenged Debussy to include some of their characteristics in his own music.

Debussy wrote *"Pagodes"* (pä-gôd′, "pagodas") in 1904, some years after he had heard the gamelan music that influenced this piano composition. Instead of imitating a gamelan ensemble, he included characteristics of gamelan music. He used scales that were not commonly found in Western music. He changed the rhythms of the melodies and added ornamental pitches to them. He also created layers of sound by having more than one melody sounding at the same time.

- Listen to *"Pagodes"* to hear how Debussy was influenced by gamelan music. Read the descriptions.

 "Pagodes," by Claude Debussy

A Section
1. Low gonglike pitches; melody 1; melody 1 with melody 2 below; altered melody 1 with melody 3 below; short melody 4
2. Altered melody 3, using high and low registers; altered melody 1; tempo slows down slightly

B Section
3. Melody 5; melody 1 reappears in part with melody 6 (very loud)
4. Melody 5 (lower); trills

A Section
   Low gonglike pitches; melody 1; melody 1 with melody 2 below; altered melody 1 with melody 3 below; short melody 4
5. Melody 3, using high and low registers; melody 6 (very loud)

Coda
   Melodies 1, 2, and 6, one after the other, with fast, high notes and low, soft gonglike pitches accompanying, to the end

Many peoples of the Far East have built pagodas. Left, below, and bottom, Borobudur Pagoda, on the island of Java, Indonesia

Left, Schwedagon Pagoda, in Rangoon, Burma

LOOKING BACK

See how much you remember.

1. Perform these rhythms from Mali and Indonesia on a percussion
   instrument with the recording.

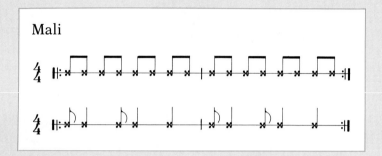

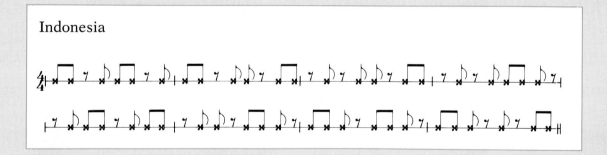

2. Pat the steady beat as you listen to *Madhu Kauns.*

3. Listen and identify the country of origin for each musical example.
   a. Japan or Turkey
   b. India or Mali
   c. Indonesia or Zimbabwe

4. Listen to this excerpt from *Kogoklaras* and identify the two cultures that contributed to this music.

5. Listen and identify the instruments you hear in these excerpts of music from three different cultures.
   a. xylophone ensemble or ney
   b. kora or gamelan
   c. nagauta ensemble or sitar

6. Listen and decide which of these examples contain repetition.

7. Listen to a portion of *Sambaso* and identify the instrument families you hear.

8. Listen to a recording of a gamelan and describe the texture you hear.

9. Listen to a portion of *Cedo* and identify the tone colors in this musical example. Identify the country where you might find this musical style.

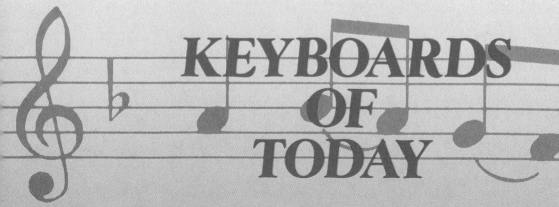

KEYBOARDS OF TODAY

The piano was invented about 1720 and developed into the familiar instrument of today during the first half of the nineteenth century. The pipe organ had its roots in ancient Greece. The electronic organ was invented in the mid-1900s.

Keyboard instruments of today include pianos, organs, and synthesizers, which were developed during the 1960s. Today's synthesizers enable players to produce an almost unlimited variety

Detail from *Harpsichord*. Johann Christoph Weigel

of sounds, even the sounds of other instruments. Through rhythm units (drum machines), sequencers (recording devices), and a variety of tone colors, the synthesizer has become more complex.

Keyboard instruments are used by many popular music groups.

• Notice the many sizes and shapes of the keyboards shown here. The arrangement of black and white keys is always the same.

KEYBOARD BASICS

- Listen to these two selections to hear the sounds of different keyboard instruments.

 "Dream of Dreams," by Joe Sample

 "Harmonic Repetition Montage"

The keyboard has sets of white and black keys. Center yourself in front of the keyboard and find each set of *two* black keys up and down the keyboard. C is always the white key to the left, D is the white key in the middle, and E is the white key to the right of the two black keys. Middle C is the C that is closest to the center of the keyboard.

Each set of *three* black keys is a reference point for finding F, G, A, and B. F is always the white key to the left, G and A are the white keys in the middle, and B is the white key to the right of the three black keys.

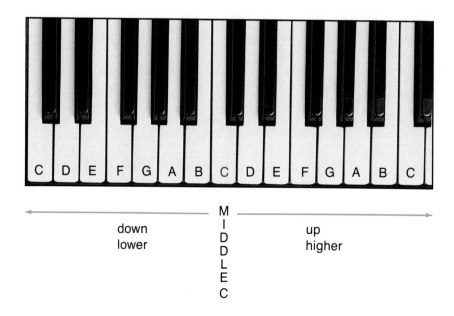

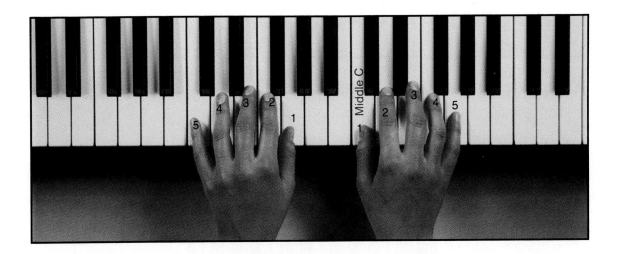

These hands show how the fingers are numbered for the keyboard. Notice that both thumbs are numbered *1*.

You can learn to play chords on the keyboard. **A chord** consists of three or more pitches played together. The twelve-bar blues is a common chord progression, or pattern, used in popular music.

To start you can play one pitch at a time.

- Find pitches C, F, and G on your keyboard. Use the fingers of your right hand as shown.

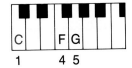
Right hand

- Play the following pitches along with the recording of the twelve-bar blues.

$\frac{4}{4}$ C C C C   C C C C   C C C C   C C C C

   F F F F   F F F F   C C C C   C C C C

   G G G G   F F F F   C C C C   C C C C

 "Twelve-Bar Blues," by Michael Treni

- Play the same pitches again with the twelve-bar blues, this time using the fingers of your left hand as shown.

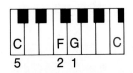
Left hand

Learning to Play the C, F, and G Chords

You can play the C chord on the keyboard.

- Start with the left hand and play C with your fifth finger.
  Skip up one white key to the right and use your third finger. You should now be on E with your third finger.
  Skip up another key and use your thumb. You should now be on G with your thumb.
  Play all three notes at the same time.

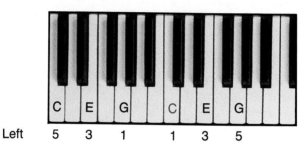

You have just learned to form and play the C chord.

- Now play the C chord with your right hand. Your thumb will be on C, your third finger will be on E, and your fifth finger will be on G.

You can play the F chord.

- Start with your left hand.
  Your fifth finger should be on F.
  Skip up one white key to the right. You should be on A with your third finger.
  Skip up another key and use your thumb. You should be on C with your thumb. Play all three notes together.

- Again, try the chord with your right hand, using your first, third, and fifth fingers.

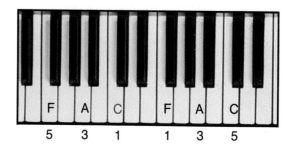

You can play the G chord.

- Start with your left hand.

  Your fifth finger should be on G.

  Skip up one white key to the right. You should be on B with your third finger.

  Skip up another key and use your thumb. You should be on D with your thumb. Play all three notes together.

- Again, try the chord with your right hand, using your first, third, and fifth fingers, the same fingers you used for the C and F chords.

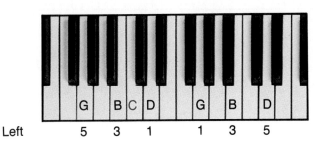

Left   5   3   1   1   3   5   Right

Now that you can play C, F, and G chords with either your left or right hand you can play the twelve-bar blues chord progression.

Many musicians play chords from chord charts. The following chord chart shows the 12 measures or bars of the twelve-bar blues. Three slashes after each chord's letter name indicate that the chord is to be played on every beat of each four-beat measure.

Twelve-Bar Blues

$\frac{4}{4}$ C/// C/// C/// C///

F/// F/// C/// C///

G/// F/// C/// C///

- Play along with the recording of the twelve-bar blues.

 CHALLENGE
Play the twelve-bar blues with both hands.

237

READING MUSIC AT THE KEYBOARD

The pitches on the keyboard are notated on the **staff** as shown in the following diagram. Pitches can be notated either on lines or in spaces.

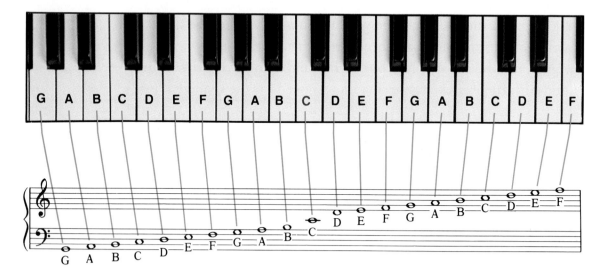

Pitches in the treble clef usually are played with the right hand.
Pitches in the bass clef usually are played with the left hand.

Reading Steps

When a melody moves *up or down* on the keyboard from one white key to the next without skipping any notes in between, it is said to move **stepwise**. The steps from one key to the next are notated on the staff as either *line to space* or *space to line*.

- Place the third finger of your left hand on G in the bass clef. Play A, the next note to the right (up), with your second finger. You have moved up a step. Play B, the next note to the right (up), with your thumb. You have moved another step.

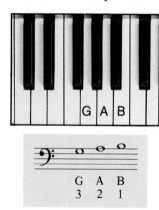

- Read and play these patterns of steps in the bass clef. Say the names of the notes before you play them and again as you play them. Notice the upward and downward motion of each melody.

1.					2.					3.							
F	E	D	E	F	F	G	A	G	F	F	G	A	G	F	E	F
1	2	3	2	1	3	2	1	2	3	3	2	1	2	3	4	3

- Place the thumb (finger 1) of your right hand on G in the treble clef. Play A, the next note to the right (up), with your second finger. You have moved up a step. Play B, the next note to the right (up), with your third finger. You have moved up another step.

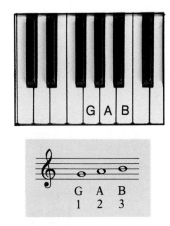

G A B
1 2 3

- Read and play these patterns of steps in the treble clef. Say the names of the notes before you play them and again as you play them. Notice the upward and downward motion of each melody.

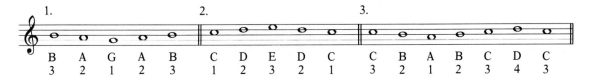

1.					2.					3.						
B	A	G	A	B	C	D	E	D	C	C	B	A	B	C	D	C
3	2	1	2	3	1	2	3	2	1	3	2	1	2	3	4	3

Reading Skips

When a melody moves *up or down* from one note to the next and skips some notes, it is said to move **skipwise**. When you skip one key on the keyboard it is notated on the staff as either *line to line* or *space to space.*

- Play C with the fifth finger of your left hand. Skip a key up to the right and play E with finger 3. Skip another key up to the right and play G with finger 1.

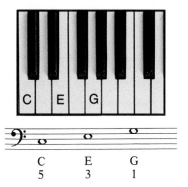

- Read and play these patterns of skips in the bass clef. Say the names of the notes before you play them and again as you play them. Notice the upward and downward motion of each melody.

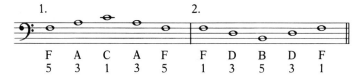

- Play F with the first finger of your right hand. Skip a key up to the right and play A with finger 3. Skip another key up to the right and play C with finger 5.

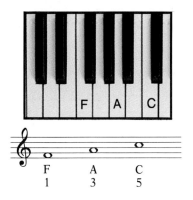

- Read and play these patterns of skips in the treble clef. Say the names of the notes before you play them and again as you play them. Notice the upward and downward motion of each melody.

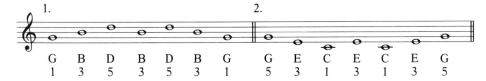

240

THE TWELVE-BAR BLUES

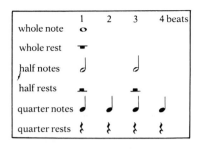

This chart shows the relationships
between notes and rests, or silences,
of different durations.

- Read and play this blues progression. Practice each part
  separately before playing them together.
- Perform this progression with the twelve-bar blues.

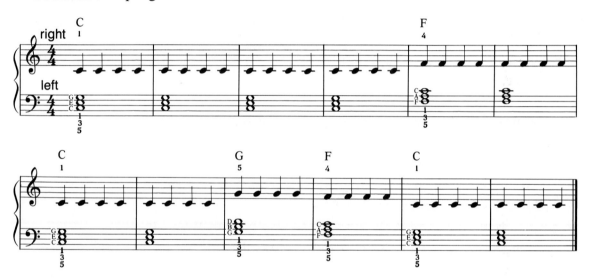

- Play these right hand melodies with the chord sequence. Pattern 1
  contains steps. Patterns 2 and 3 contain skips.
- Choose pattern 1, 2, or 3. Play it with the twelve-bar blues. Be sure
  to play each chord enough times to fit the twelve-bar blues progression.

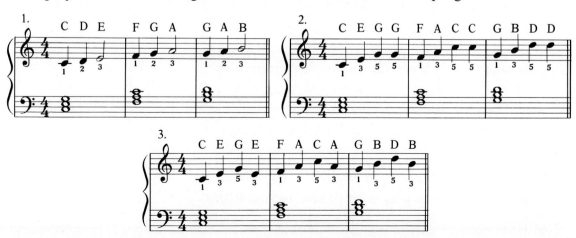

241

You can read and play this blues progression. Note that the chords are in the treble clef, and the melodic patterns are in the bass clef.

- Practice each part separately. Play the chords with your right hand. Play the melody with your left hand. Then play both parts together.
- Perform with the twelve-bar blues.

- Play these left hand melodies with the chord sequence. Pattern 1 measures contain steps and skips. Pattern 2 measures contain steps. Pattern 3 measures contain skips. Notice that when the chord changes to F or G, the beginning note of the left hand melodic pattern changes to F or G.
- Choose pattern 1, 2, or 3. Play it with the twelve-bar blues. Be sure to play each chord enough times to fit the twelve-bar blues progression.

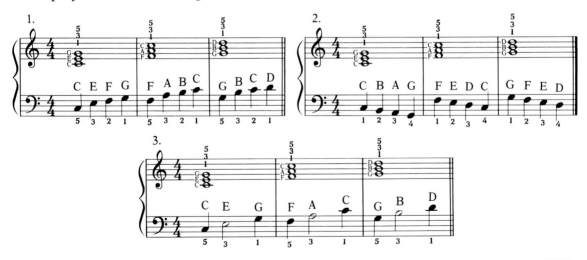

 CHALLENGE Create your own melodies by combining right and left hand patterns to play with the twelve-bar blues.

TRIADS

The chords you have been playing are based on skips. The three notes are called a **triad**. The bottom note of the chord or triad is called the **root**, the middle note is called the **third**, and the top note is called the **fifth**.

Each measure of melodic pattern 1 below begins on the root, each measure of pattern 2 begins on the third, and each measure of pattern 3 begins on the fifth of each chord.

Two eighth notes (♪♪) have the same duration as one quarter note (♩).

- Find the starting pitch of each melodic pattern before you play each chord change.

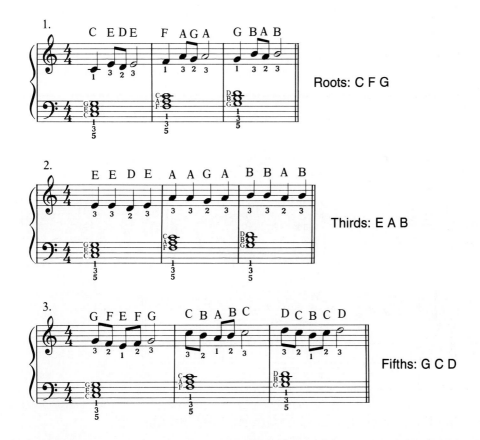

- Play the twelve-bar blues with each pattern.

SEVENTH CHORDS

The triads you have been playing contain three pitches. When a chord contains four pitches, the fourth pitch is usually one skip above the fifth. It is the seventh scale tone above the root, called the **seventh**.

- Look at this version of the twelve-bar blues and identify which measures contain chords with four pitches or seventh chords.
- Play the left hand part shown.
  B♭ (B-flat) is the black key to the *left* of B.

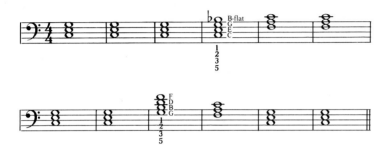

Melodic pattern 1 begins on the root, pattern 2 begins on the third, and pattern 3 begins on the the fifth of each chord. E♭ (E-flat) is the black key to the left of E.

- Name the starting pitch of each melodic pattern. Refer to the chart on page 241 if necessary.
- Play each pattern with the twelve-bar blues.

"Several Shades of Blue"

The keyboard selection "Several Shades of Blue" uses the twelve-bar blues progression and several of the melodic patterns you have learned.

- Follow the suggestions in Part I through Part IV to prepare to play "Several Shades of Blue."

Part I: Play the individual notes in each measure all at the same time to form the chord.

Part II: Practice playing fingers 1, 2, and 5 in the right hand on all notes of the chord (Example 1). Later add finger 3 to form a four-note chord (Example 2).

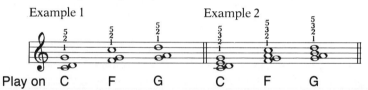

Part III: Practice moving the left hand from the root to the fifth.

Part IV: Practice with descending quarter notes (Example 1) and then add the root in the right hand (Example 2).

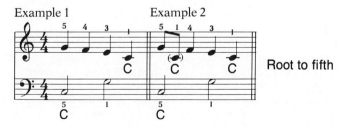

The mark ——————— stands for **crescendo** (kre-shen′ dō), meaning to play gradually louder. The mark ——————— stands for **decrescendo** (dā′ kre-shen-dō), meaning to play gradually softer. The term **simile** (sim′ i-lē) means you should continue to follow the marks for crescendo or decrescendo.

Several Shades of Blue

246

- With a group, perform "Several Shades of Blue" by:
  1. playing the root of each chord on guitar, bass, or bells (or synthesizer)
  2. improvising a percussion accompaniment on classroom instruments
  3. playing along with the rhythm section of your keyboard

If you are using a synthesizer with a sequencer, record the root of each chord on your sequencer and replay in repeat mode. Change the keyboard voice on your synthesizer and play along with the sequencer.

247

A NEW CHORD PATTERN

There are some new chords in this progression. They are shown in both the treble and the bass clef.

- Practice these chords.

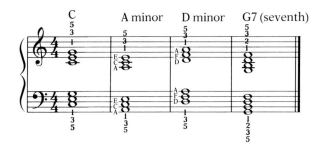

- Find and name the starting pitch of each melodic pattern below before you play it.

In pattern 2, two notes of the same pitch are connected by a curved line called a **tie**. Hold that pitch for the *combined* value of the two notes. In pattern 3, F♯ (**F-sharp**), D♯ (**D-sharp**), and G♯ (**G-sharp**) are the black keys to the *right* of F, D, and G, respectively.

- Play this chord progression with each melodic pattern.

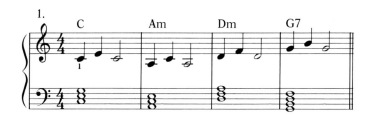

Start on the highest pitch of the chord

RESHAPING CHORDS

The pitches of a chord can be rearranged to make changes between chords smoother. This is called **revoicing**. It makes transitions from chord to chord sound smoother. It is important to remember that the names of chords do not change when they are revoiced.

- Practice this revoiced chord progression with the left hand.

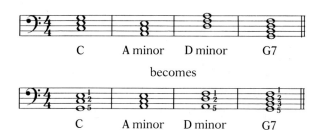

- Create your own melodic pattern in the right hand to play with the left hand chords. Use melodic patterns you have already learned.

- Practice this revoiced chord progression with the right hand.

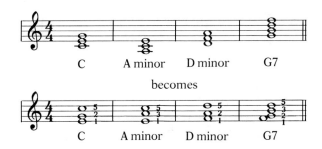

- Create your own melodic pattern in the left hand to play with the right hand chords. Use melodic patterns you have already learned.

"Blue Heart"

"Blue Heart" contains parts of the chord progressions you have learned, along with several of the melodic patterns you have learned. The **fermata** (⌢) in the last measure tells you to hold those notes slightly longer than usual.

- Practice patterns 1 and 2 before you perform "Blue Heart."

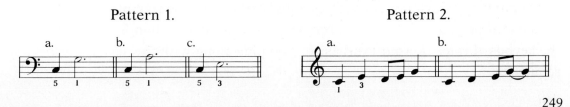

Blue Heart

- With a group, perform "Blue Heart" by:
  1. playing the root of each chord on guitar, bass, or bells (or synthesizer)
  2. improvising a percussion accompaniment on classroom instruments
  3. playing along with the rhythm section of your keyboard

If you are using a synthesizer with a sequencer, record the root of each chord on your sequencer and replay in repeat mode. Change the keyboard voice on your synthesizer and play along with the sequencer.

ANOTHER FAMILIAR CHORD PROGRESSION

This chord progression uses chords from the twelve-bar blues. It is frequently found in popular music.

- Practice the chord changes before you play this progression.

- Practice the left hand melodic patterns below. Find the starting pitch of each measure before you play it.

Fine (End)

Da Capo al Fine
(Go back to the beginning and play to Fine)

The **natural** sign (♮) cancels a previous sharp or flat in the same measure.

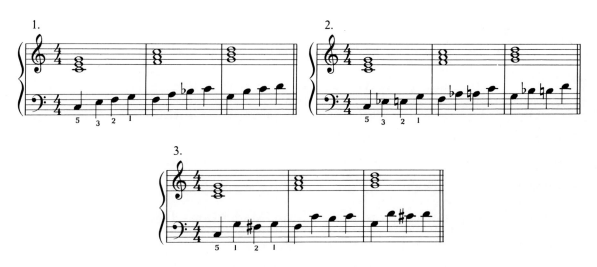

 CHALLENGE Reverse the parts so that the right hand plays the melodic patterns while the left hand plays the chords.

"Mama Don't 'Low"

You can play the American folk song "Mama Don't 'Low" as a solo or with other keyboard instruments or guitars.

• Sing the song first to become familiar with it.

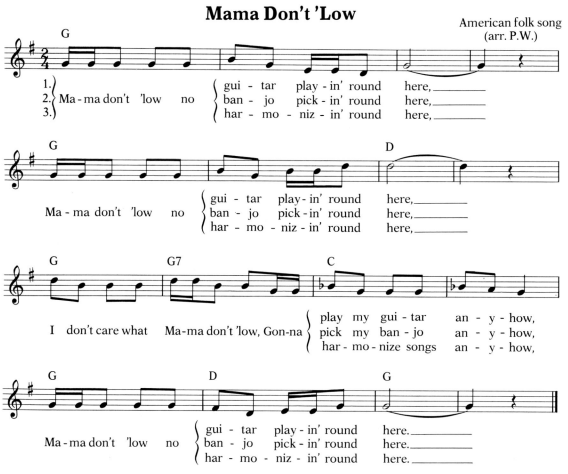

Mama Don't 'Low

American folk song
(arr. P.W.)

The keyboard accompaniment to "Mama Don't 'Low" is based on chords G major and C major, which you have learned, and new chord D major.

• Practice these patterns before you perform "Mama Don't 'Low."

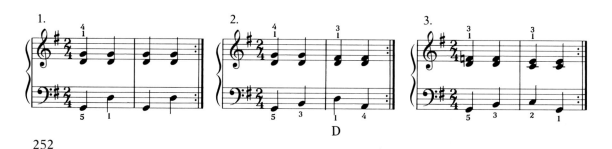

Notice that the music has a new meter signature: $\frac{2}{4}$. In $\frac{2}{4}$ meter, the the quarter note has the steady beat, with two beats in each measure.

- Pat the steady beat and clap the eighth notes to prepare for playing "Mama Don't 'Low."

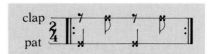

Keyboard Accompaniment to "Mama Don't 'Low"

You can also play this accompaniment with the version for guitar on page 263.

- With a group, perform "Mama Don't 'Low" by:
  1. playing the root of each chord on guitar, bass, or bells (or synthesizer)
  2. improvising a percussion accompaniment on classroom instruments
  3. playing along with the rhythm section of your keyboard

If you are using a synthesizer with a sequencer, record the root of each chord on your sequencer and replay in repeat mode. Change the keyboard voice on your synthesizer and play along with the sequencer.

PLAYING THE GUITAR

- Listen to these compositions for guitar. How do they sound alike?
How do they sound different?

 Concerto in D Major for Guitar and Orchestra, Third Movement,
by Antonio Vivaldi

Detail from *Presentation in the Temple*, Vittore Carpaccio, ACCADEMIA, Venice

 "Hickory Hollow," performed by Banks and Shane

255

PARTS OF THE GUITAR

In this section you will learn to play strum patterns, chords, and bass parts on the guitar. The four lowest strings of the six-stringed guitar can be tuned to the same pitches as the four strings of the electric bass. You can play bass parts on either instrument.

tuning machines

frets

nut

neck

fingerboard

strings

sound hole

tuning machines

nut

body

bridge

neck

frets

fingerboard

body

bridge

pickup

controls

TUNING YOUR GUITAR

The tuning most often used for guitar and bass is pictured here as it relates to the keyboard. The four strings of the electric bass are tuned to the same pitches (one octave below) as the four lowest strings on a six-stringed guitar.

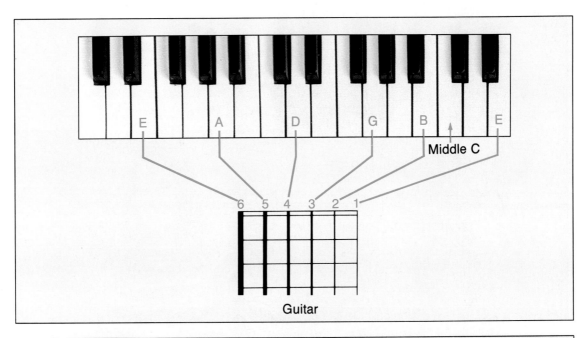

Guitar

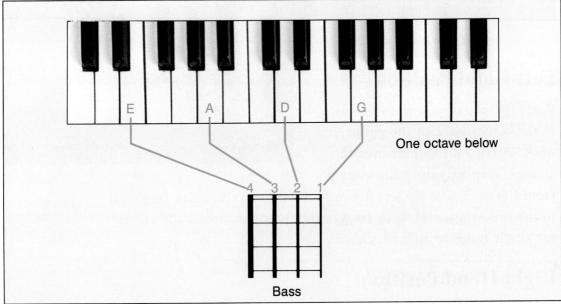

Bass

You can use two alternate tunings for some of the songs in this section. You will find these tunings, as well as chord frames for the songs, on pages 276–277.

HOLDING THE GUITAR OR ELECTRIC BASS

Left-Hand Position

Place the pad of your left thumb
in the center back of the guitar
neck. Curve your fingers over the
strings, keeping your palm away
from the neck. The fingers are numbered from the index finger (1)
to the little finger (4). Your fingers **fret**, or press down, the strings
for single notes or to form chords.

Right-Hand Position

Curve the fingers and **strum**, or brush down across the strings with
your fingernails. A down strum is indicated by this sign ⌐ .

Brush up across the strings with your thumbnail for an up
strum (∨).

258

Strum Patterns for Guitar

Practice these rhythm patterns on **open** (unfretted) strings, or with any chords you already know. Play the downward (⌐) and upward (v) strums where indicated.

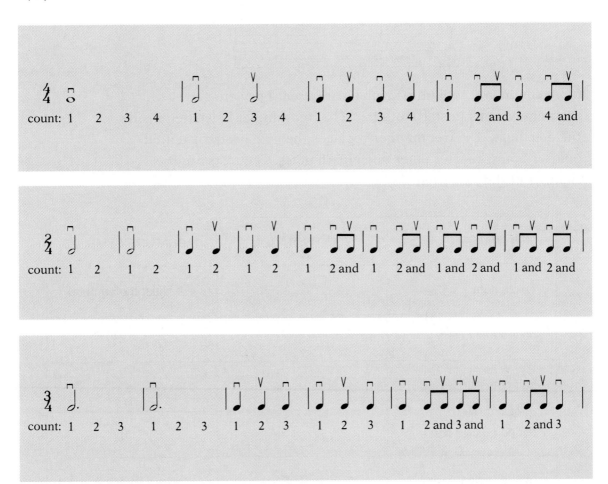

READING A BASS PART IN TABLATURE

Bass parts for either the six-stringed guitar or the electric bass can be written in *tablature*. **Tablature** is a picture of the guitar strings divided into measures of music.

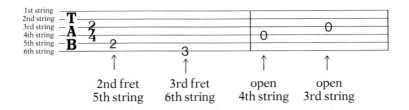

The six lines represent the six strings of the guitar. The numbers on the line indicate the frets. An *O* indicates an open, or unfretted, string. In some tablature the rhythms are shown above the fret numbers. Here the rhythm is ♩ ♩ | ♩ .

More commonly, tablature symbols are used. They are shown with their equivalents in staff notation. The fret number is written inside the note head. The fret number replaces the note head for dotted quarter notes, quarter notes and eighth notes. The rests are the same as in staff notation.

NAMES	STAFF NOTATION	TABLATURE SYMBOLS
whole note	𝅝	2 (just the number)
dotted half notes	𝅗𝅥. 𝄽.	②.
half notes	𝅗𝅥 𝄽	②
dotted quarter notes	♩. 𝄾.	2.
quarter notes	♩ 𝄾	2
eighth notes	♪ 𝄾	2
eighth notes	♫ 𝄾	2 2

This is how the symbols look in tablature.

Unless otherwise indicated, the left hand fingering is the same number as the fret.

260

PLAYING CHORDS

A chord diagram or frame shows where to place your left fingers on the fingerboard to fret, or form, a chord. The number in the circle indicates which finger to use. The circle shows you where your finger belongs. An *X* means that a string is not played.

- Practice the E minor and D major chords and the accompaniment patterns for "Drunken Sailor." Then play them with the song.

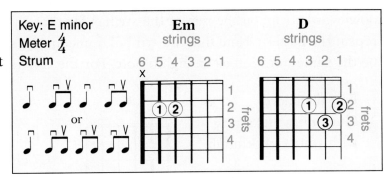

Drunken Sailor

Traditional

Em — What shall we do with a drunk-en sail - or, D — What shall we do with a drunk-en sail - or,

Em — What shall we do with a drunk - en sail - or, D — Ear - lye in the Em morn - ing?

    Refrain   Way, hey, and up she rises, (*3 times*)
                  Earlye in the morning.
       2. Throw him in the longboat till he's sober, (*3 times*)
           Earlye in the morning.
       3. Pull out the plug and wet him all over, (*3 times*)
           Earlye in the morning.

ADD A BASS PART

You can play a bass part for this song on the four lowest strings of a six-stringed guitar or on the electric bass. The top line shows the part in staff notation.

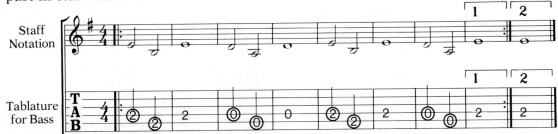

Staff Notation

Tablature for Bass

261

BASS PATTERNS

Bass patterns involve playing the lowest notes of a chord separately from the other notes. In "Mama Don't 'Low," the chords are G major, G7, D7, and C major.

To play a bass pattern, first fret the chord. Then pluck *only* the single bass note shown in the tablature. Follow that with a downward strum on the rest of the strings for that chord. Then repeat the pattern. Note that the symbol ♪ means the strum should be the same duration as an eighth note. For the G major chord:

1. Fret the chord
2. Pluck *only* this string with your right thumb

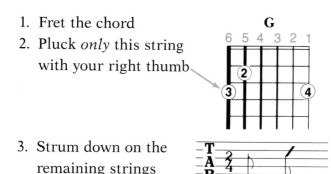

3. Strum down on the remaining strings

The left hand fingering for G and G7 chords is *not* the same as the fret number. The left hand fingering is shown in parentheses above the tablature.

Note that the G7 chord has the same bass note as the G major chord.

- Fret the D7 chord, pluck the fourth string bass note, and strum all the strings *except* the sixth string.

- Fret the C major chord, pluck the fifth string bass note, and strum all the strings except the sixth.

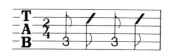

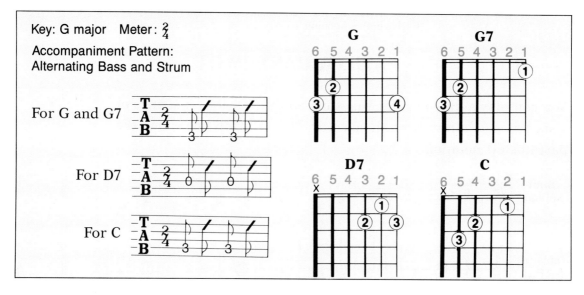

Mama Don't 'Low

American folk song (arr. P.W.)

BASS RUNS

A **run** is a stepwise pattern of notes that connects two chords in a song. Runs can be played on the six-stringed guitar. Each note in a run is played individually, usually in an even rhythm. The symbol ⌐ means the strum should be the same duration as a quarter note.

To play Bass Run 1:

1. Fret and play the bass note and the chord in the previous measure.
2. With your right thumb, pluck the single notes shown in the tablature. Change the left hand fingers as necessary.
3. Fret and play the next bass note and chord.

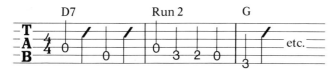

Play Bass Run 2 in the same way:

- Practice these runs until they sound smooth, then play them where they are indicated in "The Wabash Cannonball."

Notice that in this song, the bass notes for each chord alternate.

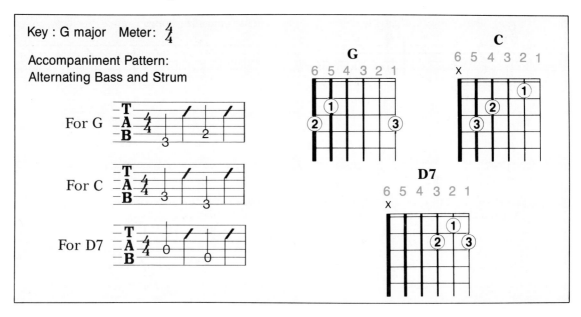

The Wabash Cannonball

Traditional

THE SLIDE

A slide is a kind of slur in which you fret two different pitches but pluck the string only once. The bass part in this song has a slide, (2-3), on the fifth and sixth strings. To play a slide:

1. Fret the string on the initial fret number indicated.
2. Pluck that string with your right thumb.
3. *At the same time*, slide the left hand finger up or down to the next fret number indicated. You will hear the pitch move up or down, too.

For example, to play (2-3), start on the second fret and slide to the third fret.

In this bass part for "The Golden Vanity," some of the left hand fingerings are *not* the same as the fret numbers. The left hand fingerings are shown in parentheses above the tablature when they are different.

This song has a meter of 4/4. The song contains two new chords: A major and B minor.

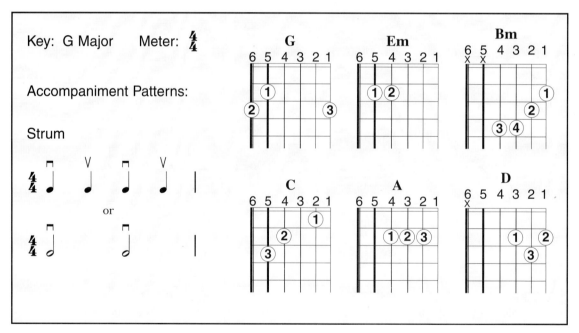

• Play "The Golden Vanity" with the bass part. Then play it again with the chord accompaniment.

The Golden Vanity

English Folk Song

1. There once was a ship, and a stur-dy craft was she; She went by the name of the Gold-en Van-i-ty. And ne'er a fin-er ves-sel did sail up-on the sea. Oh, she sailed up-on the Low Lands Low. She sailed up-on the Low Lands Low.

2. One day on the ship of the Gold-en Van-i-ty The captain raised his spy-glass to see what he could see. And lo___ and be-hold, he did spy the en-e-my As they sailed up-on the Low Lands Low. As they sailed up-on the Low Lands Low.

You will find the rest of the verses to this song on page 132.

267

PLAYING THE BLUES

One basic rhythm pattern for the blues is

- Play it with a relaxed swing of long and short sounds.

- Practice this rhythm with the G, C, and D chords.
  You can play an accompaniment to "Worried Man Blues" using
  the rhythm pattern shown above.

The Blues Shuffle

The **blues shuffle** pattern combines the rhythm you have learned
with two alternating chords, a root chord, and the same chord with
an added tone, called the sixth.

root chord   **G**

root chord with added sixth   **G 6**   added sixth

Play the root chord (G, C, or D) on the first and third beats of the
measure. Play the sixth chord (G6, C6, or D6) on the second and
fourth beats of the measure. You need to move only one finger back
and forth to make the change from one chord to the other.

- Play the blues shuffle with these chords from "Worried Man Blues."

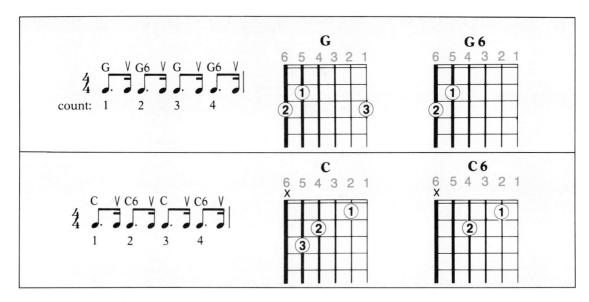

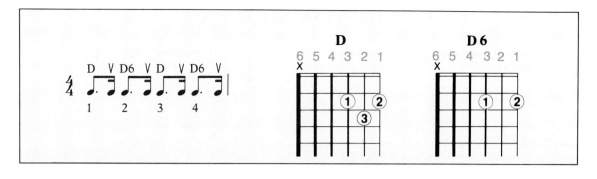

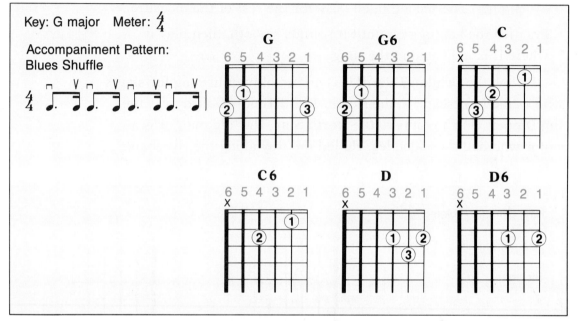

Worried Man Blues

Traditional

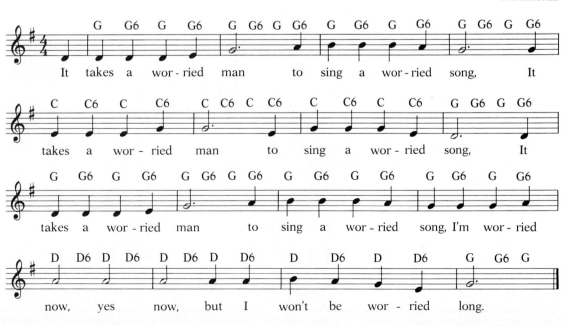

It takes a wor-ried man to sing a wor-ried song, It

takes a wor-ried man to sing a wor-ried song, It

takes a wor-ried man to sing a wor-ried song, I'm wor-ried

now, yes now, but I won't be wor-ried long.

269

THE HAMMER-ON

In a **hammer-on**, you pluck an open string, then fret it, to play two pitches. The bass part to this song includes a hammer-on .

To play this hammer-on:

1. Pluck the open fourth string with your right thumb.
2. *Quickly* fret ("hammer") the second finger of your left hand onto the second fret of the fourth string. You will hear two pitches. The second pitch lasts for the rest of the measure.

- Practice the hammer-on until it sounds smooth, then play it where it is indicated in the song.

"Follow the Drinkin' Gourd" was a kind of map in song for slaves who wanted to escape to the North. The "Drinkin' Gourd" was the Big Dipper, which points to the North Star. The "old man" was a sailor who had a wooden leg. He led the way along the riverbank.

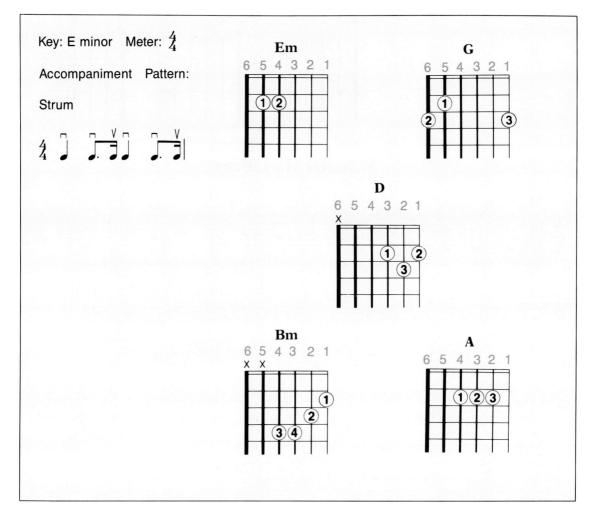

270

Follow the Drinkin' Gourd

Traditional

Verse 1. When the sun comes back and the first quail calls,_____
2. Now the riv-er bank-'ll make__ a might-y good road;____ The
3. Now the riv - er ends__ be - tween two hills;_____

Fol - low____ the Drink-in' Gourd.__Then the Old Man is a-wait-in' for to
dead trees____ will show you the way. And the left__ foot, peg - foot,__
Fol - low____ the Drink-in' Gourd. __ And__ there's an-oth-er riv - er on the

car - ry you to free-dom, Fol - low the Drink - in' Gourd.
trav - el - in'____ on, _____ Fol - low the Drink - in' Gourd.
oth - er____ side, ____ Fol - low the Drink - in' Gourd.

Refrain Fol - low_____ the Drink - in' Gourd,_ Fol - low____ the

Drink - in' Gourd,_ For the Old Man is a - wait - in' for to

car - ry you to free - dom, Fol - low the Drink - in' Gourd.

SETTING THE MOOD OF A SONG

Try to catch the mood of "The Ghost Ship" as you play the guitar part or the bass part. This song has one new chord: B7.

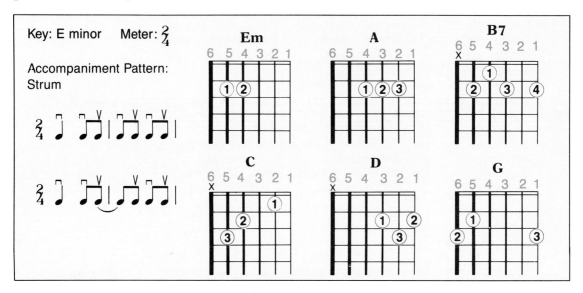

The Ghost Ship

Words and music by
Don Besig and Nancy Price

1. Now lis-ten well as a tale I tell of a night I shook with fear. We were sail-ing west on the o-pen sea, head-in' home from a long, long year. I was stand-ing

2. 'Twas then I spied off the starboard side a strange, mysterious sight.
   I froze with fear as it drifted near like a ghost in the dark of night.
   I could see a sail on a broken mast and deserted decks below.
   From all around came a mournful sound, but I saw not a living soul!

3. Well, I held fast to the forward mast as the ship moved slowly on.
   And I watched that way 'til the break of day, when I knew that it fin'lly
      had gone.
   Oh, they laughed and joked as I told my tale to the captain and the men.
   But the story's true, I can promise you, and it's sure to happen again.

AN ARPEGGIO ACCOMPANIMENT

An **arpeggio** is a chord whose notes are played one at a time, rather than all at once.

To play an arpeggio:

1. Fret the chord.
2. Pluck the strings indicated, one at a time and in rhythm, with your right hand fingers. Finger numbers for the right hand are shown in parentheses *below* the arpeggio. They are the same as for the left hand.

• Practice these arpeggios. Notice that the bass note changes from the fourth to the fifth to the sixth string. The upper strings remain the same for all the chords.

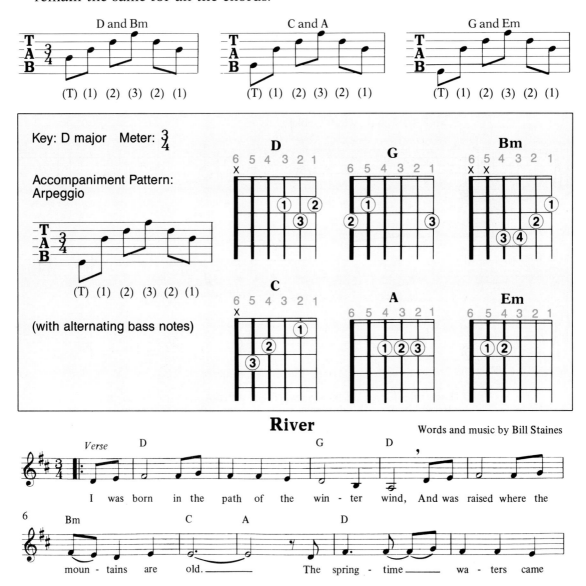

2. I've been to the city and back again;
   I've been touched by some things that I've learned,
   Met a lot of good people, and I've called them friends,
   Felt the change when the seasons turned.
   I've heard all the songs that the children sing
   And I've listened to love's melodies;
   I've felt my own music within me rise
   Like the wind in the autumn trees.

   Refrain

3. Someday when the flowers are blooming still,
   Someday when the grass is still green,
   My rolling waters will round the bend
   And flow into the open sea.
   So here's to the rainbow that's followed me here,
   And here's to the friends that I know,
   And here's to the song that's within me now;
   I will sing it where'er I go.

   Refrain

ALTERNATE TUNING: D MAJOR

You can use this tuning to play "The Wabash Cannonball" and "Worried Man Blues."

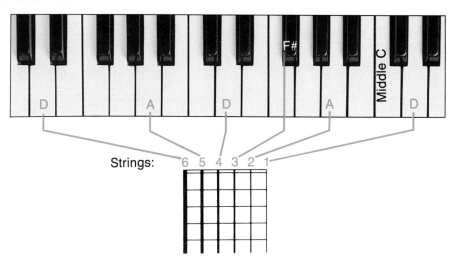

"The Wabash Cannonball"

To play the alternating bass and strum with your right hand, pluck the sixth string with your right thumb for all three chords, then strum the rest of the strings. Omit the bass runs in this tuning. G and C are bar chords. To fret a bar chord, press your index finger down firmly across *all* the strings on fret indicated.

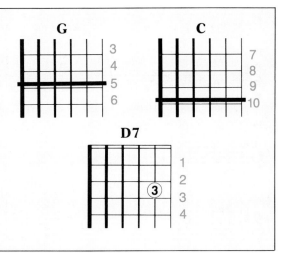

"Worried Man Blues"

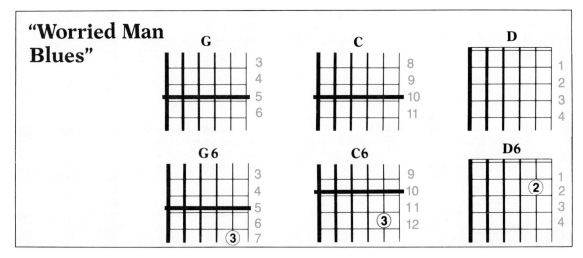

ALTERNATE TUNING: D MINOR

You can use this tuning to play "Drunken Sailor" and "Follow the Drinkin' Gourd."

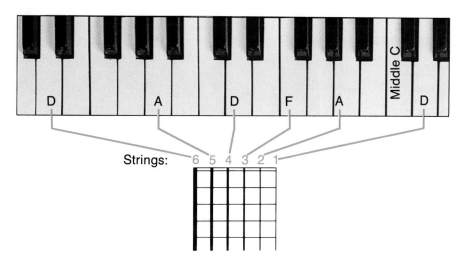

"Drunken Sailor"

E minor is a bar chord (as are A minor and G major below). To fret a bar chord, press your index finger down firmly across all the strings on the fret indicated.

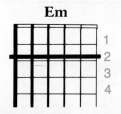
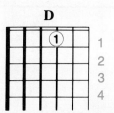

"Follow the Drinkin' Gourd"

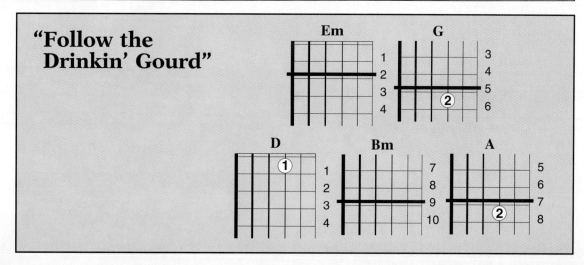

MUSIC IN

YOUR LIFE

The Participants

How many times a day do you hear music? Think of each musical encounter listed below. Which ones offer an opportunity to participate by singing or by playing an instrument? By clapping or moving?

Your favorite group is performing at the mall.

You're waiting for a haircut. Background music is playing.

You stop to listen to the pep band practice for the big game.

You tune in to your favorite music television channel.

You get out your guitar and practice a few new chord changes.

You probably have many musical encounters every day. Some of them you will ignore. Some you will enjoy by listening. Others will invite further participation.

- Participate in active music-making by performing these rhythmic accompaniments.

 "Participation Music"

Participation Music

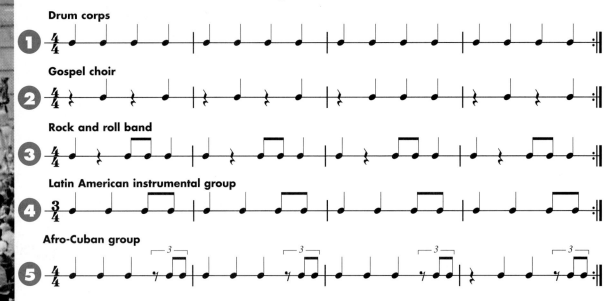

Which musical group did you most enjoy participating with? Why?

Create your own rhythmic accompaniment for one of the groups in "Participation Music." Perform your accompaniment with the group.

People who love to participate in music often consider it as a possible career. Like any career in the arts, a career in music requires talent, hard work, persistence, and a great deal of training. A career as a musical performer is very demanding.

GLORIA ESTEFAN
VOCALIST

Gloria Estefan was the lead singer for Miami Sound Machine before launching her own career. She can project many moods to her audience—from energetic dance songs to slower, more serious selections. Her ability to do both reflects her versatility as a performer.

- **Play this rhythmic accompaniment part as you listen to Gloria Estefan sing "Get on Your Feet."**

 "Get on Your Feet" Words by John De Faria, Music by John De Faria, Jorge Casas, and Clay Ostwald.

Introduction   *Verse 1: play 5 times.*
                  Verse 2: play 3 times.

Refrain 1: play 2 times.
Refrain 2: play 4 times. Last time improvise to end.   *Go back to verse 2.*

THINK IT THROUGH

Imagine what the career of a performer might be like in the future. What personal qualities and abilities will be needed? How might the training of a musician change over the next 50 years?

Choosing Your Music

Because of the advances in recording and broadcasting technology, many more types of music are available today than ever before.

When you go to a record store, what types of music do you look for first? Which ones do you never look at? How important is each of the following in choosing music?

I heard this music on the radio.

A friend told me this music was good.

I want to learn to play this type of music.

I saw a video or TV show featuring this singer or group.

I saw a movie I like and want to get the soundtrack.

After thinking about these questions, take a class poll. Which is the strongest influence in your choice of music?

Look at these posters advertising musical events. Which performance would you like to attend? What factors influence your choice? Describe what you might hear and see at the performance you choose. Include in your description the type of music, number of performers, number of instruments and vocalists, and reaction of the audience. Will the music be loud or soft? Fast or slow? Dramatic or restful?

 Musical Performances

- Listen to "Musical Performances Medley." Match each of the five short excerpts with one of the posters.

Appalachian Music Festival
Come on down for a hand-clapping good time with your favorite country music groups.

JULY 3-5
County Fairgrounds

Skiffle Bands
Dulcimer Soloists
Jug Bands
Fiddling Contests

Admission FREE

ROCK FESTIVAL

JULY 30
UNIVERSITY STADIUM

Re-live the story of Rock and Roll through 50 years of classic rock.

ADMISSION FREE

• Perform a rhythmic accompaniment with each of the excerpts.

Musical Performances

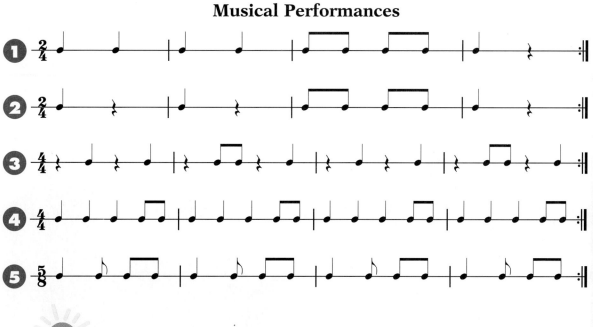

THINK IT THROUGH

Did you change your mind about which performance to attend after you heard the music? After participating as a performer? What is the biggest influence in your choice of music?

283

Influencing Choices

Commercials advertise a wide variety of products. Advertisers use commercials to persuade people to choose a particular product.

- Listen to this commercial. What is being advertised? What age group is being targeted? How is music used in the commercial?

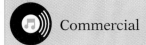 Commercial

Create Your Own Commercial

Design a commercial to sell a product. What will your product be? What age audience are you trying to reach? What strategies will you use to sell the product?

- Write a script for your commercial.

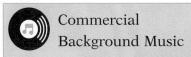 Commercial Background Music

- Listen to three types of music that might be used as background for an advertisement. Choose one to use in your commercial. Read your commercial with and without the background music. How did the music contribute to the commercial as a whole?

Celebrating Choices

Each year millions of people purchase CDs of their favorite music. Each time they do this, they cast a "vote" for their favorite recording. The music industry keeps track of the best-selling recordings and publishes a "Top 10 List" every week. The Grammy® awards, sponsored by the National Academy of Recording Arts and Sciences, are annual awards that recognize commercial success and other achievements in the recording industry.

Meet David Kahne Record Producer

David Kahne is a Grammy®-award-winning record producer. David studied music and engineering in college and on the job. He has had a varied career as a keyboardist, composer, high school teacher, producer for a major record label, and as an independent producer. It is in this last role that he is currently working with his own company in New York City.

A record producer directs the recording process. Acting as an artistic collaborator, a record producer uses the technology of the studio to create recordings that best show the artistic and entertainment qualities of the performer.

Mr. Kahne has worked with many performing artists including Tony Bennett, Shawn Colvin, Sugar Ray, and The Bangles. In 1995 Mr. Kahne won the Grammy® for "Album of the Year," with Tony Bennett's *MTV Unplugged*.

• Listen to David Kahne describe his career as a record producer.

THINK IT THROUGH

Create a "Top 10 List" of your favorite recordings. Arrange your list in order, starting with your favorite. Write a short statement describing why you chose a particular recording to be "Number 1."

Enriching Your Entertainment

Music plays a role in many kinds of entertainment. Sometimes it is the featured entertainment. At other times it heightens the excitement or creates a mood. Imagine your favorite kind of entertainment. Is music a part of it?

- Look at these pictures. How is music used to enrich each event? List other kinds of entertainment that music enriches.

Music Enhances Mood

Music can be used to create or reinforce a mood. Here are two musical excerpts that might enhance the mood of a scene in a movie.

• Choose adjectives that describe the mood of each selection, for example: sad, mournful, lively, calm, happy, sorrowful, gleeful, spirited

 Adagio for Strings by Samuel Barber

 "Spring," from *The Four Seasons*, First Movement by Antonio Vivaldi

What musical characteristics contribute to the mood of each selection?

short sounds	long sounds
smooth sounds	detached sounds
slow tempo	fast tempo
loud dynamics	soft dynamics
thick texture	thin texture

• Choose one of the selections and imagine that it is background music for a movie. What kind of movie does the music suggest? Think of a theme for an imaginary film. Then give it a title. Read your title and description of the film as the music plays in the background.

Selecting Film Music

During a film, the music helps to set many different moods. The music may enhance the mood of the current scene. It may also set the mood for a scene to come. The film director and composer work together to ensure that the music sets the appropriate mood for each scene. Feature films are often preceded by a movie promotion. The five selections below can be used in a movie promotion.

- Listen to each selection. Describe the mood and musical characteristics of each.

 Five Musical Moods

Follow these steps to create a movie promotion.

1. Think of an idea for a movie plot.

2. Think of two or more scenes, with different moods, that might be in this movie.

3. Write a few lines of dialogue for each of the scenes.

4. Decide on the mood of each scene. Select one of "Five Musical Moods" as background music for each scene.

5. Write a narration to introduce your movie promotion, connect the scenes and close it.

6. Revise the final promotion to be about 30 seconds long, including both narration and excerpts from the film music.

Composing Film Music

Film music used to be recorded live. The conductor watched the film while conducting the orchestra. Today many film composers use computer programs that allow the composer to view the film as they compose.

MEET
ALAN MENKEN
Theater and Film Composer

Alan Menken is known for his theater productions such as *Little Shop of Horrors* and Disney's animated movies. His first movie success was in 1989 with *The Little Mermaid*, on which he collaborated with lyricist Howard Ashman. A string of other successful Disney movies followed: *Aladdin, Beauty and the Beast,* and *Pocahontas.*

These animated films are done in the tradition of Broadway musicals. For this reason the music is a crucial element in bringing the story to life. For example "Under the Sea," a lively calypso number sung by musical crustaceans in *The Little Mermaid,* helps "animate" a scene in the film. Due to the tremendous success of Alan Menken's music, versions of his songs have been recorded by popular artists such as Vanessa Williams, Jon Secada and Celine Dion.

- Listen to Alan Menken as he describes the work of a film composer.

T HINK IT THROUGH

The next time you go to the movies or watch a TV show, evaluate the background music. What worked well? What would you change? Why?

Do It Yourself:
Music Through Technology

Wherever music is heard today, technology was probably involved to create it, perform it, or record it. The influence of technology is especially strong in popular music.

- Think of your favorite popular recording. Describe some of the sounds and special effects in the recording. To what extent do you think technology played a part in creating these musical effects?

Creating Music Using Technology

Much as the word processor has helped writers to work, music technology has helped composers to work more quickly. Sequencers use digital language to allow any computer or electronic keyboard to act like a tape recorder. Unlike the tape recorder, however, a sequencer allows composers to hear and revise any part of the composition as soon as it is composed. Using sequencers, composers create, edit, store, and play back music digitally. Electronic sound banks are combined with sequencers. These sound banks give composers access to a wide variety of instrumental sounds.

Many electronic keyboards designed for home use have sequencers and sound banks built in. This new technology allows people to create their own music.

Peter Gabriel is a singer and a composer who has worked on a wide variety of projects that combine music from around the world. He established his own company to promote world music. The ability to combine musical ideas from distant parts of the world is made easier by today's rapidly advancing music technology.

- Listen as Peter Gabriel tells you about using technology to create his recordings. Which of these ideas can you try by using technology in your classroom or home?

In "Don't Give Up" Peter Gabriel uses an innovative mix of synthesized sounds, bass, and percussion to create a complex texture. Listen to how the instrumental and vocal tracks are layered to create a rich blend of sounds.

"Don't Give Up" (excerpt) by Peter Gabriel

MEET PETER GABRIEL
VOCALIST AND COMPOSER

The chart below shows some of the key people involved in any recording. Which of these people use technology? Which career interests you most?

THE COMPOSER

writes the music. Using notation software, the composer can enter music directly into a computer and

THE ARRANGER

determines vocal combinations, the style of the accompaniment, and the instrumentation to help present the song to its best

THE PERFORMER

rehearses and records the arrangement, giving it his or her own artistic interpretation.

THE RECORDING ENGINEER

handles the technical aspects of a recording session: mike placement, sound levels, and effects such as reverb.

THE RECORD PRODUCER

directs the recording session by helping the musicians with creative decisions and by working with the engineer to get the desired sound.

291

Create and Share Your Music

MIDI (Musical Instrument Digital Interface) allows people to connect musical instruments to computers. Computers may be networked to allow users to share information. With MIDI, electronic instruments and computers may communicate digital-musical information. A typical MIDI system consists of five components:

1. a *controller* (a MIDI keyboard, guitar, saxophone, or other instrument)

2. a *MIDI interface* (a device that allows the controller to "talk" to the computer)

3. a *sequencer program* (software that enables a person to create, record, edit, and play back music)

4. a *tone generator* (a collection of different sounds)

5. a *sound output device* (speakers or headphones).

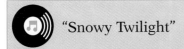 "Snowy Twilight"

MIDI systems are used for all types of music making. "Snowy Twilight" was created using a MIDI setup like the one pictured. The 128 sounds available on General MIDI enabled the composer to combine electronic sounds with percussion instruments such as marimba and timpani. Notice the combinations of contrasting tone colors as you listen to "Snowy Twilight."

Create Your Own Music

In each period of history, music and other art forms express ideas and impressions that are important to people of that time. Imagine that you are the music representative on a time-capsule team. Your task is to create a short composition called "Sounds of My Time."

 Create

1. Make a list of sounds that you will include. These could include excerpts from current music, environmental sounds, new music that you compose, or any other sounds.

2. Arrange your list of ideas in a pleasing order.

3. If original music is involved in your composition, plan and rehearse it.

4. Record the sounds and music that you want to use.

5. Revise your recording and share it with the class.

Share Your Music

Technology allows us to share music in ways we could not even imagine just a few years ago. Musicians can easily download and send music files via a computer on the Internet or World Wide Web.

T HINK IT THROUGH

What ways can you share music in your community? Throughout the world? What ways do you think will be invented in the future?

Music Library

Song Anthology

Each of us has a unique voice. Together our voices can produce rich harmony. The harmony in this song is created by singing three different melodies at the same time.

Harmony in C

Words and Music by M.J.

Create a routine for using dynamics and voice assignments in this folk song from Zaire.

Boat Song

Zairian Folk Song

THINK IT THROUGH: Evaluate the routine you created. Recommend ways to improve the routine to enhance the song.

This well-known Nigerian folk song is performed to celebrate life's highlights.

Osebaba

Nigerian Chant

O - se, O - se - o, O - se - o, O - se - ba - ba.

Al - le - lu, Al - le - lu - ia, Al - le - lu - ia, O - se - ba - ba.

Zol Zain Sholem

Eastern European Jewish Song
Arranged by Joshua Jacobson

Refrain

I and II

Ya pa pa pa ya pa pa pa yam pam pam

III and IV

Ya pa pa pa ya pa pa pa yam pam pam

ya pa pa pa ya pa pa pa yam pam pam yam pam pam.

ya pa pa pa ya pa pa pa yam pam pam yam pam pam.

Verse Solo

Sho - lem, sho - lem, zol zain zol zain
Free - dom, free - dom, let us live in

I, II

Sho - lem, sho - lem, zol zain zol zain
Free - dom, free - dom, let us live in

III, IV

Sho - lem, sho - lem, zol zain zol zain
Free - dom, free - dom, let us live in

298

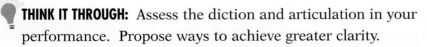

THINK IT THROUGH: Assess the diction and articulation in your performance. Propose ways to achieve greater clarity.

Exploring Your Voice

Your voice is a complex musical instrument. Have you heard suggestions such as the following in your music class? What do you think is the purpose of each?

"Your pronunciation is great!"
"Stand tall."
"Try emphasizing the vowel more."
"Make a big sound here."
"Is your voice lower?"
"You have a very clear voice."
"Light on the top please."

Vocal Exercises

Explore your voice by practicing each of the following. After singing each exercise, choose the statement that best matches the exercise. Explain your choice.

Breathing

Sink - ing sun in ___ the sky, down ___ it comes, night ___ is nigh.

Diction

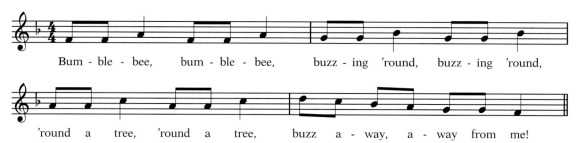

Bum - ble - bee, bum - ble - bee, buzz - ing 'round, buzz - ing 'round,

'round a tree, 'round a tree, buzz a - way, a - way from me!

Range

High _ low, High _ low, High _ low, High _ low, High _ low, High _ low.

Vowels

You, me, may I go? You, me, may I go? You, me, may I go?

Changing Voice

O ____ say, can you see, O ____ say, can you see,

As a singer, it's important to know your voice. As you grow older your voice will change. Continue to practice these and similar exercises as a way of monitoring and developing the most expressive instrument of all, your voice.

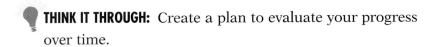 **THINK IT THROUGH:** Create a plan to evaluate your progress over time.

PREPARING *to Sing "In the Mix"*

Some melodies move quickly between high and low pitches. To sing these melodies the singer must be able to place the tone comfortably from low to high pitches.

- Sing this pattern, moving higher and lower. The hum and vocal slide will help you place the tone over a wide vocal range.

Good vocal tone is produced when proper breathing and posture are combined with proper placement of the tone.

- Sing this short song while standing or sitting tall to help with your breathing. Stress the vowel sounds in each word to help develop your vocal tone.

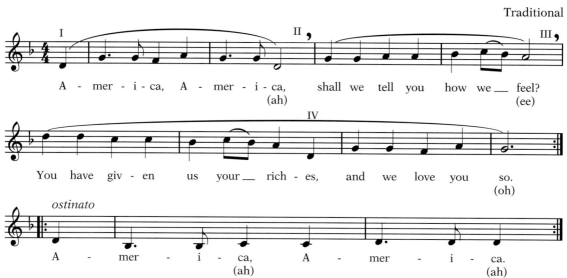

"In the Mix" contains melodies that cover a wide vocal range. Concentrate on placing your voice correctly to produce a good vocal tone while you sing.

In the Mix

"I Get Around," by Brian Wilson;
"Book of Love," Words and Music by Warren Davis,
George Malone, and Charles Patrick;
"Only You," Words and Music by Buck Ram and Ande Rand

"I Get Around" *(falsetto ad lib. throughout)*

Oo _____

Get a-round, round, round, I get a-round _ Get a-round, round, round,

I get a - round, _____ from _ town to town,

I get a-round. _ Get a-round, round, round, I get a-round, _

_____ I'm a real cool head, _____

Get a-round, round, round, I get a-round, _ Get a-round, round, round,

Second time to 𝄊

_ I'm mak-in' real good bread. _____ I'm get-tin'

Second time to 𝄊

I get a-round, _ Get a-round, round, round, I get a-round.

bored driv-in' up and down the same old strip, I got-ta find a new place where the kids are _ hip.

My bud-dies and me are get-tin' real well known, Yeah, the

THINK IT THROUGH: Evaluate the consistency of the tone quality in your vocal range. Recommend ways to improve the tone quality.

PREPARING *to Sing "Freedom Is a Constant Struggle"*

Vocal range describes the highest and lowest pitches a person can sing comfortably.

- Sing the opening passage of "Freedom is a Constant Struggle" in three different ranges. Listen to the quality of your voice in each range.

1. They say that free - dom is a con - stant strug - gle

2. They say that free - dom is a con - stant strug - gle

3. They say that free - dom is a con - stant strug - gle

THINK IT THROUGH: Which example contains the highest and lowest pitch you can sing comfortably? Which example is the most appropriate for your vocal range? Describe your vocal range. Compare your range to the range of others in your class.

Freedom Is a Constant Struggle

American Freedom Song

PREPARING *to Sing "Big Ben"*

In a round, one group of singers starts before the others. When all groups have entered the round, harmony is created. The round "Big Ben" has four parts, one for each group of singers.

- Speak this rhythm to feel the dance-like quality of the **6/8** meter, then speak the round in four parts.

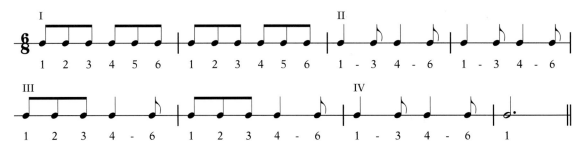

Big Ben

Music by Louis Köhler
Words by MMH

I hear Big Ben from far a - way, I hear it chime, I hear it say, "E - lev - en o' - clock, Or sev - en o' - clock, I'll chime the time of day." _____

The round "In Harmony" also has four parts. Compare and contrast the styles of these two rounds. Describe the mood of each.

In Harmony

Music by Thomas Tallis
Words by MMH

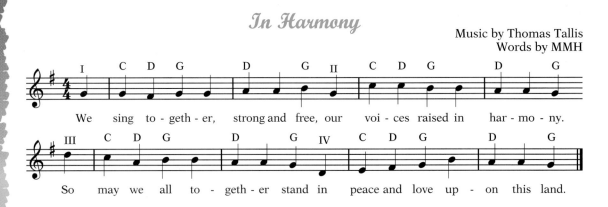

We sing to - geth - er, strong and free, our voi - ces raised in har - mo - ny.

So may we all to - geth - er stand in peace and love up - on this land.

💡 **THINK IT THROUGH:** Assess how well your performance reflects the mood. Explain your point of view.

308

PREPARING *to Sing "Red Iron Ore"*

"Red Iron Ore" has various rhythm patterns in $\frac{6}{8}$ meter.

- Speak these rhythms from the melody.

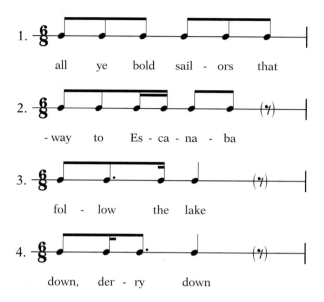

1. all   ye   bold   sail - ors   that
2. - way   to   Es - ca - na - ba
3. fol - low   the   lake
4. down,   der - ry   down

Most of the pitches in the melody of "Red Iron Ore" are in the range of a boy's changing voice, or **cambiata**.

- Sing this part of "Red Iron Ore" to help you focus your sound in the cambiata range.

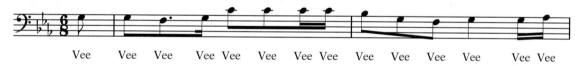

Vee   Vee   Vee   Vee Vee   Vee   Vee Vee   Vee   Vee   Vee   Vee   Vee Vee

The **refrain** section of "Red Iron Ore" is arranged for two vocal parts. One is for treble voices, and the other is for baritone. The cambiata voices can sing either part.

- Sing each part individually. Then sing both parts together.

Treble/Cambiata

Down,   down,   down   der - ry   down.

Cambiata/Baritone

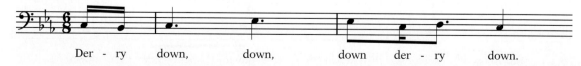

Der - ry   down,   down,   down   der - ry   down.

309

Red Iron Ore

Boat Song from the Great Lakes Region
Arranged by M.J.

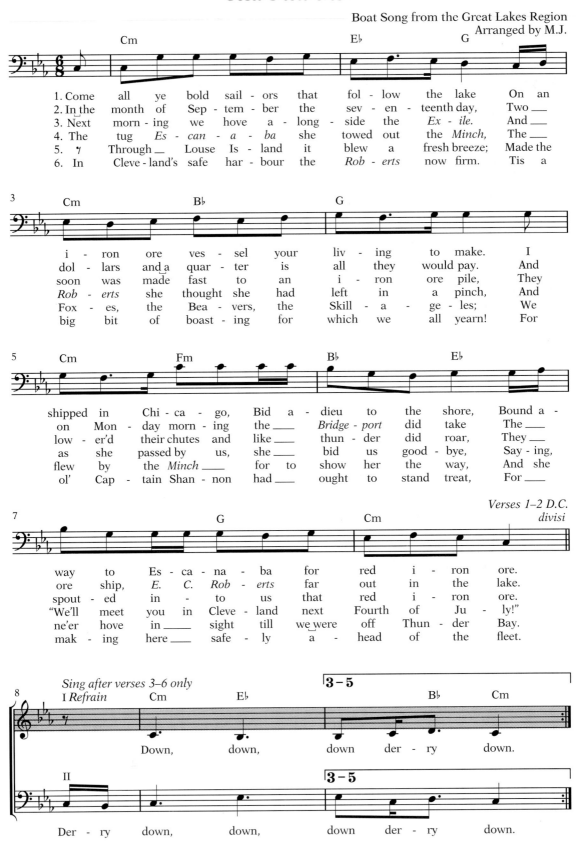

1. Come all ye bold sail - ors that fol - low the lake On an i - ron ore ves - sel your liv - ing to make. I shipped in Chi - ca - go, Bid a - dieu to the shore, Bound a - way to Es - ca - na - ba for red i - ron ore.

2. In the month of Sep - tem - ber the sev - en - teenth day, Two dol - lars and a quar - ter is all they would pay. And on Mon - day morn - ing the Bridge - port did take The ore ship, E. C. Rob - erts far out in the lake.

3. Next morn - ing we hove a - long - side the Ex - ile. And soon was made fast to an i - ron ore pile, They low - er'd their chutes and like thun - der did roar, They spout - ed in - to us that red i - ron ore.

4. The tug Es - can - a - ba she towed out the Minch, The Rob - erts she thought she had left in a pinch, And as she passed by us, she bid us good - bye, Say - ing, "We'll meet you in Cleve - land next Fourth of Ju - ly!"

5. Through Louse Is - land it blew a fresh breeze; Made the Fox - es, the Bea - vers, the Skill - a - ge - les; We flew by the Minch for to show her the way, And she ne'er hove in sight till we were off Thun - der Bay.

6. In Cleve - land's safe har - bour the Rob - erts now firm. Tis a big bit of boast - ing for which we all yearn! For ol' Cap - tain Shan - non had ought to stand treat, For mak - ing here safe - ly a - head of the fleet.

Verses 1–2 D.C.
divisi

Sing after verses 3–6 only

I *Refrain*

| 3 – 5 |

Down, down, down der - ry down.

II

| 3 – 5 |

Der - ry down, down, down der - ry down.

310

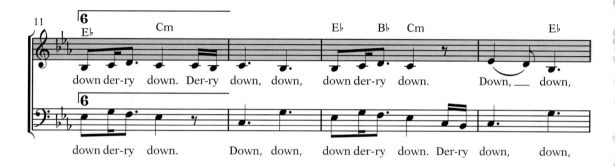

down der-ry down. Der-ry down, down, down der-ry down. Down, ___ down,

down der-ry down. Down, down, down der-ry down. Der-ry down, down,

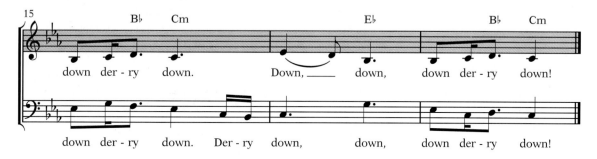

down der - ry down. Down, _____ down, down der - ry down!

down der - ry down. Der - ry down, down, down der - ry down!

THINK IT THROUGH: Evaluate the balance between the two parts in "Red Iron Ore." Suggest ways to attain better balance.

PREPARING *to Sing "Goin' Down to Cairo"*

The parts of "Goin' Down to Cairo" contain many repeated melody patterns. After practicing each pattern separately you'll be able to sing the entire composition more easily.

- Sing these melodic patterns. Find them, and similar patterns, in "Goin' Down to Cairo."

| so | fa | mi | so | fa | mi | do | la, | so, | do | re | mi | so | fa | mi | so | fa | mi | mi | mi | re | re | do |
| 5 | 4 | 3 | 5 | 4 | 3 | 1 | 6, | 5, | 1 | 2 | 3 | 5 | 4 | 3 | 5 | 4 | 3 | 3 | 3 | 2 | 2 | 1 |

| la | so | | la | so | | so | so | fa | fa | so | la | | la | so | | la | so | | so | so | fa | fa | mi |
| 6 | 5 | | 6 | 5 | | 5 | 5 | 4 | 4 | 5 | 6 | | 6 | 5 | | 6 | 5 | | 5 | 5 | 4 | 4 | 3 |

| do | so, | | do | so, | | do | mi | re | re | mi | so, | do | so, | | do | so, | | do | so, | la, | ti, | do |
| 1 | 5, | | 1 | 5, | | 1 | 3 | 2 | 2 | 3 | 5, | 1 | 5, | | 1 | 5, | | 1 | 5, | 6, | 7, | 1 |

Goin' Down to Cairo

Illinois Play–Party Song
Arranged by M.J.

1. Go - ing down to Cai - ro,
2. Oh, how I love her,

Good-bye and a bye, bye.

Good-bye and a bye, bye.

Go - ing down to Cai - ro,
Oh, how I love her,

Good - bye, Li - za Jane!

Good - bye, Li - za Jane!

Black your boots and make them shine,
Old cow died and how I cried,

Good - bye, and a bye, bye.

Good - bye and a bye, bye.

Black your boots and make them shine,
Old cow died and how I cried,

Good - bye, Li - za Jane!

Good - bye, Li - za Jane!

Make them shine,
Old cow died,

Good - bye, Li - za Jane!

Good - bye,

Good - bye, good - bye, good - bye, Li - za Jane!

The Cahuilla (kä-wē´yə) tribe has lived in what is now south-central
California for centuries. They still maintain many of their traditional
ceremonies, songs, dances, and other forms of cultural expression.
"Powama" comes from the body of Cahuilla songs
known as "Bird Songs."

Powama

Traditional Cahuilla Indian Song

The Seasons

Music by William Byrd
Words by MMH

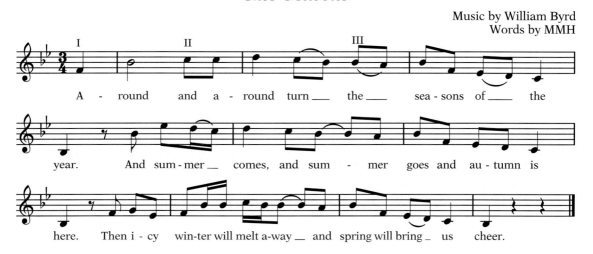

A - round and a - round turn ___ the ___ sea - sons of ___ the

year. And sum - mer ___ comes, and sum - mer goes and au - tumn is

here. Then i - cy win-ter will melt a-way ___ and spring will bring ___ us cheer.

💡 **THINK IT THROUGH:** Experiment with varying tempos, dynamics, and word colors in "The Seasons." Choose an expressive combination for your performance. Justify your choices.

PREPARING *to Sing "La Cigarra"*

"La Cigarra," is a favorite song in Mexico. The title refers to a cicada, an insect with a colorful song. This song has a characteristic $\frac{6}{8}\left(\frac{3}{4}\right)$ Mexican beat. Practice these rhythms to help you feel the beat.

La Cigarra (The Cicada)

Words and Music by
Ray Perez y Soto

1. Ya no me can-tes ci-ga-rra que a-ca-be tu___ son-so-ne-te___ que tu can-to a-quien el al-ma co-mo un pu-ñal se me me-te sa-bien-do que cuan-do can ___ tas ___ pre-go-nan-do vas tu muer-te. ___

2. Un pal-o-mi-to al vo-lar___ que lle-va-ba el pe-cho he-ri-do___ ya ca-si pa-ra___ llo-rar me di-jo muy af-li-gi-do ya me can-so de bus-car ___ un a-mor co-rres-pon-di-do. ___

Ma-ri-ne-ro, ma-ri-ne-ro di-me si es ver-dad que sa-bes por-que dis-tin-guir no pue-do

Ba-jo la som-bra de un ár-bol y al com-pás de mi gui-ta-rra can-to a-le-gre es-te hua-pan-go

316

28 E7   Am

si en el fon - do de los _____ ma - res _____ hay o - tro co - lor más _____
por - que la vi - da se a - ca - ba _____ y quie - ro mor - ir can -

31 G   F   E7

_ ne - gro que el co - lor de mis pe - sar - es. _____
- tan - do co - mo muer - e la cig - a - rra. _____

34 E7   **2**

_____ Hay, _____ la, la,
_____

A   D   E7   A   D   E7   A   D   E7
39

la. _____

45 E7   **3**   D   D

_____ Hay, _____ la, la, la. _____

53   E7

_____ Hay, _____ la, la, la. _____

60

_____ Hay
      Y

1
67 D   E7   A   E7   A

o - tro col - or más ne - gro que el col - or de mis pe - sar - es. _____
quier - o mo - rir can - tan - do co - mo

2
73 E7   *Freely*   A *a tempo*

mu - er - e la ci - ga - rra. _____

317

Choral Anthology

Careers on Broadway

People come from all over the world for the bright lights of Broadway in New York City. Broadway musicals have thrilled audiences for decades. Large-scale musicals involve many people with diverse careers, each bringing a variety of talents to the project.

Musicals start with story ideas. Often these ideas come from other plays or from books which are then adapted to create a musical. *Les Misérables* of Shönberg and Boublil was based on the novel of the same name by Victor Hugo. Andrew Lloyd Webber's musical *Cats* was based on poems of Nobel Prize winner T. S. Elliot.

When the story ideas have been developed, the words for the songs are written by the lyricist and set to music by the composer. Once the words and the music are written, the **director** works with the **music director** and **choreographer** to bring the musical to life, combining many elements to create a balanced whole. The music director helps the **actors** learn their songs, and often conducts the **orchestra**. The choreographer creates the dance routines and teaches them to the actors and **dancers**.

Many people work on the look and sound of the production. The **set designer**, **lighting designer, sound technicians, costume designers, make-up artists** and **hair stylists** have the ideas that will help to transport the audience to a different time and place, and help the actor create a character that comes alive on stage. All work together to prepare for opening night. When it finally arrives, a hush falls in the theater, the lights are dimmed, and as the curtain rises, the audience is led on a journey of imagination and delight.

As you sing the following choral selections, think of a favorite book or movie that might work well as a musical. Decide how each of the songs could fit into your musical, and write new lyrics, adapting them to your story-line. Once you have the songs, create dance steps, costumes, and a set design. When you have rehearsed your musical, give a performance for your friends. Who knows? With time and effort, you might end up with a career under the bright lights of Broadway.

PREPARING *to Sing "Milk and Honey"*

The Broadway musical *Milk and Honey* depicts the strong spirit and determination of the people of Israel. This spirit can be heard in the song "Milk and Honey," which describes the plentiful land of Israel.

Practice Your Music Reading Skills—Sight-reading

- Sight-read this rhythm pattern.

   The following patterns are similar to sections of the melody in "Milk and Honey."

- Clap, tap, and sing these patterns.

- Sing these patterns, then find them in "Milk and Honey."

A.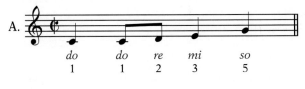

B.

C.

Milk and Honey
from *Milk and Honey*

Words and Music by Jerry Herman

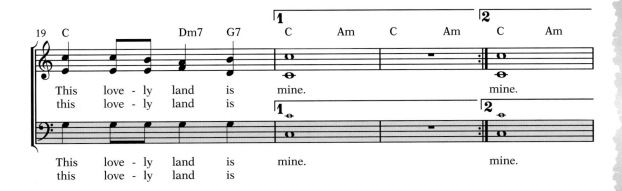

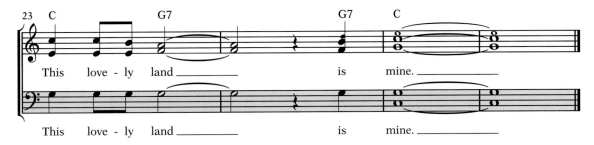

Music and Lyric by Jerry Herman

 THINK IT THROUGH: Determine ways to highlight the syncopated rhythms best. Evaluate how effectively your performance conveyed the energy of the song.

Practice Your Music Reading Skills — Syncopation

"Milk and Honey" contains syncopated rhythm patterns. Syncopation emphasizes beats or parts of the beat that are not normally emphasized.

- Read these rhythm patterns to yourself. What words in "Milk and Honey" match these rhythm patterns?

- Clap each pattern as you say the words. Which part of the rhythm pattern contains syncopation? You can tell because it feels catchy and uneven.

- Practice these syncopated exercises. Tap a steady beat with your foot as you speak and clap the syncopation.

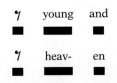

PREPARING *to Sing "Together Wherever We Go"*

Ethel Merman's performance in *Gypsy* helped make her a Broadway legend. Jule Styne and Stephen Sondheim worked together to create the music and the lyrics for *Gypsy*. As with many musicals, there have been different versions on both the stage and in the movies. Many other great stars, such as Angela Lansbury, Natalie Wood, and Bette Midler have helped make *Gypsy* a well-loved classic. The song "Together Wherever We Go" expresses the friendship of the characters, who vow to stick together through "thick and thin."

Practice Your Music Reading Skills — Syncopation

• Clap this syncopated rhythm pattern.

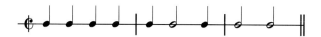

• Clap this pattern. A tie between the two quarter notes makes this syncopated pattern more challenging.

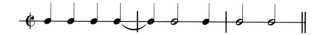

In "Together Wherever We Go" this rhythm pattern is combined with a melodic pattern that contains many leaps.

• Sing this melody from "Together Wherever We Go" to experience the melodic leaps.

gon - na go through _ it   to - geth - er.

THINK IT THROUGH: Assess the accuracy of your performance of the rhythms and melodic leaps. Recommend ways to improve the precision.

Together Wherever We Go
from *Gypsy*

Words by Stephen Sondheim
Music by Jule Styne

PREPARING *to Sing "Food, Glorious Food"*

The musical *Oliver!* is based on Charles Dickens' novel *Oliver Twist.* Lionel Bart reworked this classic story about the orphan Oliver into a successful musical. It opened in London in 1960 and ran for 2,628 performances. This set a record for the longest running musical ever. In "Food, Glorious Food," Oliver Twist and his friends at the orphanage dream about how nice it would be to have delicious food, instead of their usual gruel. It is this strong craving for "glorious food" which sends Oliver on his wild journey where he encounters the evil Sikes, the mischievous Fagin, and the slow-witted Bumble.

Practice Your Music Reading Skills — ¾ meter

Dotted half notes are often found in ¾ meter. A dot after a note means that one-half the value of the note is added to the original value. Since a half note equals two beats, a dotted half note equals three beats.

- Clap this ¾ rhythm pattern from "Food, Glorious Food."

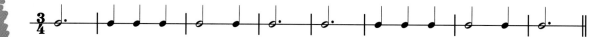

- Sing this melody with the rhythms you just practiced.

do'	*so*	*mi*	*do*	*mi*	*fa*	*so*	*so*	*so*	*la*	*ti*	*ti*	*do'*	*do'*
1'	5	3	1	3	4	5	5	5	6	7	7	1'	1'

There are three different meter signatures in "Food, Glorious Food." As you listen to the song, locate and identify the meter changes.

THINK IT THROUGH: In "Food, Glorious Food," the mood changes when the meter changes. Describe how the change of meter supports the new musical mood of each section.

324

Food, Glorious Food
from *Oliver!*

Words and Music by Lionel Bart

(solos and groups alternate)

Is it worth wait-ing for? If we live 'til eight-y-four, All we ev-er get is

gru - el! Ev-'ry day we say a pray'r, will they change the bill of fare?

Still we get the same old gru - el! There's not a crust, not a crumb can we find, can we

beg, can we bor-row or cadge. But there's noth-ing to stop us from

get-ting a thrill when we all close our eyes and im-ag-ine;

Food, glo-ri-ous food! _____ Hot sau-sage and mus-tard! _____

While we're in the mood, _____ cold jel-ly and cus-tard! _____

325

Pease pud-ding and sav - e - loys! What next is the ques-tion? _____

Rich gen - tle - men have it, boys, in - dye - ges - tion! _____

Food, glo - ri - ous food! _____ We're an - xious to try it, _____

Three ban-quets a day, _____ Our fav - or - ite di - et! _____

Just pic - ture a great big steak, fried, roast - ed or

rit.

stewed, oh, food, won-der - ful food, glo - ri - ous food, mar - vel - ous

Brightly, in 2
mf

Food, glo - ri - ous food! _____ Don't care _____ what it looks like, _____

Burned, un - der-done, crude, _____ Don't care _____ what the cook's like, _____

Just think - ing of grow - ing fat, Our sen - ses are

reel - ing, _____ One mo - ment of know - ing that

full - up feel - ing! _____ Food, glo - ri - ous

food! _____ What would - n't we give for, _____

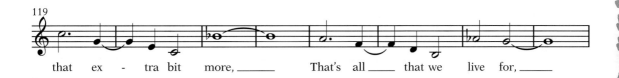

that ex - tra bit more, _____ That's all ___ that we live for, _____

Why should __ we be fat - ed to do noth - ing but brood on

cresc.

food, mag - ic - al food, won - der-ful food, mar - vel-ous food, fab - u-lous

f

fab-u-lous food, glo - ri-ous food, glo - ri - ous ___ food! _____

PREPARING *to Sing "Freedom"*

The musical *Shenandoah* tells the story of a household struggling with life during the American Civil War. In the song "Freedom," Gabriel, a youth who has recently been freed from slavery, sings about his new life. He says that freedom isn't a place to go, but a way of thinking about life.

Practice Your Music Reading Skills — Patterns

• Clap or tap the rhythms in these patterns from "Freedom." Then find these patterns in the song and sing them with the song text.

A.

B.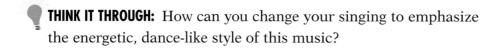

💡 **THINK IT THROUGH:** How can you change your singing to emphasize the energetic, dance-like style of this music?

Freedom

from *Shenandoah*

Words by Peter Udell
Music by Gary Geld

of mind. You can't get to free-dom by rid - in' on a train.

The on-ly way to free-dom is right on through your brain. __ wo-wo wo - wo wo

wo, The way is right on through your brain. __ Wo-wo-wo - wo-wo

(claps)   of   mind!   Free - dom!

PREPARING *to Sing "Lift Ev'ry Voice and Sing"*

James Weldon Johnson, a founder of the National Association for the Advancement of Colored People (NAACP), wrote these words in 1900 to commemorate the birthday of Abraham Lincoln. His brother J. Rosamond Johnson set the words to music. Many people refer to "Lift Ev'ry Voice and Sing" as the African American National Anthem.

Practice Your Music Reading Skills — 6/8 meter

• Practice 6/8 meter by clapping the following:

• "Lift Ev'ry Voice and Sing" has two different melodies. Sing both melodies and notice similarities and differences.

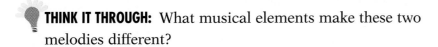 **THINK IT THROUGH:** What musical elements make these two melodies different?

Lift Ev'ry Voice and Sing

Music by Rosamond Johnson
Words by James Weldon Johnson

1. Lift ev'- ry voice and sing, till earth and heav - en ring,
2. Ston - y the road we trod, bit - ter the chas - t'ning rod

Ring with the har - mo - nies of lib - er - ty.
Felt in the days when hope un - born had died.

Let our re - joic - ing rise high as the list - 'ning skies,
Yet with a stead - y beat have not our wea - ry feet

Let it re - sound loud as the roll - ing sea.
Come to the place for which our fa - thers sighed?

Sing a song full of the faith that the dark past has taught us;
We have come, o - ver a way that with tears has been wa - tered,

Sing a song full of the hope that the pres - ent has brought us;
We have come, tread - ing our path through the blood of the slaugh - tered;

Fac - ing the ris - ing sun of our new day be - gun,
Out from the gloom - y past, till now we stand at last

Let us march on till vic - to - ry is won.
Where the white gleam of our bright star is cast.

PREPARING *to Sing "La Borinqueña"*

"La Borinqueña" achieves its unique rhythmic style by alternating two and three sounds to a beat.

Practice Your Music Reading Skills—Two and Three Sounds to a Beat

- Tap your foot to create a steady quarter-note beat.

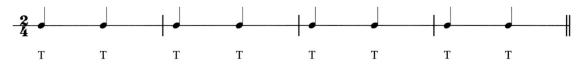

Tap the steady beat with your foot while you clap two sounds to a beat to perform a duple division of the beat.

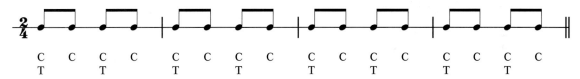

- Snap your fingers, alternating hands, three times to a beat to perform a triple division of the beat.

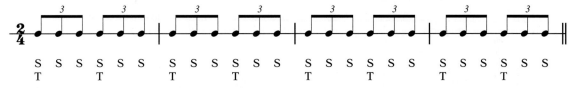

- Perform this rhythm which contains both duple- and triple-beat divisions.

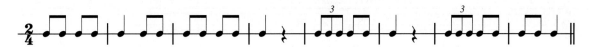

- Create your own body percussion patterns that alternate between two and three sounds to a beat.

La Borinqueña

Words by Manuel Fernandez Juncos
Music by Felix Astol
English Words by MMH

La tie - rra de Bor - in - quen don - de he na - ci - do yo
Oh, land of Bor - in - quen, The ___ land my child - hood knew.

Es un jar - dín flo - ri - do de má - gi - co pri - mor.
There in your fra - grant gar - dens, flo - wers of ev - 'ry hue.

Un cie - lo siem - pre ní - ti - do le sir - ve de do - sel,
Heav - en - ly bree - zes blow - ing lul - la - bies soft and sweet.

Y dan a - rru - llo plà - ci - do Las o - las a sus pies.
Peace - ful and calm your sun - lit face, Waves at your grace - ful feet.

Cuan - do a sus pla - yas lle - gó Co - lón, ex - cla - mó lle - no de ad - mi - ra -
When to your bea - ches Co - lum - bus came, in ad - mir - a - tion he loud - ly

ción: ¡Oh! ¡Oh! ¡Oh! Es - ta es la lin - da tie - rra, Que bus - co
cried: Oh! Oh! Oh! Now in this love - ly land my voy - age is

yo. Es Bor - in - quen la hi - ja, la hi - ja del mar y el
done. Oh, Bor - in - quen, the daugh - ter, the daugh - ter of sea and

sol, del mar y el sol, del mar y el
sun, of sea and sun, of sea and

sol, del mar y el sol, del mar y el sol.
sun, of sea and sun, of sea and sun.

PREPARING *to Sing "A la Nanita Nana"*

Listen to "A la Nanita Nana" to find the musical characteristics that give it a dreamy, lullaby quality.

Practice Your Music Reading Skills—Singing in Minor

- Sing this minor melody from Part I of the song.

la,	la,	ti,	do	re	mi	mi	mi	fa	re	mi	mi	mi	fa	re	la	mi
6,	6,	7,	1	2	3	3	3	4	2	3	3	3	4	2	6	3

- Tap and sing these minor patterns from Parts II and III of the song.

la,	la,	ti,	do	re	do	do	do	re	ti,	do	do	do	re	re	mi	do
6,	6,	7,	1	2	1	1	1	2	7,	1	1	1	2	2	3	1

la,	la,	la,	la,	la,	la,	la,	la,	la,	la,	la,	la,	la,	la,	ti,	do	la,
6,	6,	6,	6,	6,	6,	6,	6,	6,	6,	6,	6,	6,	6,	7,	1	6,

- Sing patterns I and III; I and II; II and III; and I, II, and III to experience two- and three-part singing in D minor.

Practice Your Music Reading Skills—Singing in Major

- Sing this major melody from Part I of the song.

mi	so	do'	ti	la	ti	so	la	so	fa	mi	fa	so
3	5	1'	7	6	7	5	6	5	4	3	4	5

- Tap and sing these major patterns from Parts II and III of the song.

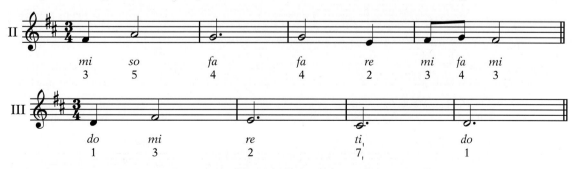

mi	so	fa	fa	re	mi	fa	mi
3	5	4	4	2	3	4	3

do	mi	re	ti,	do
1	3	2	7,	1

- Sing patterns I and III; I and II; II and III; and I, II, and III to experience two- and three-part singing in D major.

A la Nanita Nana

For Three- Part Choir, with Keyboard

Traditional Cuban Carol
Arranged by Michael Braz

flow - ing, song - birds are sing - ing.

flow - ing, _____ song - birds sing - ing. _____

flow - ing, _____ song - birds sing - ing. _____

Rip-pling wa - ters and bird - song flow through my dream - ing.

Rip-pling wa - ters bird - song _____ through my dream - ing.

Rip-pling wa - ters bird - song _____ through my dream - ing.

Hush now, be ver - y si - lent, he slum - bers so deep - ly.

Hush now, be ver - y si - lent, he slum - bers so deep - ly.

Hush, now, be ver - y si - lent, he slum - bers so deep - ly.

Sleep, oh my lit - tle ba - by, slum - ber so sweet - ly, Ah, __

Sleep, oh my lit - tle ba - by, slum - ber so sweet - ly, Ah, __

Sleep, oh my lit - tle ba - by, slum - ber so sweet - ly,

__ Ah! __

__ Ah! __

Ah, __ Ah! __

PREPARING *to Sing "Take These Wings"*

One of the characteristics of harmonious choral singing is **blend**. Notice the blending of voices as you listen to the recording of "Take These Wings."

- Listen to the choral blend as you sing the three-part section of "Take These Wings." What words can you use to describe the concept of choral blend?

Practice Your Music Reading — Choral Blend Skills

- Practice these patterns by singing them using pitch syllables or numbers. Then sing the following portion of "Take These Wings" on *loo*. Add each part one at a time, listening to the other parts as you sing.

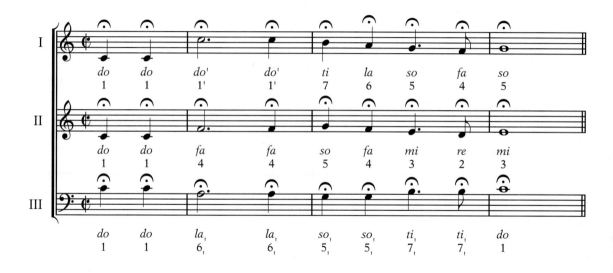

💡 **THINK IT THROUGH:** How can you change your voice to match the voices of others and create a pleasing blend in your choir? How can you sing the vowel sounds in the lyrics to improve the choral blend?

Take These Wings

Words by Steve Kupferschmid
Music by Don Besig

I found a spar-row ly-ing on the ground: ____ Her

life I knew would soon be at an end. _____ I knelt be-

fore her as she made a sound, ____ and lis-tened as she said: "My

friend, _____ Take these wings _____ and learn to fly ____

Take these wings ____ and learn to

____ to the high-est moun-tain in the sky; _____ Take these

fly to the high-est moun-tain in the sky; _____ Take these

eyes _____ and learn to see _____ all the things so

eyes _____ and learn to see _____ all the things so

342

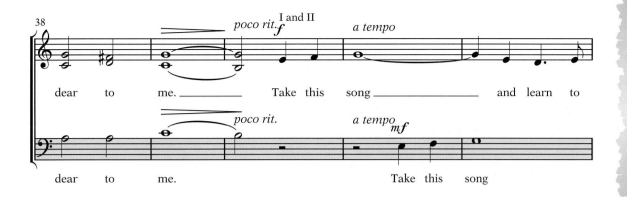

dear to me. _____ Take this song _____ and learn to

dear to me. Take this song

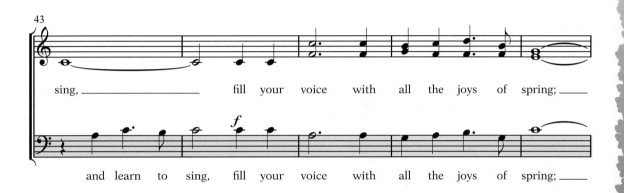

sing, _____ fill your voice with all the joys of spring; _____

and learn to sing, fill your voice with all the joys of spring; _____

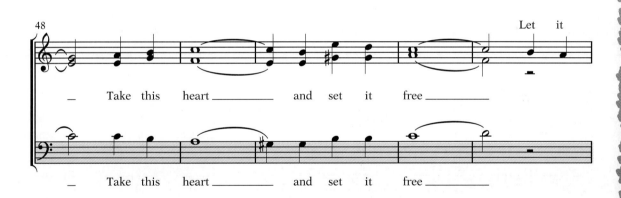

_ Take this heart _____ and set it free _____

_ Take this heart _____ and set it free _____

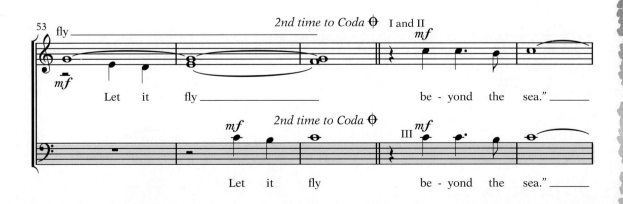

Let it fly _____ be - yond the sea." _____

Let it fly be - yond the sea." _____

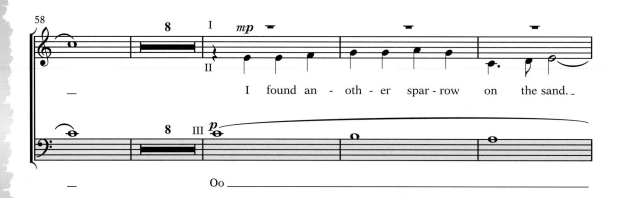

I found an-oth-er spar-row on the sand.

Oo

Oo

a tin-y bird whose life had just be-gun.

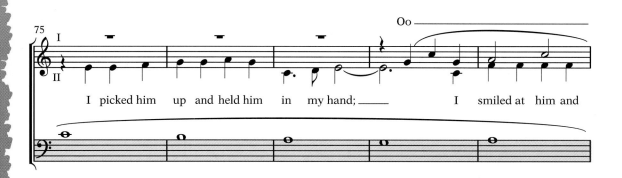

Oo

I picked him up and held him in my hand; I smiled at him and

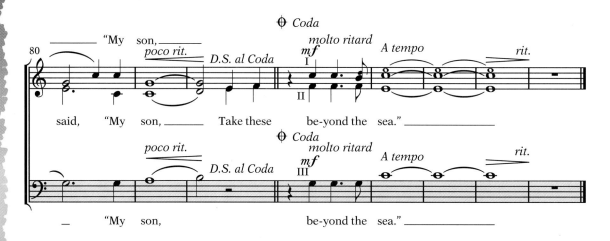

"My son, Take these be-yond the sea."

"My son, be-yond the sea."

PREPARING *to Sing "All the Good People"*

"All the Good People" has the quality of a folk song. This quality is due partly to the repeated patterns in the song, which help to make the song easy to sing and remember.

Practice Your Music Reading Skills — Rhythm Patterns

- Play these patterns from "All the Good People."

- Create new rhythm accompaniments by combining two or more of these patterns.

- Find all of these rhythm patterns in "All the Good People."

All the Good People

Words and Music by Ken Hicks

This is a song for all the good peo - ple,

All the good peo - ple who touched up my life. _____ This is a

song for all the good peo - ple, Peo - ple I'm thank - in' my

stars for to - night.

This is a song for

pick - ers and sing - ers whose tunes and whose voi - ces have blend - ed with

mine, __ On back - steps and sta - ges, for love and for wa - ges, it's

one kind of giv - in' and one kind of fine.

This is a song for all the peo - ple

This is a song for all the good peo - ple, All the good

This is a song for all the good

💡 **THINK IT THROUGH:** How can you change your singing to emphasize the energetic style of this music? Suggest a place and time that might be appropriate to sing "All the Good People." Justify your answer.

70 Times the Speed of Sound

Bluesy, swinging sound

Music and Lyrics by Linda Worsley

1. Ba - by said she loved me, ___ then she made me feel so bad,___
2. Ba - by sent a let - ter, She mailed it from the moon.___
3. I can see my ba - by, ___ see the one I love the best,___

I made him ___ feel so bad. ___
I mailed it ____ from the moon. _
I know that ___ he loves me best. _

When she went and left me, ___
It said "I real - ly miss you, ___
see her go - ing o - ver in an

Right there on ___ the launch-ing pad. _
I wish I ____ could see you soon! _
I'm fly - in' o - ver ___ from east to west. _

there on the launch-ing pad. ____
wish that I could see you soon!___
or - bit from East to West. ___

My

And

Last time to Coda ⊕

at sev en ty times the speed of sound._
I'll go sev en ty times a round the sun. ___
at sev en ty times the speed of light. _

Last time to Coda ⊕

ba - by left the ground ___ at sev-en-ty times the speed of sound._
But be - fore I'm done, _ I'll go sev-en-ty times a - round the sun. ___
then she's out of sight, ___ at sev-ent-y times the speed of light. _

1 **2** *go on to* Ⓑ **3** *Instrumental Interlude* **23**

___ ___ A A

1 **2** *go on to* Ⓑ **3** *Instrumental Interlude* **23**

348 ___ ___

💡 **THINK IT THROUGH:** Compare and contrast two performances of this song. First, sing the song with straight, even rhythms as notated, and short, staccato articulation. Then try singing the song in a freer, jazzier style. Which style suits this song best? Are there parts of the song that might sound better in one of these styles? Create a style performance plan. Evaluate the effectiveness of your performance.

Can You Hear the Music?

Words and Music by Linda Worsley

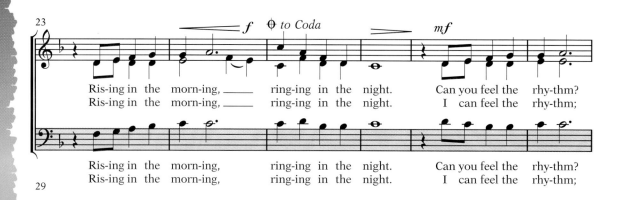

350

💡 **THINK IT THROUGH:** Are the questions in the text of this song ever answered? What performance techniques can you use to highlight the question and answer phrases in the text? Evaluate the effectiveness of your question and answer phrases.

PREPARING *to Sing "In Stiller Nacht"*

"In Stiller Nacht" was composed by one of the most famous musicians of the 19th century, Johannes Brahms. This piece is one of many vocal works he composed in his native German language. The music is notated in $\frac{3}{2}$ meter. In $\frac{3}{2}$, the half note receives the steady beat.

Practice Your Music Reading Skills — $\frac{3}{2}$ meter

In $\frac{3}{2}$ meter:

the ♩ will sound for one-half of a beat

the 𝅗𝅥 will sound for one beat

the 𝅗𝅥. will sound for one and one-half beats

- Sing this rhythm pattern on one pitch using the syllable *loo*. Try to feel three beats to a measure. Be sure your singing is *legato*, or sustained in quality.

- Sing this dotted rhythm found in the melody of "In Stiller Nacht." How can you emphasize or stress this new dotted rhythm?

Find this rhythm at the beginning of all three parts in the music.

- Sing the third part in unison, stressing the dotted rhythm. Then divide into parts. Start with only Part III, then add Part II and finally Part I, maintaining the stress on this rhythm.

In Stiller Nacht

Words and Music by
Johannes Brahms
Arranged by David L. Weck

Blü - me-lein,   mit Trä - nen rein   hab ich sie all be - gos - sen.

Blü - me-lein,   mit Trä - nen rein   hab ich sie all be - gos - sen.

Blü - me-lein,   mit Trä - nen rein   hab ich sie all be - gos - sen.

THINK IT THROUGH: Choral composers often write melodies and rhythms in a way that places emphasis on certain words. Which words are stressed in this music? What do these words mean in English? What vocal skills can you use to emphasize these words?

PREPARING *to Sing "Cum Sancto Spiritu"*

The majority of early church music in Western civilization was composed and sung in Latin. "Cum Sancto Spiritu" composed by Antonio Lotti (1667-1740), comes from this tradition. Composers in Lotti's time often wrote using **polyphony** or independent melodic parts in the style of a round or canon. Popular forms of polyphonic music were the round and the **fugue.** "Cum Sancto Spiritu" is written in polyphonic style. Each part enters and imitates the previous part.

Practice Your Music Reading Skills — Imitation

- Sing Part I from "Cum Sancto Spiritu."

Cum   Sanc-to   Spi - ri - tu,   in   glo - ri - a   De - i   Pa — tris

- Sing Part II, noting how it imitates Part I.

Cum   Sanc-to   Spi - ri - tu,   in   glo - ri - a   De - i   Pa — tris

- Sing Part III, noting how it also imitates Part I.

Cum   Sanc-to   Spi - ri - tu,   in   glo - ri - a   De - i   Pa — tris

- Find all three parts in "Cum Sancto Spiritu." Can you find other examples of imitation in "Cum Sancto Spiritu"?

THINK IT THROUGH: How can you use the expressive elements in music to highlight the independent polyphonic parts? Experiment by varying the tempos, dynamics, and word colors. Then create a plan that best highlights the important melodic lines in "Cum Sancto Spiritu." Justify your choices.

Cum Sancto Spiritu

Traditional Latin text
Music by Antonio Lotti

PREPARING *to Sing "I Hear America Singing"*

The rhythm used in "I Hear America Singing" can be described as strong and syncopated. This helps to give the composition energy and vitality.

Practice Your Music Reading Skills — Syncopated Rhythm

- Perform this syncopated rhythm pattern from "I Hear America Singing" by clapping the eighth notes and patting the quarter-note durations.

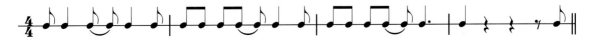

- Clap and pat the syncopated rhythm in the bottom voice starting in measure 25, "Great camp meeting." Add the upper parts, one at a time. Find and practice other measures that contain syncopation.

 THINK IT THROUGH: Assess the accuracy of your rhythmic performance as a group. Recommend ways to improve the rhythmic precision.

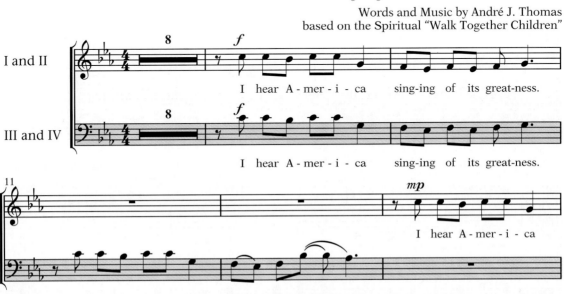

I Hear America Singing

Words and Music by André J. Thomas
based on the Spiritual "Walk Together Children"

I hear A-mer-i-ca sing-ing of its great-ness.

I hear A-mer-i-ca sing-ing of its great-ness.

I hear A-mer-i-ca

I hear A-mer-i-ca sing - ing strong. _____

nev-er   tire, _____   sing and   nev-er   tire. _____   There's a   great camp meet-ing,

nev-er   tire, _____   sing and   nev-er   tire. _____

And A - mer-i-ca's sing - ing!   Great camp meet - ing,

great camp meet - ing

Land! _____

great camp meet - ing   in   the Prom - ised   great camp meet - ing,   A -

great camp meet - ing   in   the Prom - ised   great camp meet - ing,   A -

_____   Prom-ised   Land!

mer - i - ca's sing - ing,   great camp meet - ing, Prom-ised   Land!

mer - i - ca's sing - ing,   great camp meet - ing, Prom-ised   Land!

PREPARING *to Sing "I've Got a Robe"*

Gospel music had its beginnings in African American church services during the 1930s. Gospel singers ornament traditional spirituals such as "I've Got a Robe" with their own rhythmic and melodic improvisations.

- Clap these rhythms from the first part of "I've Got a Robe."

I've Got a Robe

Traditional Spiritual
Arranged by David Parker

363

walk _____ a - round hea - ven all day!
talk _____ and spread __ the news!

walk _____ a - round hea - ven all day!
talk _____ and spread __ the news!

walk _____ a - round hea - ven all day!
talk _____ and spread __ the news!

a - round hea - ven all day!
and spread __ the news!

When I get there how hap-py I will be, When I get

When I get there how hap-py I will be, When I get

When I get there how hap-py I will be, When I get

When I get there how hap-py I will be, When I get

there my Sav-ior's face I'll see. Well!

there my Sav-ior's face I'll see. Well! Walk _

there my Sav-ior's face I'll see. Well!

there my Sav-ior's face I'll see. Well!

Rest first time through
Sing second and third times through

Hea - ven! all day!

Solo, first time through (sing these four measures three times)

_ a-round hea-ven all day! Walk ___ a-round hea-ven all day! Walk _

Rest first and second times through
Sing third time through

talk, and tell the sto - ry,

Rest three times through

Hea - ven! all day!

_ a-round hea-ven all day! Walk ___ a-round hea-ven all day! Walk _

Talk, 'bout how I made it o - ver.

365

💡 **THINK IT THROUGH:** What expressive musical elements can you use to engage your audience in your performance of "I've Got a Robe"? Create a chart of musical elements and create plans for adding expressive elements. Evaluate the success of each plan.

PREPARING *to Sing "Drum Song"*

This traditional Chinese "Drum Song" is remembered by many as the triumphant song sung as soldiers marched home at the end of World War II. The vocables, or syllables, mimic the loud banging and clashing of the drums. These noises are associated with driving away evil and setting the stage for a joyful and triumphant celebration.

Practice Your Music Reading Skills — Rhythms

"Drum Song" has combinations of quarter-, eighth-, and sixteenth-note rhythms in both the melody and percussion parts.

- Clap the following rhythms in preparation for reading "Drum Song," then find them in the song.

We're com - ing home   and we   all   are   full   of   joy

Drum Song

Traditional Chinese
Translation by Lucy J. Ding and Julian Harvey
Arranged by Julian Harvey

368

Men and wo - men, ev - ery-one you see, Young and old are hap-py as can be.

sfz *sfz*

sfz *sfz*

p cresc.

p cresc.

f sfz

f sfz

mf (second time f)

sfz

Man and wo-man, girl and boy, Now we sing our songs of joy, (shout) Heh!

mf (second time f)

sfz

mf second time f

sfz

mf second time f

sfz

Songs of __ joy and songs of __ tri - umph, songs of __ tri - umph songs of

joy!

💡 **THINK IT THROUGH:** Many of the words in the text of "Drum Song" imitate percussion sounds. What interesting vocal tone colors can you use to imitate the drum and cymbal sounds in the text? Plan a performance that uses both real and vocally imitated percussion sounds. Evaluate the effectiveness of your performance.

PREPARING *to Sing "Psallite"*

"Psallite" expresses the joy that surrounds the Christmas season. Michael Praetorius was a composer and musician who lived during the late Renaissance. Like many composers of that era, he often alternated between polyphonic style with its independent melodic parts, and homophonic style with its chordal parts. Look for passages in "Psallite" that show both of these ways of writing.

Practice Your Music Reading Skills — Rhythm Patterns

Perform each:

- Clap this pattern.

1.

- Tap this pattern.

2.

- Snap this pattern.

3.

- Say this pattern using an *sss* sound.

4.

- Create your own musical composition by combining two or more of these patterns.

THINK IT THROUGH: Perform all four patterns together. Then think of performance techniques that would help to keep each pattern distinct and clearly separated.

Psallite

Words and Music by
Michael Praetorius

THINK IT THROUGH: Evaluate the clarity of each part. Try singing the imitative sections using a sustained bell-like vocal quality. Sing the fast-moving sections in a light and detached manner. How does this plan change the quality of the performance? Create a plan for your performance and decide the most appropriate techniques for this style of music.

TIMELINE

Michael Praetorius **1571**–1621
Thomas Weelkes **1576**–1623

1600

Jean Baptiste Lully **1632**–1687
Johann Pachelbel **1653**–1706
Henry Purcell **1659**–1695
Antonio Vivaldi **1678**–1741
Johann Sebastian Bach **1685**–1750
George Frederick Handel **1685**–1759

1620 Mayflower lands at Plymouth Rock
1643 Louis XIV becomes king of France at age 5

1666 Newton discovers Law of Gravity

1700

Franz Joseph Haydn **1732**–**1809**
John Stafford Smith **1750**–**1836**
Wolfgang Amadeus Mozart **1756**–**1791**
Ludwig van Beethoven **1770**–**1827**

1707 United Kingdom of Great Britian formed

1769 James Watt patents his steam engine
1775 American Revolution (ended 1783)
1776 American Declaration of Independence
1787 American Constitutional Convention
1788 John Fitch invents steamboat
1789 French Revolution; George Washington
     first president of United States
1791 Bill of Rights
1793 Eli Whitney invents the cotton gin

Franz Schubert **1797**–**1828**

1800

Fanny Mendelssohn Hensel **1805**–**1847**

Felix Mendelssohn **1809**–**1847**
Frédéric Chopin **1810**–**1849**
Robert Schumann **1810**–**1856**
Richard Wagner **1813**–**1883**

1803 Louisiana Purchase
1804 Napoleon crowned emperor; Lewis and
     Clark expedition
1807 Robert Fulton builds first commercial
     steamboat; London streets lighted by gas

1812 War of 1812
1815 Napoleon defeated in Battle of Waterloo
1819 First steamship crosses Atlantic
1825 Opening of the Erie Canal
1825 First public railroad opened in England
1838 Daguerre takes first photographs

1825

Johannes Brahms **1833**–**1897**
Georges Bizet **1838**–**1875**
Modest Mussorgsky **1839**–**1881**
Peter Ilyich Tchaikovsky **1840**–**1893**
Edvard Grieg **1843**–1907
Nicolai Rimsky-Korsakov **1844**–1908

1844 First telegraph message transmitted
1846 First use of ether as an anesthetic
1848 California Gold Rush; first Women's
     Rights Convention

1850

John Philip Sousa **1854**–1932
Cécile Chaminade **1857**–1944
Giacomo Puccini **1858**–1924
Claude Debussy **1862**–1918

1860 Lincoln elected president;
     Civil War (ended 1865)

		1863 Gettysburg Address; Emancipation Proclamation
		1865 Abraham Lincoln assassinated
Scott Joplin 1868–1917		1869 First American transcontinental railroad; opening of Suez Canal
James Weldon Johnson 1871–1938		
Ralph Vaughan Williams 1872–1958		
W.C. (William Christopher) Handy 1873–1958		
Arnold Schoenberg 1874–1951		
Charles Ives 1874–1954		
Robert Frost 1874–1963	**1875**	1876 Alexander Graham Bell invents telephone
		1877 Thomas Edison invents the phonograph
		1879 Edison invents improved incandescent electric light bulb
Igor Stravinsky 1882–1971		1885 Louis Pasteur develops milk "pasteurization"
Ferdinand ("Jelly Roll") Morton 1885–1941		
Gertrude ("Ma") Rainey 1886–1939		1886 Statue of Liberty unveiled in New York Harbor
Ernst Toch 1887–1964		1889 Completion of Eiffel Tower in France
T.S. (Thomas Stearns) Eliot 1888–1965		
Sergei Prokofiev 1891–1953		
Bessie Smith 1894–1937		1895 Wilhelm Roentgen discovers X-rays
William Grant Still 1895–1978		1898 Spanish-American War
George Gershwin 1898–1937		
Duke Ellington 1899–1974		
	1900	
Louis Armstrong 1900–1971		1901 Guglielmo Marconi transmits wireless telegraph signals across Atlantic
Harry Partch 1901–1974		1902 Pierre and Marie Curie discover radium
Langston Hughes 1902–1967		1903 Wilbur and Orville Wright make first successful airplane flight
Ogden Nash 1902–1971		1904 First sound moving picture
		1905 Albert Einstein offers Theory of Relativity
Harold Arlen 1905–1986		1906 San Francisco earthquake and fire
		1908 Model T Ford produced
		1909 Robert Peary and Matthew Henson reach North Pole
Milt Hinton 1910–		1910 Discovery of the South Pole; discovery of protons and electrons
		1912 Titanic disaster
John Cage 1912–1992		
Morton Gould 1913–1996		1914 Opening of the Panama Canal; World War I (ended 1918)
Benjamin Britten 1913–1976		
Lester Flatt 1914–1979		
Milton Babbitt 1916–		
Eve Merriam 1916–		1917 Russian Revolution
Lou Harrison 1917–		
Leonard Bernstein 1918–1990		1920 First commercial radio broadcast; suffrage (19th Amendment)
Dave Brubeck 1920–		
Katsutoshi Nagasawa 1923–		
Earl Scruggs 1924–		
Paul Desmond 1924–1977		1927 Charles Lindbergh's flight across the Atlantic; first television transmission
Pierre Boulez 1925–	**1925**	
		1928 Sir Alexander Fleming discovers penicillin
Burt Bacharach 1928–		1929 New York stock market crash; beginning of worldwide depression
Claude Bolling 1930–		

Stephen Sondheim	1930–	
Shel Silverstein	1932–	1932 Franklin D. Roosevelt elected president
Isao Tomita	1932–	
John Williams	1932–	
Krzysztof Penderecki	1933–	1933 Nazi Revolution in Germany
Terry Riley	1935–	
Philip Glass	1937–	
Leo Brouwer	1939–	1939 World War II (ended 1945)
Trevor Nunn	1940–	
Bob Dylan	1941–	
David Fanshawe	1942–	
George Harrison	1943–	
Vangelis	1943–	
James C. Pankow	1947–	
Elton John	1947–	
Andrew Lloyd Webber	1948–	
Stephen Schwartz	1948–	
Stevie Nicks	1948–	
Billy Joel	1949–	

1950

Peter Gabriel	1950–	1950 Korean War (ended 1953); Vietnam War (ended 1975)
Bernie Taupin	1950–	
Dewey Bunnell	1952–	
Bruce Hornsby	1954–	1954 First polio vaccine developed by Jonas E. Salk
Gloria Estefan	1957–	1957 Launching of Sputnik, first earth satellite
		1961 First successful manned orbital space flight
		1962 Cuban missile crisis
		1963 President John F. Kennedy assassinated
		1965 First "walk" outside spaceship by an astronaut
		1968 Martin Luther King, Jr., and Robert F. Kennedy assassinated
		1969 First men land on the moon
		1971 Voting age lowered to 18 years

1975

1976 U.S. celebrates its bicentennial on July 4; Viking I and II landers set down on Mars

1981 Sandra Day O'Connor becomes first woman appointed to the Supreme Court; first reusable spacecraft, space shuttle Columbia, travels into space and returns to earth

1983 Sally Ride becomes the first American woman to travel in space

1984 First mechanical heart implanted in a human

1985 Worldwide Live Aid concert to benefit famine victims in Ethiopia

1986 Statue of Liberty centennial celebration

1987 Voyager makes first nonstop flight around the world without refueling

1990 Germany reunited; dissolving of the Soviet Union; spacecraft Magellan maps Venus

GLOSSARY

ABA form a three-part form in which there is repetition after contrast, **21**

absolute music makes no attempt to tell a story, describe an event, or paint a picture, **153**

accent (>) placement of emphasis or stress on certain beats, **3**

aria solo song from an opera or oratorio, **196**

arrange to re-set a composition for a different combination of musical resources, **206**

art song music written for solo voice and instrumental accompaniment, usually keyboard, **111**

atonal music characterized by the absence of a tonal center and equal emphasis on all twelve tones of the chromatic scale, **92**

ballad a song that tells a story, **130**

bar lines lines separating measures, **18**

baroque style the common musical characteristics reflected by the music composed between 1600 and 1750, **17**

bitonality harmony created by playing two different tonalities at the same time, **108**

blues a melancholy style of American music characterized by flatted notes and a syncopated, often slow jazz rhythm, **104**

cambiata the range of a boy's changing voice, **309**

calypso style of folk music from the Caribbean Islands, **10**

canon a form of music in which different vocal or instrumental parts take up the melody, successively creating harmony, **82**

chamber music compositions for small groups, **194**

chord three or more pitches sounding together, **4**

classical style the common musical characteristics reflected by the music composed between 1750 and 1830, **17**

coda concluding section, **20**

composer writes the music, **290**

compound meter meter whose beat is divided into threes and/or sixes, **61**

consonance the sounding of a combination of tones that produces little tension, **80**

controller element of the MIDI system on which the music is played, **290**

crescendo (⎯⎯⎯) getting louder, **13**

dancehall melodic form of rap music from the Caribbean Islands, **5**

decrescendo (⎯⎯⎯) getting softer, **13**

development the expanded treatment of a musical idea, **147**

dissonance the sounding of a combination of pitches that creates harmonic tension and sounds incomplete, **108**

dominant chord a chord built on the fifth tone of a scale, **11**

dotted quarter note (♩.) a symbol for a sound equal in length to three eighth notes; represents the basic beat in compound meter, **60**

dotted quarter rest (𝄽·) a symbol for an interval of silence lasting as long as a dotted quarter note, **60**

duple meter beats grouped into sets of two, **18**

dynamics levels of loudness and softness, **12**

eighth note (♪ or ♪) a symbol for a sound in music that is one eighth as long as the sound of a whole note, **8**

eighth rest (♪) a symbol for an interval of silence lasting as long as an eighth note, **8**

episodes sections of a baroque concerto played by the solo player, **192**

études term meaning studies or exercises, **199**

expressionism a movement in the arts characterized by the artist's concern with the expression of feelings about an object or event rather than realistically depicting the object itself, **93**

fermata (⌢ or ⌣) indicates that a note should be held longer than usual, **249**

forte (*f*) loud, **13**

found objects sources of tone color that are ordinary items that wouldn't usually be thought of as musical instruments, **181**

free form a composition that changes from one performance to the next, **158**

fugue a form of polyphonic music using imitation, **356**

gospel style of religious music which was originated in the South by African Americans; influenced by rhythm and blues and soul music, **99**

half note (♩ or ♩) a symbol for a sound in music that is one half as long as the sound of a whole note, **4**

harmony a musical combination of tones or chords, **80**

home tone the focus or tonal center of a scale, or system of tones, **80**

homophonic music having one melodic line with the other parts providing harmony, **83**

imitation occurs when one voice repeats, or varies slightly, a melody in another voice, **356**

irregular meter a mixture of duple and triple meters, **48**

jazz style of American music that originated in the South by African Americans, characterized by improvisation and syncopated rhythms, **52**

key scale or system of tones in which all the notes have a definite relationship to, and are based on, the **tonal** center or keynote, **100**

key tone the focus or tonal center of a scale or system of tones, **11**

legato music that sounds smooth, **141, 194**

lyricist writes the words to be set to music for a song, **318**

measures groups of beats, **18**

meter the organization of beats into recurring sets, **18**

minimalism compositional style that emphasizes repetition of short rhythmic and melodic patterns, **129**

modulation transition from a section of music based on one scale to a section based on a different scale, **100**

monophonic music having a single melodic line with no accompaniment, **83**

MIDI (Musical Instrument Digital Interface) a system which connects instruments to computers, **290**

MIDI interface a device which allows the controller to "talk" to the computer, **290**

motive a short musical idea, **127**

natural (♮) symbol indicating that a sharp or a flat should be canceled, **25**

neoclassical style of composition exhibiting the characteristics of classical piece, but composed after the close of that period, **149**

opera a drama with scenery and costumes in which all or most of the words are sung to the accompaniment of an orchestra, **196**

oratorio a dramatic musical composition usually set to a religious text and performed by solo voices, chorus, and orchestra, without action, special costumes, or scenery, **83**

ostinato repeated pattern, **54**

phrase a complete musical idea, **120**

piano (*p*) soft, **13**

pipe organ keyboard instrument whose sound is produced by wind moving through pipes, **172**

pizzicato music played by plucking the strings of a stringed instrument with the finger instead of bowing the strings, **106**

polyphonic music having two or more independent melodic parts sounding together, **83**

polyrhythm a combination of two or more different rhythm patterns played at the same time, **70**

prepared piano piano whose sound has been altered by placing items of wood, metal, rubber, between the strings of the piano, **175**

program music a composition whose title or accompanying remarks link it with a story, idea, or emotion, **50, 152**

quadruple meter beats that are grouped into sets of four, **40**

quarter note (♩ or ♩) a symbol for a sound in music that is one fourth as long as the sound of a whole note, **3**

quarter rest (𝄽) a symbol for an interval of silence lasting as long as a quarter note, **3**

record producer directs the process of making a recording, **290**

recording engineer handles the technical aspects of the recording session, **290**

reggae style of popular music from the Caribbean Islands, **5**

register the high to low range of a voice or instrument, **102**

Renaissance style the common musical characteristics reflected by the music composed between 1450 and 1600, **17**

repeat sign (𝄇) play or sing the pattern again, **3**

retrograde a backwards version of a melodic pattern, **88**

ritardando gradual slowing of the tempo, **20**

ritornello section of a baroque concerto played by all the players, **192**

rock and roll style of music combining the styles of many other forms including rhythm and blues, blues, rockabilly and others, **30**

romantic style the common musical characteristics reflected by the music composed between 1830 and 1900, **17**

root the lowest pitch of each chord, **11**

salsa style of Latin dance music characterized by exciting rhythms and tone colors, **70**

sequencer program software that enables one to create, record, edit, and play back music, **290**

serial music atonal music written using a technique based on the successive repetition of all twelve tones of the chromatic scale in a fixed order, **90, 238**

ska fast, lively style of music originating in Jamaica, **5**

skipwise melodic movement using skips between pitches, **240**

sonata allegro a musical form that uses the overall design of exposition, development, and recapitulation, **149**

sound output device speakers or headphones, **290**

staccato music that sounds crisp and detached, **141**

steady beat an unchanging beat or pulse, **3**

steel drums "homemade" percussion instruments found in the West Indies, **182**

stepwise melodic movement using only adjacent pitches, **238**

stratification layering of melody or sound, **226**

strophic form form in which the music is repeated with each new verse or stanza of text, **130**

style quality that is characteristic of a culture, individual, or historical period, **2**

subdominant chord chord based on the fourth tone of the scale, **104**

suite a musical composition consisting of a succession of short pieces, **24**

symphony long orchestral work organized into three to five movements, **149, 194**

syncopation off-beat rhythm pattern that has unexpected sounds and silences, **10**

synthesizer an instrument for producing electronic music that combines sound generators and modifiers in a single control system, **178**

tempo the speed of the beat, **8**

ternary form (ABA) a three-part form in which there is repetition after contrast, **21**

texture the character of the different layers of sound in music, **83**

Theremin first electronic musical instrument, invented by and named for Leon Theremin, **178**

tonality the relation of melodic and harmonic elements to a home tone, **80**

tone color the unique sound of each instrument or voice, **13**

tone generator collection of sounds to be accessed by the computer, **290**

tonic chord a chord built on the first tone or key tone of a scale, **11**

triple meter beats grouped into sets of three, **18**

twelve-bar blues chord pattern often used in blues music based on the I, IV, and V chords, **104**

twelve tone row a type of pitch organization made up of all of the tones of the chromatic scale that has no tonal center and in which all pitches are equal, see also **serial music**, **90**

twentieth-century style the common musical characteristics reflected by the music composed since 1900, **17**

whole note (o) a symbol that represents a sound that lasts for four quarter notes, **4**

CLASSIFIED INDEX

LISTENING SELECTIONS

ALPHABETICAL SONG INDEX